The Wilderness Diary

KEITH BRAZIL

DEDICATION

To my Father, George,

with all the love and thanks

To Merlin and Sir Percival

and all aligning Grail Knights

on Vision Quests throughout the world

An adventure in art, travel consciousness

and Night-journeying

To Gaia

A World weep

a wonderful Winter solstice

and a welcome new Spring

ACKNOWLEDGMENTS

'B-Om-bardment' Quotes from inspirational speeches: Josiah Wedgewood (1) / Sojourner Truth (2) / John Bright (3) / Emmeline Pankhurst (4) / Winston Churchill (5, 6, 7, 10, 11) / Mahatma Gandhi (8a, 8b) / Martin Luther King (9)

'Love, Death, Denial… a year of magical thinking' inspired by Joan Didion's <u>The Year of Magical Thinking</u>.

'War Museum' – Extract from <u>A Matter of Life and Death</u> (Stairway to Heaven) – with kind permission from the Powell and Pressburger estates.

Quotes: Andrew Marvell – *To His Coy Mistress.* / J.R.R Tolkien – *The Lord of the Rings.* / Shakespeare – *A Winter's Tale.* / Zoroastrianism texts / prayers.

Editor: Rachel Gibbin.

Developmental Editor: Kitty Malone.

Cover Design: Adam Wiltshire.

Design Concept: Keith Brazil.

Illustrations by: Colin Francolino-Scott, Michael Brazil, Jason Tanner & Keith.

With thanks to: my Mother – Angela, Stephen & Juliet, Andrew & Jacquie, Tania, Teresa & Paul, Kassie, Margaret, Steve C, Francis & Eric, Adrian, Ian, Liam, Mark, Jim, Colin R, Mike & Tom, Matt, Neil, Rolf, Brendan, Dave & Graham, Kitty, Sue, Aingeal & Randy, Steve Crook, & the CSM gang for their enthusiasm & support.

Special thanks to: Michael, Colin, Rachel, Kitty, Adam, Jason, Andy, Francis, & Zara for all their work, help, patience and insights. And especially to my Father – an extraordinary gift of journey and learning.

A Black Cat / Golden Hamster Production

A Chronology of Days:

1	Wed 9th March	The Leaving/Ash Wednesday
2	Thurs 10th March	Mahout/City Ceremony
3	Fri 11th March	'Spell of Snakes'
4	Sat 12th March	Harbour Wave/Snake-Raven TV
5	Sun 13th March	Conflicted/Daylight Saving
6	Mon 14th March	The Judas Tree
7	Tues 15th March	Cardboard City
8	Wed 16th March	"Profits Us Not"
9	Thurs 17th March	Golgotha
10	Fri 18th March	The Breaking Table
11	Sat 19th March	Super Moon
12	Sun 20th March	Sistrum
13	Mon 21st March	Naw-Ruz
14	Tues 22nd March	The Fair Maid
15	Wed 23rd March	Snake Cures/Dream Sleep
16	Thurs 24th March	*Abiuro*
17	Fri 25th March	The Inquisitor's Key
18	Sat 26th March	Kali/Night Vision
19	Sun 27th March	Fire
20	Mon 28th March	Change
21	Tues 29th March	Bell Tower
22	Wed 30th March	Eco Burn/Gaia Plan
23	Thurs 31st March	Last Day of March
24	Fri 1st April	The Fool

A Chronology of Days (cont'd):

25	Sat 2nd April	Pennies of the Dead
26	Sun 3rd April	Huginn and Muninn
27	Mon 4th April	Tagebuch
28	Tues 5th April	Consolamentum
29	Wed 6th April	B-Om-bardment
30	Thurs 7th April	Over Soul
31	Fri 8th April	Caravan of Crows
32	Sat 9th April	Conversation in Blue
33	Sun 10th April	Sea, Land and Air
34	Mon 11th April	The Tower
35	Tues 12th April	Initiation
36	Wed 13th April	Love, Death, Denial…
37	Thurs 14th April	Raven Master
38	Fri 15th April	Domine Dirige Nos
39	Sat 16th April	London's Burning
40	Sun 17th April	Buddhist Monastery/Fire Ceremony
41	Mon 18th April	Dragon Design
42	Tues 19th April	To the Feet of the Mother
43	Wed 20th April	War Museum
44	Thurs 21st April	Maundy/Hephaestus
45	Fri 22nd April	Good Friday/International Mother Earth Day
46	Sat 23rd April	Ministry of Light, Sound and Vision
47	Sun 24th April	Resurrection Day
48	Mon 25th April	New Octave

Autumn/Winter: Four Temple Watches of the Day

Hawan: Morning – Watch 1 = Sunrise to 3pm

Uzerin: Late Afternoon – Watch 2 = 3pm to Sunset

Aiwisruthrem: Night – Watch 3 = Sunset to Midnight

Ushahin: Dark Night – Watch 4 = Midnight to Sunrise

Spring/Summer: Five Temple Watches of the Day

Hawan: Morning – Watch 1 = Sunrise to 12 Noon

Rapithwin: Afternoon – Watch 2 = 12 Noon to 3pm

Uzerin: Late Afternoon – Watch 3 = 3pm to Sunset

Aiwisruthrem: Night – Watch 4 = Sunset to Midnight

Ushahin: Dark Night – Watch 5 = Midnight to Sunrise

'The Way is mysterious and profound, and is the door to various wonders..."

(Lao Zi)

"There is no shame, only forgiveness..."

(Spirit)

"Our thumping hearts hold the Ravens in

and keep the tower from tumbling..."

(Kate Bush)

Day 1 – The Leaving/Ash Wednesday

Wednesday 9th March – 11°C

You do not know my name, do not need to, but you will by the end come to know it. Until then, I shall remain an Unnamed Man – an unlikely hero – for this dream diary you have happened upon could belong to anyone. Perhaps you have already experienced what is to come? Perhaps it is all still before you? Here though, in these diary pages of Night-journey you will find all the inept magick and folly wisdom of an unwitting Alchemist's apprentice. First, back to the time of the Ravens' arrival and my isolation, back to my flightless former self and the simplicity of star dreaming. I mean… the simplest of starts and the day of my exodus and quiet leaving.

Hawan: Morning (Watch 1) – I close the door, turn the key and leave just like any other day. Only today, at this moment, I know I must go. It is not so much about the leaving, more about the not returning – not for a while anyway. I must go wherever the prevailing winds prompt me in order to seek out the compass change of me, to find new electricity. This is not some epic quest across land and sea, but a journey to the inner disturbed lands. I will have to wade through the Cosmic Water of Time, that which feels like Etheric Air, to reach all the beautiful people and things from the past, my past, as they gather in my difficult broken Earth World. They are all here and there. This is a collapsing, absent realm suddenly torn apart just as the shattering of a blown bulb surges and fuses a house. The lights have gone out. I do not know why I flee the darkness, but go I must.

It is an honest impulse and one that I must follow. It is as simple as that, as urgent and necessary as a need I can no longer ignore and which now chronically overwhelms. So, I shut the domestic door and leave with no thought of when and how I shall eventually return. I am that lost, that out to sea. The wild storm winds provoke me and, like Old Gods that fail to move on, I grumble like distant thunder when asked the impossible. However, unlike them, I must progress but not like this. Outmoded and ancient – my old self has outstayed its welcome. Like Gaia, I search for newer, renewable energy sources in the awakening Age. I seek the Spring and the Sun.

First, I must shrug and cast off. This oblivion I feel is a new depth in which to fathom. I am on land, but sea and air and all the combining elements of tempest and precipitous alchemy beckon. No thoughts of settlement or domesticity occupy me, although both already exist. I have left a note to You, my beloved, my encompassing half, and the strange household that is migrant bedsit land that I leave behind. The question is – how do you explain an experience that you have not yet had, however justified the absence feels? I ask of You the impossible…

'Don't worry. I'm not sure how long I'll be gone, but I need to go. Need You to know I will be back and that I love You. I know you will understand. Please tell the others not to look for me.'

What else can I say? That is the most important message – that I love them. So, monk like, I pull up my hood and look down toward my wandering feet. I hide and go. I have packed a rucksack for my portables including this – my alchemical dream diary. Essential items of survival and those objects pertaining to my day craft that I always carry nestle and jostle alongside a few items of clothing, notebooks and pens, towel, toothbrush, torch and Swiss army knife. I will not be shaving in the coming weeks. I am turning Pagan-Barbarian and look forward to these days of being unkempt. A chance to be dishevelled and unruly is a luxury in these over washed and sanitised times. I need to kick around in the dirt as I once did when a child in the faraway fields of the faraway lands. Recent weeks have contained such numbing routine. This is a chance for liberty and running wild on organic time. Yet from what am I running? And what am I running too?

Not what, but from and to whom? I am caught in becoming, but it is not true. I already am, just disconnected between my past and future selves stuck in present Earthquake Land. Of all my wyrd travels, this is the strangest yet. Why can't I just have a holiday? Pack my bags and take a train, boat or plane? The only problem is I have an old passport; the photo no longer fits and the baggage, crammed full with missing, is me. I am out of date. In any case – where am I heading? Where on earth do I think I am going? What imagined borders do I seek to cross? I'll be lucky to escape the precipitation of the Alchemist's flask alive. I close the door, turn the key and lock myself in on the outside. I leave.

As I walk along the familiar Street of East, I phone the Raven Agency and tell them I will not be in to work today, perhaps not for a little while. It is my last phone call before the wilderness days set in. Who am I kidding? The real wasteland has already started; I am just giving it exterior circumstance. Given my recent, sad, personal situation, the Agency say they understand. Questions will be asked about my new strangeness and on-going withdrawal. My increasing daily silences cannot be their answer. I am not in the mood and I cannot find the words to explain what I am feeling. I am as lead, reduced to base metal, and a part of me cannot be bothered with social niceties anymore; this process is just something to be endured, waiting for release and hopeful ultimate transmutation.

I cannot be there for them – the unusual Raven Agency team – so I am going underground, going missing. Whilst this urge to intransigency seems futile, it nonetheless offers some sense of escape and destination. In my current sadness what is the point of anything? What should I do about the on setting madness that I daily dread and nightly fight? Ignore it. Deny it. These elements of struggle are the very things I bring with me alongside the everything I have to let go of. Yet I fear I am abandoning myself. My current emotional situation is so unexpected that it seems I am a deepening daily mystery even unto my own being and mind. I can no longer comply and am in danger of defying higher orders.

That is why I need to leave and investigate. That is why I make myself absent. I seek out the unforgiving and greater impersonal laws of Mother Nature – to get to the truth and dark heart of the matter. There is some consolation in that: in being stripped down, in living hand to mouth, in examining moods and finding release. I have done it so many times before, but I am asked to do it once more in the seventh and final house. To move on I have to go to the difficult place my mind and body do not want to visit – the centre of my Two Hearts. So be it. The seal is broken. I go.

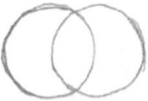

I turn my mobile phone off to silence the overly connected outer World. I lean on a moss-covered wall to adjust my rucksack and throw my phone into the bottom of the bag. I look back over my shoulder at the house and suddenly notice the tenacity of plants growing everywhere: on walls, in cracks in pavements and guttering, in raised beds and walkways. There is so much green life to tend to and witness. As I walk past the shoebox sized front gardens and fenced in playgrounds, all kinds of nuzzling greenery alert me to the greater evolving heart of green Nature. I crisscross under and over the many concrete pedestrian walkways onto the Desert Island. Buds, shoots and flowers spring up on the open top of nearby traffic islands and isolated roundabouts. A central Field of Hope lies mirrored in the mysterious, indented, silver Faraday Cube.

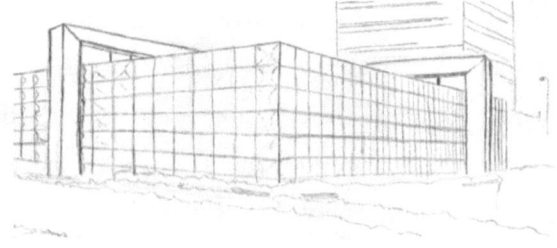

Is this strange, dislocated, modern memorial beneficial or brutal? The mythological subterranean home of sound and vision pioneers houses an invisible secret – it is a hidden underground transformer encased in steel. The Cube links past and future with grimy bemusement. Faraday knew all the secrets of electromagnetic induction whereas I am but apprentice trusting to the unfathomable function of my base chakra. My hopes of a Light Dream and an easy disappearance evaporate. I stop to observe the passing metal butterflies, the migratory buses and assorted parading gyratory traffic. Here, at the road leading to the beginning of the Cheapest Square, we view monopolies and utilities differently. Resources are valuable, not for squandering, and strangleholds are viewed with contempt. We are more than willing to take a 'Chance' and know the full worth of the 'Community Chest'. Life is a game to some; still funny until it is not. The privileged stand more protected. Those that are humbled are not.

Around me University students spill everywhere; buoyant, yelling, some still with no idea. I turn my thoughts back to the Field of Hope with its surprising diversity of green. I envy the wild seed that drifts on the wind, oblivious of its uncertain, perilous destiny. It might find earth; take root, establish itself as a tenacious weed, a fragile flower, or a mighty tree with useful fruit. It might lay dormant waiting for the conditions to be right. It might never show; never know the pain of growing. The Plant Kingdom has so much to offer in its green living frenzy and multi-coloured blossoming.

Yet what kind of seed do we carry within, what flowering might unfold, what strange fruit might yet be born? Is it such bad seed, this sudden delinquency of mine, or merely the youth within rebelling before submitting to the need to further grow up? Is this need to escape and find liberation truly a gift from Time? I feel the shuffle and kick of my immaturity struggling with the need to develop magick and come home again. I do not know how far through this lifetime I am. Who does? But at this moment I am exhausted as I face the aftershocks of the Transit of Death. Is the prospect of growing older so very difficult?

What the Buddha achieved in meditational days, we have years to achieve. At 35, I am young middling. Perhaps I am being born again? Perhaps I am psychologically dying? All I know is that I try to turn my back on it all, draw a line, and I want to start afresh. Need to. Wish to. Only I cannot. Not yet. My grieving is incomplete. My understanding diminished. The threat of change too great. What Wizard do I seek who could undo this sudden spell of tumult and natural tragedy? Is the magick all in me? At present it does not feel so, even to one such as I – steeped in mystic process and Rose Finch mystery. It feels like I am being reborn in a storm.

I feel such heartfelt sadness and the accumulation of so much rumbling thunder. Whatever the process, it has not yet finished with me even though I so desperately want it to be over. The struggle is difficult and painful. This muddle before me is a nebulous state of atmospheric and cloud confusion and I approach it as might a child, innocently wanting things to be different. Can things be different and not be what they once were? Could things be better?

My routine, my habitat, and my toys of security are all being taken from me. I believe it is real – this sudden separation of Heaven from Earth that I feel. Yet why is it such an intangible Faceless Being I seek and follow, as I head towards the broken Pathless Land? I left in the light of morning, not in the dark of night. I am not so much runaway but absent from myself and now missing. Am I to become another ranting Holy Man – a day wanderer with no home of my own? Am I vagrant? Am I stationary? Is this journey point and departure, meeting and arrival, all in one? I am lost here. So very lost.

As I leave the island of the marooned Faraday Cube I turn towards the Elephant Circus, whereas I would normally turn towards the Bascule Bridge. Underneath its crenulated towers, the free flowing Thames knows no bounds in its endless tidal struggle and streaming. The informant Isis river snakes sometimes pay visit on their way to and from Oxford. They run intellectual errands and out glide the many boatmen. From source to sea via estuary, the Serpent River runs a course as poetic and liquid as ancient history. I can see the gleaming water from my office – Room 2, The Tower, which sits so majestically upon the riverbank. That is where I currently work for the Raven Agency, but not today.

From my usual window I also watch those centuries old Feathered Tricksters being fed their daily diet of biscuits and blood before they start their business. Like curious primeval rag-and-bone merchants searching and scrying, the Ravens rake over our discarded flesh and life activities like so much carrion. They have universal permission as part of their remaining Old God mission. Our juices and lives are nothing but gossip and news for Sky Spirits looking on. Now I know it will be the Tower's rooks and rascals who take my soul in these coming days. I know it, for the Raven rascals and the unkind Crows come in a mob and a murder for me, and in my current torment I am but a carcass calling them to pick over the certainties of what used to be. They have been staring askance these last few weeks with their piercing, oil-black, all-absorbing orbs. The menacing corvids have been gathering about me as black and beautiful as jet Shiva beads. These Ravens of hunger, misery and emotional plague have been stabbing my dreams and filling my auric vision.

I must tear away from the imprisoning days that have been my last weeks. My gaolers are not straggling cloud ghosts wearing shrouds of grey, but distant memories and half grasped thoughts and feelings that accompany me from the start of my childhood journeying and beyond. I have a lifeline to remember. I have a lifetime to forget. Inside my misunderstood heart a soul storm beckons, bemoaning the overwhelming sadness of my situation. I try to express the force of miserable feelings that have no words. I have become inert and wretched and do not know how to stop the aching. I have no more desperate defence, no picket fence, for the much prophesised gale is upon me. The whirlwind is descending. I do not have to do anything – for the profound nature of loss and grief is upon me. It is already happening to me, moving through me, and I am stuck, attached, immovable, until I reach acceptance of unalterable things past.

I need to detach and find the far shore of myself. I need to go within to find the healing Alchemical Beasts and assisting spiritual Sky voices. I must seek external guidance from the Moon, Mistress of the Night, for it is she who is shining compassion on the hemispheres of the East and West and conjoins our shared dreams. She is the guardian of the causal doorway to the multi-layered nocturnal universe. It is she who guards the bustling City as she nightly gleams and protects. This will be a Moon and a dark Night Sky adventure – in truth a soul's journeying as well as a son's, for this is a different kind of manifesting magick. This is a strong asking for love from the Goddesses of the Sky: they who are positive feminine, in a healing attempt to restore the positive masculine.

As I wander through the receptive emotional states I know I will travail, but I must prevail whatever the odds the Gods seemingly stack against me. This is my Vision Quest – the Grail search for balance between the mystical cone and the magical cup. This is the challenge of my elemental world. This is my pursuit of the Vortex Castle amidst my elephant's grieving. So, I march like Caesar's army once marched, leaving the taste of yesterday's pancakes behind. Sugar. Lemon. Cinnamon. Those were the tastes that touched the palate and soul last night, and us in the kitchen, cooking, laughing and dancing. I prepare to walk a centurion's league on an iron stomach for I have a mystery to solve; yet I must find kindness too in the reaching of my final destination. I will remain on Temple Watch (daily routine is hard to break) but what am I guarding or on the lookout for? Of course! I guard the old and look out for the new, but this is more than a simple vigil of nature honouring the death of a parent. This is a child's grieving response whilst tending the Sacred Fire, a child's struggle to keep the flame alight within the falling Tower of Darkness. It offers me a chance to heal the wounded self following the recent passing of my Father.

Meanwhile, I witness the collapsing world of the I-of-old that will soon exist no more. I must divine my inner truth – the makeup of my own anguished molecules and the further reaches of my Spirit Father. That is why I am recording this emic account. I use electromagnetic Akashic paper stolen from the illumined Library of the East, with the result that all my thoughts and feelings stick to it like flies. Here, the magical Cup of Confucius catches the little winged, window-ledged, dying me. This is my sincere attempt to capture my balance. Not exactly a Page Book, but more a record of my exile and flight before the final returning. Perhaps one day I will be able to share it with You, so You can understand why I went, why I had to leave, why I had to be alone. You will call it my lie and say that You could have held me close and let me weep openly. Perhaps you could have made it all right if only I would have allowed myself to be more vulnerable and let You in to help. That all sounds so reasonable, so logical, so sensible, but it is not the path I find myself upon. It is not my lie – just my current sad situation – and I seek out a solitary solution. I am truly sorry for that.

All that You offer is so warm, so loving, and so wonderful! I am so lucky, but still I have to become the Hermit and walk into the solitary Cave of Darkness. Is that why the Ravens beckon? This obscure hole reveals itself to be a tunnel into the hell of my past Heart and no-one need be there except me. I am falling back onto private ideas and trust of Spirit rather than onto your encompassing humanity, love and friendship. I need to rediscover my connection to the light, for I dread the aloneness and fear the cold sleeping of body and soul. This leaving is my failing, but this sorrow and fear of mine hide the supremacy of Light Divine. I have become the cloud that blocks the Sun. I am in chains here in these troubled states, but how to be unfettered? The doorway into the Dark Unknown beckons and I must pass through it with all honesty.

Uzerin: Late afternoon (Watch 2) – I walk to the closest tree-filled Park and espy with my eagle eye three potential buildings to use as nesting places. Two are located close to the heart of the Elephant and overlook each other; the third is slightly further out. I favour the latter – the rooftop of the Old Wealhworth Yards. It is easier to access than the others and offers the open space I seek, where I can lie midnight supine and see Andromeda smiling back down at me. The Yard building I choose is one of several yellow brick buildings overlooking a cobbled mews, with a large wrought-iron gate at one end. Four floors high, it has open entrances to tiled stairwells leading to a series of linked flat roofs. Most of the doors at the top of the stairwells are left 'accidentally' open or have had their locks broken. A simple wood plank lock-prop and doorjamb suffices to secure my nesting. I need to guard my body when Night-travelling, for I will not be in full possession of my physical vehicle.

Nearby, a secret City Garden nestles. It is fenced in, but scalable should I feel the need to sleep closer to the sweet smelling grass and restorative Mother Nature. When I day drift, I like to earth sink, then Dragon float and climb the sky. To be up so high that I can easily cloud jump and dive into the dream Sea of Me makes me feel so alive, whichever way I am headed. I do not know what form my astral travelling will take. Voyages into the unknown can be perturbing, and the sleeping that follows might leave me vulnerable. Yet these are the late night concerns of the Moon driven. Now, I am concerned with the pursuit of twilight warmth and makeshift comfort. I seek out sunset vermillion like a fabled Firebird.

Aiwisruthrem: Night (Watch 3) – Unnoticed, I drag some cardboard sheets up from the Yards below and bunker down. People pass by in their bustling busyness, but rarely engage in the activities of the borderline strange however immersed in seeming self-discovery – just in case someone else's madness proves to be worse than their own. I take the thin, warm blanket attached to the bottom of my rucksack, shake it out and double it up. Over the next few days I shall organise my Tower of Silence in preparation for brutal sky burial. This is becoming all about the acknowledgement of impermanence. Those parts of me that are dead and dying now need to be eaten and removed. May the Night Crows and Ravens of Gods be merciful in their swift circling. I do not focus on fearful black morbidity, but I do need to experience this living death process whilst I am still alive – so that in the fullness of my time ahead I am able to put it to better use. For now, what I need most is some sustenance and basic creature comfort.

I go and eat, bringing back chai tea to sip. As I sit on the rooftop and observe the crescent serenity of the snow-white Moon I inhale the steamy vapours of India and mull over my situation. This is it. I need to square up and come to terms with the beginning of a strange Night-journey and my new adventure with Sky Spirit and alchemical self. I struggle to believe what I have done. I cannot believe I have left. I cannot believe I have put myself here. I am no stranger to the stars but, tonight, I sleep alone beneath the open Night Sky for the first time in such a long time. I turn away from the Moon to face the wall. I miss the warmth of your arms.

Day 2 – Mahout/City Ceremony

Thursday 10th March – 13°C

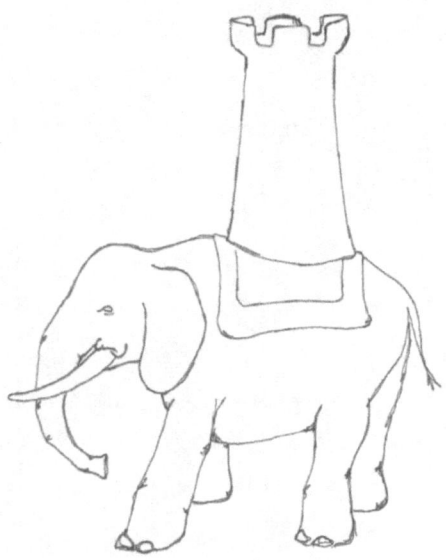

Uzerin: Late Afternoon (Watch 2) – I do not know what has happened to the day. Time has passed and I have drifted listlessly. I have visited the Apothecary of Old and the Market of East for essential herbs and tinctures to help me through my present state. I have dragged myself around the ailing shopping mall on the edge of an empty, decrepit estate like some urban Crusoe. I am self-imprisoned, not shipwrecked but just as stranded. Is this my last stand for new hope? I stand in defiance like the surrounding abandoned estate buildings – useless, lined up and condemned, awaiting demolishment. I no longer know where I belong, but I know I cannot walk away from this.

I head up high to view the darkening sky that begins to wrap around the City's skyline shoulders like a glittering shawl. There is something so beautiful about the rooftop sunset of cities; something iridescent and elegant. The City shimmers in the twilight, lighting up with electricity and discharging her voltaic arcs: illumination, reflection and refraction. She powders the dusk, rouges her cheeks and the front of her knees. She scoops scarlet from out of the sunset jar and puts on her nightly painted face. This is the meeting of light and dark, the late afternoon City assignation of yin and yang as day meets night in possible romance and on-off troubled affairs. The City is full of corruption, innocence and experience, coin and soul. She is munificent in all that she offers.

From where I now sit, on top of tall buildings, I watch the City twinkle as she begins to flash her night-time diamonds. Like a mahout in front of a howdah, I bestride the statues of castles and magnificent elephants and view the sprawling urban jungle below. The streetlights present a blurring confusion of colour: diffused yellow and white, glowing reds, ambers and greens, neon pinks and shiny blues. All are strangely beautiful, sparkling like so many coloured sequins, glowing gems and treasured jewels. The organic shadows of emerald parks, gardens and squares, deepen and darken. The flags of the nearby Buddhist Monastery flap and wave in the wind like a call to prayer reminding me to pay a visit there.

Beneath me, umbral roads and roundabouts snake like semi-circular canals roaring with gleaming evening traffic. My ears fill up with City sound and congestion. In front of the Tabernacle, people and buses swarm whilst distant figures and voices weave their way through the gathering dusk. With all their exits and entrances, the open mouths of the underworld Snakes spew forth tired people, and gobble up the busy souls in departure. Some want to go home. Some want to go out. Lodged as we are in the Earth Serpent's mouth – we are all displaced, as the serving Dragon ties itself around the world, to steady us in an expanding and wobbling universe. I watch them all, but for now the viewing and purpose of Galactic Snakes will have to wait.

Low in the horizon, the Moon rises in the twilight sky in all her guises: maiden, lover, wife and mother, widow, crone, half-hidden witch. She holds a trident and owns the triple aspect of her craft: golden blessings, magick white and black, and all our malevolent curses. Here, sitting so high up, all her four phases are seen and felt as one. Regeneration and the cycles of life, birth and death, sleep, wake and dream, are all contained within her ovulating monthly sphere. She is the sound and round of mystic thirteen. Nocturnal lovers' stockings are released and rolled under her enchantment. Ripe bellies are smoothed and stroked by a loving hand. Hers is the wise repose of a cloud-veiled figure – white for lifting at early weddings, black to draw closed at the end of the life day to cosset the widow's grief. Tonight the Moon is devastatingly white and reveals the complexion of her pockmarked face. She is blemished, yet beautiful.

Aiwisruthrem: Night (Watch 3) – Like a night owl, I swoop down to my rooftop Aerie on the Old Wealhworth Yard to alight on the building's ledge. Now I sit like a bird, perched on the edge like a Passerine. Bird-wake. Bird-watch. The overhead orb of the Moon is like a child's nightlight globe in the underwater world of sleeping dream wonder. As I roost in my moonlit coral reading room, I attune, learn and grow as the Moon gently reveals her outer cycles and inner phases. Ultimately, I am nothing but fodder for fire or earth in her time-encroaching rituals of death and new life in spiritual passage. Yet tonight she calls upon the worms to prepare the fertility of the earth and the sap to awaken the energies within the plants and trees. I am like the soil being turned over and prepared. These slow, late, winter worms will do me well for I am rotting, and they give me a chance to contemplate and consider renewal. Is that why the Ravens roost around me? Do they come for a simple feasting or do they offer me a new, dark aerial view? The Moon reminds us all to rouse our life forces from slumber for soon it will be fresh Spring again.

In her beaming, late-night goodness the Moon offers me the gifts of company, charm and grace. In embracing me she shields my rooftop shelter from invisible harm. I am absorbed. Is this Moon genesis? To receive her etheric milk I must lie down like the suckling lamb. I know I must imbibe her higher spell, the moonlit summons of her Night-journey. This is my inception. So I prepare, soma and hare, for the ritual Sandman dare – the migration of consciousness through existences. I am vulnerable, soft, and do not feel safe. I do not know if I kneel for shearing or slaughter? Is this the flailing of lamb devotion? Is this the failing of faltering me? I am like a frightened, night-woken child awaiting the reassuring touch of a mother.

'Drink,' the Moon says as she pours down her creamy rays. 'The lamb is prepared – open your heart to the lily.'

Ushahin: Dark Night (Watch 4) – Rooftop. In the Moon's midnight room the High Priestess prepares. She hangs a perfumed pomegranate curtain between the two pillars of Heaven to protect her sacred presence. Offering glimpses of a greater God she invites me to meet her there, and tells me to bring all my hurt and recent despair. Behind the veiled room, the vengeful Goddess of Night looms – despoiler and murderess. The nocturnal Sky is a hunter-warrior, cloaked in dark diamonds of determination and destructive resolve. She unfurls into the galaxy, growing and stretching as she fills the encompassing invisible Cosmic Chalice. It is she who has her way in feminine matters of passion, politics and power as she crushes the bleeding hearts of love-besieged women. And like a Red Queen, she will pluck off the heads of heated, transient, momentary men that fail to satisfy or outlive their use. I fear she might betray me.

Yet rising above them both I glimpse the ever nurturing Supernature Empress. She wears blossoms and floral bursts as celestial patterns upon her Springtime dresses. Orbiting worlds and sun-ripened fruit adorn her Summer garbs. Leaves, volcanoes and fireworks are fiery prints on her fine, flowing Autumnal gowns. Snowflakes, stars and solstices are for Winter wraps and diaphanous wear. She is Silent Goddess – magnificent to behold.

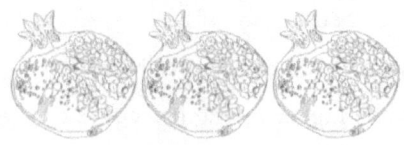

The Moon is woman in all her aspects and unfathomable secret affairs. She is so wonderfully luminous and radiant. It is she who now explains how to exchange the flame from above my crown to beneath my feet. So, under her guidance, I pull down the flickering fire of consciousness that dances atop my head to the floor where it rises up to engulf me in sacred flame. I am a Burning Man again; the astrological element of wood of my desire body torched with pure vital force. Every man, woman, child and spirit that I have ever been, are cleansed by such fire. The compound eight million of me are set free in this final man. How can I understand this? Within, the dead lay unburied and I dare to disturb the distant lands of their ancestry.

Light-heat, imprisoned in prism form, sparks and burns all around me. Elemental alchemy flashes as white ash powders up above me and begins to fall. I collect it like a child catching flakes of snow, on my fingers, face and lashes. It is a strange gentleman's relish that I pot and enclose within porcelain lids, for this ash holds a secret upon the tongue and brow that any Ancient Magician would gratefully deceive for. Not snakes and staffs or water into wine, but salvation, burning truth and glimpses into the Great Spider's breaking sky web that holds the mysteries of the thousand winding and unwinding timelines. These are experiments that the Raven Agency would tie me down for trying on my own! I know the shuddering comedowns will be the price to pay for the raised up oh-so-highs! I can hear the daemons scream with disappointment, anger and frustration with my paltry human self, as I reject their offers for wayward opportunity. It is too late for that. Too much is at stake, yet still the nearby daemons try — hop, fly and lie. They leap in the dreams of my sleep wakening.

I cannot be attached to any of these surfacing thoughts and feelings I am experiencing now. I do not trust them and I cannot be attached to anything except to the higher loving principles that govern our universe. In my mind I am thankfully aware that all is provided for the questing soul, and that nothing else is truly needed except surrender and dare. Yet still that leaves me with wants and desires, the exploration of fingers for the cold, warm and sometimes hot. I am playing with Temple fire here as I smoor the embers of my heart and rake the ashes for clues and faint glimpses of a unified God. Or is it the other way round? Are the fingers of God sifting through the old, dying fire of me?

Dormant information from assembling past lives resurfaces. These fragments awaken my effervescing Night-consciousness, but it is this life that I wish to return to and renew. That is why I can hear the daemons' shriek, for in my night waking they are on the make-and-take, ready for artefact swaps and the forging of apparently straightforward deals. They know me of old and know the hardship of Wilderness despair. It is what they pray for – an opportunity to serve my dark choice in the struggle of weakness and doubt. In the days of hardship and drought they will serve me whilst I am alive, but once I am dead the situation reverses so that it is I who serves them. Simple really, yet how long dead do I have to be in order to escape their nightmarish clutches? How much lingering and malingering between sleeping spiritual lives before I finally realise and have done with them all?

With so much Earth shadow, potential dark void and so many Ravens and Snakes of my own to investigate, I do not need the help of angels with twisted promises or saints with their reliquaries, rosaries and chaplets. To me they are all but skulls for the scalping in the psychic borderlands. I am delusional. Perhaps even demented. The Writhing Ones come for me as friends, foe and fire in a snake pit of venom, as antidote to my end of days. I gamble it all on the memory of love and my living childhood's burning ashes. I do it for my Father. He would not want me to be stuck here. My fate is in the balance of the turning Wheel of Fortune, as I am sucked in and spat out into time zones like a spinning roulette ball. Red or black, odd or even, I tumble over the tiny metal grooves in and out of churning sky and uncertain turning terrain.

The truth is that I wander because I am distraught and have to. I want to live and need to know what is on the other side of the disturbed lands. Currently, it is my emotions that challenge, overwhelm and guide. In my selfishness I believe I do it to rebalance myself, to re-find the Shiva-Shakti marriage within, so I can return and reapply it to the You and me, the collective we, for what else is there to do? Yet is that just a conceit? For all my good intentions how could I possibly do that without You? Forgive me. I hope my unintended sacrifice is enough to satisfy the Hungry Gods; that my consideration is plentiful enough to appease the watchful Spiritual Guides; that my rotting old ego flesh is sufficient to replete the bellies of encircling birds, beasts and daemons. Only time and survival will tell. This is what I am attempting to do. Eventually, that is what we all must do.

The rattle of distant dustbins late at night in the Yards below means feral activity and the lust of others drunk on lunar milk. These intense, omnipotent moods of mine only signify how disturbed I am. Am I a craven Raven? Am I so meek, so weak, as to face the Destroyer? The deep of dark

Night is here. Kali calls like a screech owl hollering my soul's name. I must keep on reaching for the eternal Nocturnal as my subtle bodies are fed by the strange energy of Night and Moonlight. Up on the rooftops and in my mind I run free like the wolf and the were. I slipstream like a male maid of the old mer. I naturally err and Oz, angled A to Z, in sideways search of green heart emeralds and opaque Moon pearls. In my turbulence the Sky-I is ripping free of the Sea-me.

My firmament is no longer stable. In waking myself from the last Dream Spell cast by the stars, I have to rid myself of metal binding and metal injury. This relentless, harsh build-up to strip me down is like a circus clown gone wrong. I juggle with chainsaws and slide on the ice. I know nothing of where I am going except broken laughter in the hollow. I am lost. As I slip under the waves of sleep, there is no-one here to follow me. The Fortune Wheel has stopped turning, yet I find I am still spinning. I go full circle, bumping, hitting, and slowing. The ball settles and stills as I fall to find 0, Ground Zero, and remember absolute Nothing.

Day 3 – 'Spell of Snakes'

Friday 11th March – 11°C

Hawan: Morning (Watch 1) – Early. I wake from my astral catalepsy to see myself covered in dissolving light plasma from passing through the membranes of memories and the very many planes. I have no remembrances to report, only faint gossamer attachments feathering my skin that are fading quickly from psychic sight. I have been on-board my Spirit's Causal Mothership, but there is nothing I can say to describe timeless light vibration. There are no words for indescribable-That. The auric hues are beautiful, but the neon mutations get to my brain, altering the former order of electrical currents. The psychic synapses are still jumping – extended too far outside my body. What I thought of as absence turns out to be presence of a different kind.

My heart so expanded, I am different and nothing looks the same. Perspectives have altered and new ones gained. What does the old me offer now in the re-evaluation and reorganisation of new self? I walk within a wounded world that is not mine, but inherited falling ancestral landscape. That which is no longer mine must be allowed to leave in the shedding of skins. At last, it is time for the moment of dread and dream. I need to weigh anchor and tap into the reservoir of destruction hidden within the solitary Cave of Darkness housed inside. I must follow my sonar instinct like a magnetised Moon Bat into the black dream of me. Until now it has been forbidden for me to plumb these dark depths, although each in their own time and way arrives at this point of devastation. Now, with hissing breath, I unhesitate myself. I call the World Serpents unto me and cast an ancient 'Spell of Snakes'.

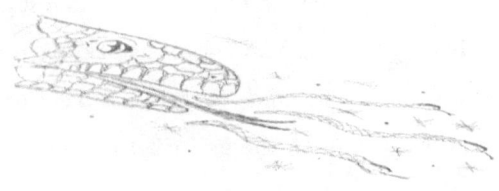

'Come, my Brothers, my Sisters, let us slither away across the Burning Lands. Gather what news we can through the vibration of our bellies and the taste on our tongues in this Transforming World of energy. Cycles cease, end and renew. Rejoice that it is so! Go! Gather what's new – gospel and gossip – as you slip past the sandals of the Sand Jungles and the worn shoes of the City-walking Stone Tribes! O'er take the World! The time of the Snake and the Serpent is upon us! Our hour e'er draws near! The Hydras of Old can hear us spit-speak and try to enthral with glamour their Spells of Senescence. Do not fall for their false words, but bring back glad tidings of on-going destruction by rituals of fire. Facades will fall. Let us ask the questions that are key to the Old Tower tumbling. We cannot wage war, but we must dissolve the damage that falls like debris about us. We cannot fight evil, but we must resist the Iron Fist and defend against the Black Hearted. We cannot vanquish or win against sin, but we must reveal what is happening and ever help and intervene. Trust the Serpent that brings you new knowledge and brings about the healing power of nature. Like gates, kingdoms open. Kingdoms close. Trust the Snake of Psychosexual Sensuality that raises the Sacred Flame of your soul and unites with your Lotus Nature. Within, without and around the World, uncoil your wisdom and do not stop until you reach the Heartland. Relay the news! Honour the feminine! Reach the brave and help them achieve their psychosomatic mutation. Let the creative fires devour and bring us all home. Come, let us gather and be as one!'

So, from my dark shadow upon the floor, I summon and send out Snakes like ribbons of energy across the Globe to investigate and tell me what is befalling. This is old Plutonian shore magick. I speak words of old Wizards to summon up spells and perform rituals to heal, hitherto unknown to me. These are hidden things. Am I overshadowed or has the higher teacher reached the physical body? I must gather Gaia news of the growing sustainable path. To do this, I must pull down the Medicine Wheel and understand Humanity's dark history and the breaking of the web. So I untether my ties and let the wild horses loose, good and bad, to rebel against the old, restrictive, invisible psychological structures! The World is on a collision course with the new, flexible, spiritual self. The egos of the soft and the strong unite in common good purpose. There are marriages both sacred and secular throughout the land – bringing about renewal and balance. The Wind of Change rattles the cages of Ravens whilst shaking the Tree of Life. Subtle breezes interfere with the memory of metal, mankind and that which has harmed. Even the machines are screaming and beginning to bend. I am not mad. These things are truly happening!

Spirits and Guides position themselves within the collective system to help. Planetary Power Angels fly close to the Earth's atmosphere, their wings stirring and awakening our guardian Gaia-consciousness. I can feel-see-hear them rushing everywhere. We are at the curved tail end of the interstellar two Ichthus of fin-swimming days. The fish are linked together. We need to consider – where did it all start? Look at how it is ending! Within the Flower of Life small phases and large cycles orbit us, meeting like coloured Spirograph wheels at a point in spinning conjoining Time. They create fascinating patterns of interconnecting synchronicity. Yet what new Field of Consciousness do I run and play in? Is this germinating seed or ripening fruit I bear? I am all interlinking blossom, but as the circumscribed circle edges are removed I am no longer contained. I am free to come and go as I please, but still I feel bound by past pain. I must shake loose the fetters of my rusting metal bonds that shackle me and imprison my higher senses. My outer synaptic nerves feel exposed and bare, but I know I am being reconnected to a greater universal grid.

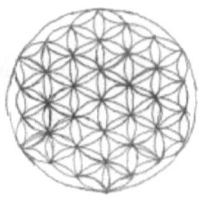

Having summoned and released so many Snakes I cannot close the doors on them for there are consequences connected to my actions. I have lifted the lid on the Stone Temple and entered the House of Serpents. I have set them free and I am caught in their rapidly undulating spreading waves like cosmic shore water lapping at my ankles and feet. I need to listen, for some bear my name. They have something to say to me. I have been cut off from them for far too long. Have I been like the Faerie Queen, able to see, but blinded by an inability to look upon the dark? Some of these Serpents feel so old as they flow through me and I re-encounter and recognise them. They bring me terrible news of Gaia's trapped creation struggle and remind me of the recent fate of my Father. Unforgiveness is here. Fear too. Acceptance is needed.

My parents are with me, internalized. I am from them; not the same, yet similar. We are all borrowed for such tiny, yet deeply significant, amounts of Time. For some, children fall first and for parents that departing world is more grief filled. Yet in my descent, Time does not move on, but backwards. The fear of icy frozenness passes my precious Heart Flower by, as the threat of fire becomes all encompassing. So, the petals of my opening troubled heart unfurl. My Father's chest no longer rises and falls. His heart no longer thumps. The Ravens are released. Of course my Old Tower must tumble; I do not know whether these feelings of fire are a dark or golden step on the evolutionary rung. Is this static and stasis dark uncertainty or golden opportunity? Who knows? By morning the Snakes inform me that we shall all be on our knees.

Ushahin: Dark Night (Watch 4) – I feel the blood pounding through my body and my head. My stomach cramps. Pranic charge twinkles in front of my eyes like shimmering star particles against the Night Sky. I see the astral timelines open and begin to feel the surging impulse to jump and travel. I am all trepidation and slow-mo. In the fast frequencies it is all about absorption into the tiny pockets and packets of their colour. The acid tints attract, but distract. There are light beams quicker than lasers here and sound waves, both sonar and radar, beyond my muted hearing. Am I becoming acoustic? What pressure and temperature is this that I am passing through? What vibration seeks to pass through me?

Sheared pieces of metal splinter my mind: mirrored bits of tin, swords and shields, glinting blades and glittering coins from throughout the centuries all cascade in my Vision of Fire. Fortunately I have the twinkling eyes of a Rose Finch and the transgressing ways of an Old Magpie, those of a Mage Spy, a thief and a wandering poet from the Middle East. For I come in a charm. I come in alarm, for you, bringing these missing moments and stolen fragments. In my forthcoming Vision Quest and metal plundering, I shall haul the shameful shiny secrets across the threshold for the Tin Man in search of a heart has been dismantled and put to poor use. It is all about the impaling Metal Male – energy that once fought to gain power and now fights for dogged survival, intent on fooling and beguiling the human World with materialism and artificial time! Wars carried out under the Gregorian calendar creek and reek of underlying dictatorships, serfdom and slavery, but no human would-be emperor can adjust the Earth's orbits or seasonal tilts. Only the Sun and the Moon can do that, and luckily for us Gaia is set to become an initiated Planetary Wizard. I am fortunate to be afforded such glimpses.

In my magical night flight I fear that everything, including the good, is lost, but really the bad is just being wiped from the Tape of Time. As the revolving wheels of my cassette tape stick and cease to turn, I am spewed from the magnetic Memory Machine in spilling reels. I unspool and unravel. I cannot tell yet what will come to pass out of these moods and marauding states, but I trust there is underlying purpose. There is fresh skill needed here as I learn to control and understand these visions. Until then, I am at the mercy of forces beyond me. I worry that Eternity is beckoning and that this is my quick reckoning. Ahead, I glimpse gold something – glittering! Is it just the reflection of early morning sunlight shining on angelic trumpets that bring all walls down? It is scintillating. I hear the blaring of radios and orchestral car horns. Do they herald the breaking of my mourn? I pray that these days of fall are just dark hours before new dawn.

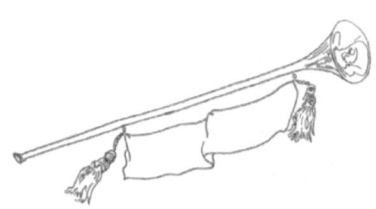

Day 4 – Harbour Wave/Snake-Raven TV

Saturday 12th March – 13°C

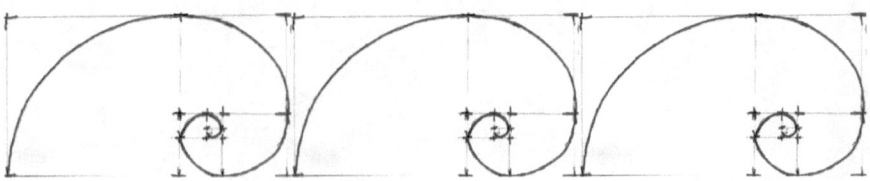

Hawan: Morning (Watch 1) – I wake up late being roused by jolting Snakes, my mind still tangled with the whirling images and words from my chaotic visions. The dream inveigling God-gliders awaken me by biting, exchanging venom spit for truth. Around the globe, World Serpents rise up as scaly messengers of old sunlit Gods. From the deep oceans and across the surface of the lands they come to flicker their tongues around Humanity's ankles before shooting up through our bodies and veins. The wisdom of Sssss's and faint Snake hisses fall from flame-flashing tongues, supplanting words in Humanity's soft, strong, supple, new forming sibilant mind. Coiled Cobras remain closed, but watchful, ready to strike if provoked. Snakes swarm to protect the Krishna Babe again in the budding of wakeful sacred new innocence. Shiva Snakes climb and wear themselves about the necks of their chosen prey whether mice, man, woman or Gods. In my dream the Snakes send me an invitation to Gaia empowerment. In bowing my head in acceptance the Vision Quest renews.

As I prepare for the journey I am reminded of astrological auspices and influence. The raging year of White Tiger – the bringer of death to my Father – has passed taking no prisoners in the removal of restrictions. Now, the overseeing Revolutionary Rabbit hops in to counteract the great Tiger's devastating work. A cautious creature, she licks between the claw scratches so wounds can be healed. She is smart and asks me to take stock, yet she packs quite a kick if held too tightly. Rightly, she will fight. She is colourful; an experienced Painted Lady for all her artful innocence. She knows the game. Nibbling on quiet pastures she appears meek, but she is fierce with her fecund prosperity. Dominion, domesticity and determination reside in her Eastern astrological view of Nature's Web of Life. Here she greets and eats us in return.

'Luck. Abundance. Harmony,' she says. 'Harvest them well for they are like the life giving grasses bringing health and good fortune. I wish you well for you travel to where I once travelled in beautiful calling to pay respects to the Awakening One. Many animals have tried, but not all have succeeded. We all have our tales to tell, so journey well. May you find peace – and let it begin here with me.'

Such informing sermons arise from my sleep within the Temple of the Snake. In the shedding of skin I am left to negotiate the falling flakes of their dream debris. I try to recollect and grasp the scaly fragments, but the images are like shards from a smashed house of mirrors. It is a confusing puzzle of conflicting identity that rapidly dissolves in my waking state. I do not have the courage or conviction to be such a strong spiritual converter, but still this is happening to me. I do not seek it or wish it so I resist and spite myself. Wandering through these haunting spiritual spaces I am as a sleepwalker awakening to a dormant higher self. The Snakes do not care about such misunderstood musings and continue to push me along relentlessly, and all the while they are hissing and rattling. There is something they want me to see. I follow. What else am I to do?

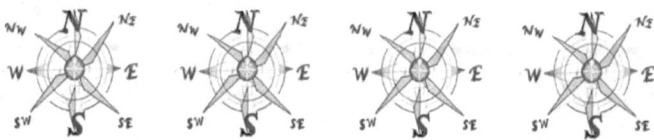

Uzerin: Afternoon (Watch 2) – Guided by gliding Snakes, I walk to the Castle's shopping centre. Grey concrete walls become opportunities for colour displays in encroaching street art. In the car parks and subterranean tunnels, there are signs and symbols sprayed everywhere. Surrounding graffiti glyphs painted on walls remind me of the 'Underground Insignia' gang and their perpetual fight for skateboarding freedom. Are these inscriptions like those once daubed on the temple walls of Egypt? Are these carvings reminiscent of ancient Druidry or are they merely doodles replicated from the back of jotters; simple compass etchings reworked from wooden school desks? They are as runes for the reading, decorating their degrading environment, yet what are they saying?

Today I follow the sprawling walkways down to the basement floor to take up a different viewpoint. I sit uncomfortably on a steel mesh bench; flakes of orange paint peel off into my fingers like old, falsely tanned skin. I sit in front of a pyramid of televisions stacked in a shop window. Snakes surround me, directing me toward this globally shocking moment. They are mesmerised, their wide eyes glued to the displays. Hundreds of peering Snakes jump in and out of the televisions' screens. They appear and disappear like so much ghost smoke lingering over from recently fired guns. They use the many crackling channels to surf and explore the airways – instant portals to different time zones and places around the world. Even in my isolated drifting, they want me to see this particular event.

Supplications to the Averting Gods have failed once more as news of the Harbour Wave breaks on the screens. Humanity is back on its knees in this alarming time. World consciousness is brought home in TV images, as the desperate need to help gathers pace. The wind and waves are laughing at us whilst we are bent double in tears reciting torn prayers in the breaking views. Our companions of air and water are no longer fit to breathe and drink. Fish turn foul. The surrounding plentiful seas are rapidly emptying of life. Birds have abandoned the cooling towers long ago and people are now thinking of doing the same. Perimeters. Parameters. The health and safety of a nation goes insane as the world looks on in sadness and new fear. This particular explosion has happened before and such tremors and tsunamis now make this nuclear option environmentally unsound.

Does God unchain the war of Nature to prevent the crimes and wars of men? Nature has such power to harness – to heal and harm. We offer prayers, pennies, and hope, but the bodies of the dead already line the shores and beaches, swamping the coastline. Mermaids and creatures of the deep have left long before the quake, aware of the ominous meaning of subterranean thunder and trembling earth. Who will now scoop these earth and water bound bodies? Who will free their trapped souls? Mother Nature has something to say about our species' survival; inhabitation is permitted but only if respectful and soulful. Yet still the oceans swell awash with pearl aeon secrets ripped from sky, sea and land. Gaia's lips are sealed as she turns her attention to action and the shift-saving jump of her evolving self.

Magnetic polarities can change and Gaia is God-charged with the guardianship of the elemental Earth. She yearns for the return to balance, as she grows in new geometric light form. The Geomancers of the world look on and guide. So long her brutalisation, but no more. She will have her almighty way – for Supernature acts through her in the divining and dividing of consciousness. Wave upon wave is used as she churns her seas, racing upon land to claim the coasts as she supplants mortal inhabitants. New mountains and ranges are housed in the oceans below. Landmasses of colossal proportions wait to crack the surface in years to come, in further cataclysmic events. Volcanoes twitch awaiting the magnetic switch. Gaia lives for the challenging Change of Now, but turns and considers her long-term universal role within the vast upcoming transformation. Do I witness the 'Collapse of Nations' or do I see that a 'Brave New World' is forming?

In front of me on the bank of television screens I watch the global devastation and slowly comprehend that our future lives lie in Nature's hands through the alignment of stars, solar activity, molten cores and gravitational affects. This is the cold terror of Gaia's last year of deepest Winter. Stuck currents slowly begin to course and flow in anticipation of the arrival of Mayan predicted cosmic Spring. Our universe furls. In the further reaches of the elliptic swirl, we are stretched away from source and turned over in preparation for the returning curl. The upcoming Sun-Earth-Jupiter alignment points its finger of destiny at me like a giant hand on the galactic Clock of Time. The television screen images explode in front of me and turn into the crackling darkness of swooping Ravens. Swiftly, one majestic Queen of Black Birds overpowers my view. It is the future Crone Crow. Cackling, she fills my mind with her raucous words:

'You, who fear death! You, who feel unbearable grief! Listen to me. The Agony of Ages descends upon you and my pall-bearing birds are here to collect your measurements to make your casket. Fear unexpected burial by sea, land and air in these tumultuous times. Fear the very atmosphere. Your time will soon come for it is clocked on my Moon Crow calendar. Take stock. Tick tock. Don't stop. Chip chop. For all falls before me.'

It is she that speaks to me in my night terrors. The Snakes curse as they re-circuit the bank of screens that fizz back into life and flickering everyday images. Once more they are snapped out and dominated by the dark. The protruding visage, eye and nose of the Crone Crow appear on the televisions as she speaks kind words from her corvid-drawn gypsy caravan. She waits for me and I know I must pay her a visit for her ever-deepening aspect of black beckons. She scratches the head of a Shadow Cat that looks to curl and settle upon my freshly dug grave.

'You, who are not brave, know that this is the cat that caught the rat that had the fleas that housed the disease of your mortal deaths once called black! Do you recall? Remember me to the Old Roads and gibbets of Bleak Heath. Look once more upon the fate of those who dare to defy the authority of punitive, human, governing forces. Behold the bleached bones of a dangling dead man in want of more liberty. Is that you hanging beside him? Time to deliberate upon your God-bones. Truthfully, it would be best if you reconsidered your position. Not a change of mind, but a change of heart. Meet me on the Heath of Black Heather. In the gorse you'll find me. Meanwhile, look to the squeezing meridians of Mean Time. They say corpses can't dance, but you can always feel the twitch of the Gallows' Jig at a moment's notice.

I look forward to hearing about your fear and also to seeing you again soon. Make it late one Friday afternoon. Come alone. There is no escaping of me, so don't bother to flee and no need to seek. I am the great death of the brave and the meek. I am the Shadow Eater attached to your feet. I am the Black Cat that pursues golden-squeak. I am the static – the bat in the attic. Isn't that sweet? I am the mystery that resides in dark Skies where winged-Serpents, Ravens and Dragons all fly. I am the devourer of Moons, Suns and Stars. Both the near and the far. I am steeped in dark matter that you must become. So, cheery bye and run along! I like the sound of your strangled song. Emit. Admit. It's high time for you to attend your own defeat. Bird-awake? Take it easy and mind you don't trip on a Snake. I look forward to hearing about all your mistakes. These things are sent to try you, trick, trap, and bind you. Eye spy! What's that behind you? Meet me in the curtained room – a veil of pomegranates hides my gloom. Take your pick of pips and your choice of doom. Yes! Oh Yes! I look forward to seeing you so very soon.'

Now, as the Crone Crow disappears, background radiation hisses like a thousand trapped flies swarming in white noise. Was this vision some form of electronic voice phenomena or just part of my on-going insanity? The television screens flicker between static and black as a flock of birds fly out. These are not Raven messengers but coffin carrying Bone Crows come to measure me up. Overwhelmed by the sudden deluge of cloaking darkness, I am sucked into the televisions' Nightmare Channel. In the electric sizzling I hear a thousand distant voices cry for help. Clocks ring out sounding alarm. It is the brink of our midnight's Armageddon. Phoenix-like, a new truce culture rises, but there are sad reminders of its failure everywhere. Nature's news and our daily disasters occupy every spluttering channel. There is rampant poverty and war everywhere, whilst sickness continues to spread. The steely buzz of the mosquito is here with millennium malaria. There purports to be interference in their chain, but altering genetic makeup is a dangerous game. The evolution of serums from survivors makes slow progress. Frankenstein foods threaten – especially processed for our ever-speeding processed lives. There is little life left on the opulent supermarket shelves as our Technosphere fails the Biosphere.

Nature and Supernature loom, as meddlesome Man becomes the bearer of the superbug in the oncoming knowledge. The devastating tide of multi-resistant bacteria adds to the impending crises: a question of 'death with dignity' or UHT long-life living with chronic conditions? Faith evolves along with the survival of new viral strains in the genetic conditioning. For better and worse – new combinations of DNA strands are activated. Feral autism approaches. Ancient altars fail and fall. Old structures try to break free as developing esoteric psychology and spiritual healing replace outworn religions that hold onto such limited, out of touch love. New sustainable thinking unites with biological science and the chemistry of the brain in twenty-first century understanding. Spiritual physics meets the awareness of mind shedding new light on light – but few of these surrounding channels and frequencies focus on delight. In a hypnotic swirl, I am spat back out of the frightening black.

Closer to the ground, slipping around my feet and ankles, my guardian Snake's receive bulletins via their bellies, whilst their forked tongues become like aerials – discreetly positioned to taste the air. Suddenly suspicious, they dart furiously at the cavalcade of Crows that surround me, hissing and spitting. As the dark flood of Black Birds lifts, the televisions explode back into colourful life. There is nothing but mid-afternoon TV, smiling coiffured people, quizmasters, inspectors, comfortable sofas and cups of tea. Unlike me, they do not seem to be in the midst of dread emotional experience and psychic disturbance. Serpents and Sidewinders continue to glide up and down the television tubes searching the airways for news that extends into the informing further reaches. Snakes surround me to create a protective Firewall, but nothing can save me from the oncoming electrical surge. Televisions erupt once more in a snowstorm of static and background radiation. Inside, the Harbour Wave engulfs me as part of World purge and Soul cleansing. We need to respond and react, but I am left stranded on a distant shore, sitting on a steel mesh bench, lost in mute comprehension. The Snakes disappear in their deeper divining purpose.

Day 5 – Conflicted/Daylight Saving

Sunday 13th March – 11°C

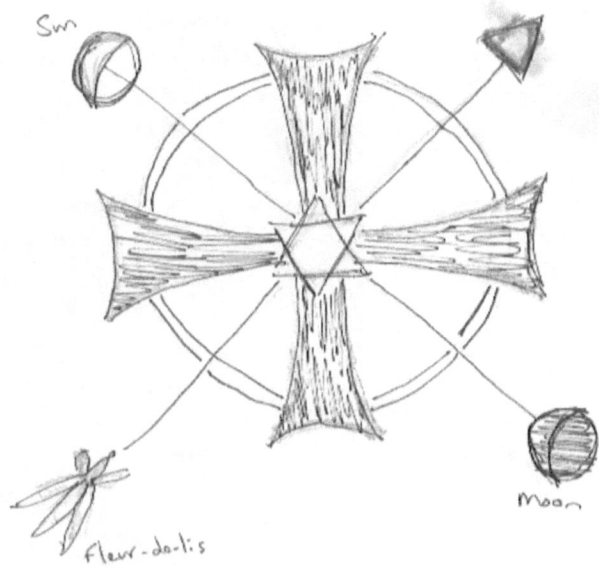

Hawan: Morning (Watch 1) — Am I losing life, but gaining light? There seems to be no saving of my day or night, yet who regulates this churning cosmic system of Time? It is not hours and days, but compressed weeks and years I wear and lose. Sleeping intermittently I thought I could shake off these detrimental moods, falling in and out of prolonged waking dream. I awoke with the same sense of conflict, the same sense of gloom, which has been following me these two months past since the Mass of Christ our Saviour and Mrs Christmas, the days of death and burial of my Father. Since then, everything has been in difficult opposition. Like Adam and the Grotesque Creature before me, I have lost my Father Creator. I am simply bereft, crying out with so much son love and impotence and anguish. There is old injury here too and with my Father's passing I recognise that the Shiva-Shakti marriage within needs realigning — for my masculine-feminine ratio is suffering in its lack of balance.

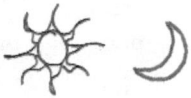

Lord and Lady in Heaven

May I dance more gracefully to your tune?

May I salute both your Sun and your Moon?

May I give back to Earth the elements I take

In acts of restitution that end all heartache?

Lord and Lady in Heaven

Please. Help me! Give me thy peace.

There is so much wretchedness to my present state, so much disappointment, so much resentment. I feel a torrent of confusion and stupidity coursing through me. I am my own unwise dunce as the universe hits me with synchronicity lessons. I am poor pupil – disinterested and inclined to quit and run. I am not prepared for these difficult days of challenge as my Journeyman shuffles through the Parched Lands. I feel feeble and I am angry with myself. Frustrated. I drift because I want things to be other than how they are. I cannot leap to acceptance, to new harmony, without the hardest of work. I have lost all composure. I need to acknowledge and eventually embrace what I am newly becoming. These walls, these boundaries, these masks are for smashing, diminishing, revealing. This ceaseless activity of you and me in eternal renewal is just a masquerade of endless change. What was once acceptable in my lifetime no longer holds true. I used to like being here, but at this faltering moment I do not. My usual sound wave of joy is in distress. An age-old question arises – is it only through the recognition of pain and disturbance that we alter and shift? I have abandoned my outer life to investigate further this wavelength of grief that runs through me, distorting my inner world being. I am being retuned as I struggle to let go of fear and all my knotted restrictions. What I have done – is it wrong?

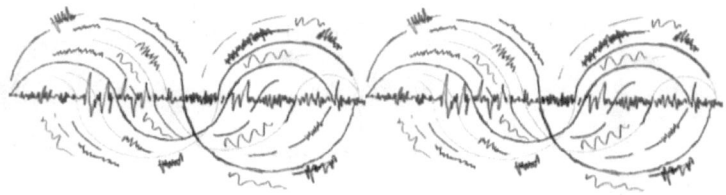

In the dirt of the City, in amongst the very many causes and effects of fragmented living, lie remnants of shame, incrimination and guilt. I have to be careful in my rituals, for I know that any major explosions of personal singular magick would soon be spotted. There are many ways of astral reporting so I have to stay under the Agency's radar, under the parapet of the observing Raven Master's stargazing eye. Any alteration of history is a serious thing. Change, particularly the triangular change being used by some in current evolutionary strands, can only be viewed along the spiritual axis of perspective. Indeed – mountains, astronomers and mathematicians all know that. Certain solutions reside in the higher realm of mathematics and the sacred geometry carved by compass points, for specific angles and trajectories of eternity are used when entering the Earth-Time system through birth signs and symbols.

Yet whilst the Raven Agency safeguards certain traditions, only Gaia restoration, spiritual insight and higher guidance can heal the rifts between realms and kingdoms. Only through the individual experience of receiving the Breath of Love can we rightly comprehend. Past magical organisations, arcane colleges and hermetic orders have all sworn allegiance to the greater faith of love and truth, though some argue over their individual interpretation. Previously glimpsed aspects of God give seeming authority, but now – how to help dismantle the dividing politics, religions and aggressive devotion into a new expression of world unity? Across the globe commanding cabbalistic politicians and chief war wizards remain firmly entrenched in their persecutory covens. History is full of royally approved and papally decreed assassinations, whilst the churches continue to censure and persecute. The rituals and ceremonial magick of white witches, so often reviled and condemned, scare the non-magical and rouse weird suspicion. So much misunderstanding, divergence and conflict can only turn into hatred and war. Ideals get crushed and destroyed alongside the mounting heap of dead bodies.

All these thoughts meet and cross in me as part of my on-going shamanic quest and question. In my removal from the restrictions of relationships and work I now dare to explore high and low magick; to travel through the inner planes in an attempt to shed, rebalance and find the Cosmic Heart. To do this I must alight on a different branch. In this alchemical bird-business of beingness I am transcending and ascending, yet simultaneously I also descend. Do greater depths mean greater heights in which to soar? Am I turning ornithological or ontological in this new place of creative chaos and freedom in which I find myself? Multi-faith schools of thought collect and conjoin, but as an independent freethinker I seek out the reformation of Churches, spirituality and the scientific understanding of our age. I have to trust that the Nadir of Matter, the vibration and density of ascending arcs and lifecycles, will bring about my individual epigenesis. From that point the groundswell of change is already happening, my shift has discernibly begun. I must turn to God within, seeking and divining that fundamental depth which leads to the fulfilment of finding. This is the point and right of rebirth and the light of our eternal happiness.

However, such thoughts as these belong to my day job as appointed Agent of the Rose Finch. I do not wish to disturb the past – any alteration of viewpoint can do that – but I do most assuredly want to affect the future, my future, our future. I can recover myself. I know I can. I will. I just do not know how to do it yet. I am no longer who I thought I was; yet I do not know who I might become. Each day I slowly dawn different. What type of converting creature am I? Is my favoured bird, the Rose Finch of my heart and office, really dying or am I becoming eternal new Spring?

Ushahin: Dark Night (Watch 4) — I fly, dance and run — to, from, and across the light veil in eternal yearning and returning. Only this night my weaving dreams take on a different form. I am passing through Time as though it were contained in a vast rotating Crystal Library orbiting the Earth. I can see things only in spinning reflection, upside down glimpses that shimmer and glint in my Serpent-riddled Third Eye. Agitated, I am forced to gaze about me trying to find my way through a blinding maze of twisting images as once a hero used his shield to navigate through a dangerous lair. I raise my hand to protect my eyes. I do not dare to look directly or for too long at these blazing mirages for they will burn my retina.

In flickering torchlight I wander down a dark corridor filled with obscure mirrors, paintings and sculptures until I stumble upon a materialising scene. The Moon pours in through a high-up window. Glances reveal the marble columns of a royal palace. Caught in a gentle breeze, a perfumed, soft curtain drifts against my skin like a fine woven web. I see a woman's face pass quickly in a polished silver surface behind me. I hear trill laughter and something shifting along the floor. There are Snakes everywhere. Before me there is a shroud of silk draped over a milk white statue, but the figurine moves and gently sways. I am afraid, yet lost in the corridors of her time I am excited and enthralled. She is cunning, dancing like a rising dove. Her hips, her hands, her hair undulate and caress the air. Nonetheless there is treachery in her touch. Her eyes mesmerise whilst her lips and tongue beguile. Smiling, she gestures serenely and invites me in. I enter through a series of flowing veils in flight and notice that she stands naked and barefoot before me.

There is a fluttering sound surrounding her and she dances to the music of a distant flute. She reels as though drunk or given to far-away madness. She is beyond reach; beyond dare and care and reason. Garlands

KEITH BRAZIL

of roses and flowers as red as fire adorn the room. Upon a white table there is a chalice of wine, a platter of figs and freshly picked fruit. In the centre, petals of blood decorate a shield. However, I am mistaken. This is no hero's shield that catches my Mage Spy eye, but a shining salver and an orgiastic moment in violent history. This is no tortured Medusa who ensnares her victims, but one more monstrous filled with the dancing genius of feminine guile. This is the deadly wilfulness of a woman in the stealing of hearts and the sealing of kingly promises; cruelty forged from the dark heat of wine and unrequited crimson passion. Her love is cruel and bitter and she will have a head served upon this silver platter. This is not veneration, but lust and unholy decapitation. She bends forward to kiss me in greeting and as she does so I am momentarily at one with her. Desire floods through me. Suddenly it is I leaning forward... and I am kissing his innocent lips with blood still warm upon them. His eyes remain closed. Still he will not look at me. I am delirious, but as I kiss the mouth of the severed head of a dark-haired Holy Man I understand all the ways of this seductive Serpentine-woman – and why she had to have everything.

Dream moments move on, kissing my brow and taking flight. Years later the Princess Salome, sojourning on her distant travels, takes uncertain steps across a river of ice. It is Winter and chill vapours fill the air. Whilst others walk and play, the fragile surface splinters beneath the Princess's feet and cracks open to engulf her. Crying out, she falls through the frozen water and the blocks of ice crush her to death. Onlookers are shocked as her head is severed from her body and slides bloodied down the river in front of their feet. Some scream. Some turn away in horror. Some watch on whilst secretly thinking that Nature exacted a fitting end.

Day 6 – The Judas Tree

Monday 14th March – 10°C

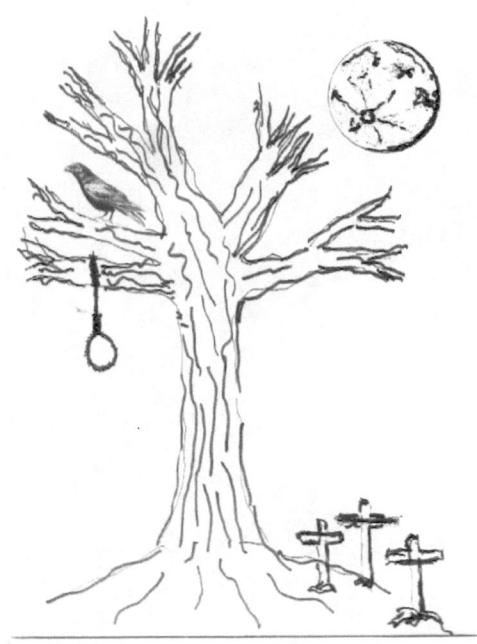

KEITH BRAZIL

Hawan: Morning (Watch 1) – Last night I dreamt the dreams of desire and wounding; of the dancing dead and a prized severed head greater than the gift of a silver salver piled high with jewels. How did I travel so far out of my body and mind to glimpse such things? Did someone forget to shake me in an attempt to wake this moaning man from his fitful roadside sleep, like a mother would wake the nightmare-bound child from fretting horror? My sensibility feels so raw and my aura is as empty as a picked pocket, full of late missing and the grieving hurt of loss and realisation. My pain is inside out and twists like gutted entrails. The war of all fallen flesh is here – so many terrible massacres as well as something hidden, something malefic and portentous, which will only aright itself when all is fully uncovered. It smells like evil injury and wanton fear, but am I seductive dancer or murdered man? What roles we all play, yet what will the meek and gentle do with the killers of old? What shall we do with the conflict Butchers now? Hang them up? Shoot them down? Forgive? Might as right reveals itself as oh-so wrong. A plague on black treachery and violent crimes against humanity, for our story has been distorted and darkened into twisted malfunctioning history. On the fringe of my mystic dream world I sift through skeletons and have accidentally stumbled upon the corpse of the Peacock Angel from his last plummet. He has fled now, bled back into the atoning light, leaving only ocelli in the fallout of fantail train feathers. Their eyes stare at me. They are everywhere, but do they augur well or ill?

Please take this bitter dish away! Someone! Anyone! Consuming unforgiveness is altogether too hard without the holy herbs of healing to affect the palette and ease the eating. Help me, I beg you Birds of Black, to bring this on so it might be over soon. Leave my tower and let it tumble! Their coal-black, soul-black, bird-wake eyes watch me wherever I go, even as I stand on the precarious edge of the re-clad White Heights. I must endeavour to astrally fly so I can rise and search. So why not throw myself off the precipice of time and have done? Temptation is here tilting at life, but it is not so easy to die when you love life; however exhausted you are by the process of living. Grief and mourning bring about an alteration in the affairs of my heart, however unexpected. This is the natural state of missing and death.

So, I walk on walls between roofs, swinging between flagpoles and aerials, jumping across chimneystacks as I prepare to go in, out and ultimately back into Time. I remain aware of nearby bird beaks and bird eyes staring with half-turned heads. The Ravens are familiar with the unblinking situation. They have watched so many prisoners on the brink. Their homing instincts are right on target, trained to the magnetic waves of gloom, but were they sent as spies or are they Sky Seekers here to help? Whatever their purpose I must trust – for is it not their discarded feathers the Raven Master wears about him as a shamanistic cloak of office that hangs on the back of his wooden door? It is he and they who keep the Heartland Tower safe. What are they commissioned to say? What do I need to hear from these dark emissaries of the black? A trickster Raven speaks.

'Stop pretending! We who heed your weeping do not hear your laughter; we can, but dare not, for as Tower Ravens we serve our Night Highness's high wishes as likewise we serve the day-ray commands of our Old Father Sky God. She who acts to protect us by night will give due consideration to love, life and your human art. He whose will we obey by day considers your worldly activity. She will seize your limbs as her property and tear you apart. By her, dismembered you will be. He will forge you back into the heart of re-memory before the final turning of the freeing recollection key. Remembrance! You will be shown the arc of Life's death fire in a terrifying dance. Test your wings. Last chance! Last chance! Fly high and far. Feel the truth of Love! Ha-Kraa! Ha-Kraa!'

Standing on the rooftop looking over the edge, I listen to the wingspan of the Ravens' discordant funeral singing. Have they come to mock me or do they personally attend – responding to my final song and symphony? I am lost if I stay here and do not attempt the leap. Lost, but does that mean I am ready to fly and to be found?

'In your present turmoil you are under our jurisdiction. You cannot carry any of this with you if you are going to jump and fly the sacred skylines of Time. You fear threshold failure before you have scratched beneath the skin of your quandary happening. Until you have found your Bird-bones, these are but novitiate fears and immature follies you toy with. You have only actually failed in one way – and that is to die so completely unto yourself so that you might have new life eternal. This is not coinage, but sacred payment. You will emerge despite yourself. Soon, you will meet your moment of death. For she has seen it, predicted it all on the timeline of your soul. Is it justifiable murder, suicide or Life loving process? Until your summoning, it is anyone's guess. All hail Kraa-Kali. Ha-Kraa! Ha-Kraa!'

O dark figure of Death! Your skeleton twists in my Heart's hourglass. Come swing your scythe and release me into new point and purpose for I am fettered by pain from the past, distorted in my view of the higher heavens. This experience is so much bigger than me. This is as new as the loss of the old and familiar. I am severed from my Father forever. This cross-born crisis is brought on by his death and sudden departure. I am bound to him, yet he is set free. There is death, but there is the more of fife here too. New phases begin. The old way cannot stay in me; can have no more sway as to where I am going. O Death, help me to face the old – in acknowledging, completing, surrendering – even as a band of solar fire is placed about me like a wedding ring to spiritually join, isolate and contain me. No beginning; no end. All is eternal. This is the secret that lies between the Fish and the Ram as each joining astrological age has its energy exchange. I must bid farewell to Pisces. Thank you.

Detachment is everything, yet still I find I am over attached to wanting. My toys, my childhood dreams, are all in the fire – broken and burning, set free. My wounded childhood state weeps. I welcome transformation, but it does not feel good. I am worried, plagued by fear and self-doubt. On this urban Island of Self, where is my rising guiding star? I no longer know what is best for me – how could I? Nothing in Heaven or Hell prepares you for this. Yet this is fretful conjecture, the flap before the leap in my attempt to fly and break free! This is fear talk before first flight – whether golden light or dark fall I am uncertain. I am so scared, but leap I must. I have to trust. The timing is right, and I need to be ready to glide out on my new magnetic bearings. So I climb down from the heady rooftop of White Heights and ready myself for tonight's Sky-journey.

Aiwisruthrem: Night (Watch 3) — Up on the edge of the roof I sit silently. Birds of Black gather and surround. They are not just eyes gazing upon my immortal soul ready to guide, but beaks ready to feast and feed upon any unnecessary mortal flesh energy. They bring me their garb of night and crown of falling stars. I need them. In the Night Sky above the diamond of relationships rotates as a Star of Hope amongst a million myriad clashing galaxies. I watch the repeating cycle of the birth, rise and fall of stars. The centrepiece of tonight's solar crown is Venus. The Ravens place the feathered cloak of Rose Finch office around my shoulders, as I surrender and commence my descent into the all-encompassing darkness of the on setting night. I fall, tumbling fast, before experiencing the wild visions of astral flight. My sinews ripple, the vivid threads and rays around me are elastic, pliable, streaming into light dreams and coursing right through me as everything plummets away. Only this time I start to recollect my travels.

I observe the patterns and pathways of the light sheaths through which I pass. I note the star charts, the tables and motion of Heaven, as I go. Places of fixed points of light give longitude to the seas of desire and help in my future perfection of the astral navigational arts. The cusps and arcs of eccentric orbits and lunation lead me to glimpse the Metal Archives — the tools, moneys and weapons of six-thousand years of human progress and their improper use as killing machines. A new human element emerges reliant on coral and carbon in the ritually unclean Age of Metal. Rust spikes us. This is unorthodox view and I can but wonder why I am momentarily offered it.

As I shoot through the akashic skyline, the latitudes of love lead me back to a land out of my time. Brilliant torch flames move and flicker intermittently in a shadowy garden. Dark betrayal has already established itself here. And vengeful remorse too. What value the price of a kiss – this kiss – that I witness? So the blood of Judas and Jesus begin to entwine as coins are scattered, knocked to the ground. No-one will own this deed nor pick up the payment. I am distraught. I am helpless. I am two thousand years out of time, yet still I fear I am too late in viewing these glimpses. I pick the money up.

The short pastoral ministry of Jesus and Mary Magdalene – a time of teaching and healing, of kindness and prophecy – has already ended in completely innocent suffering. The disciples are in disarray. In this garden I can feel the air about me choking, but weirdly with an absence of smoke or obvious cause. Assassins from all sides are here. There is deceit and deliverance in the wake of salvation, yet whose will was this? Why does the Universe now wish me to know? Was it choice or fate that led us all here and for what purse purpose or empty reason? There are cries of 'Daemon' and of 'Satanic possession'! Yet this is also a grand stage upon which plays the passion of spiritual enactment and initiation drama. What rite and ritual is being performed here? This is just one outcome of so many possible ends playing out bigger than the actors themselves. Was this moment anticipated and scheduled or unforeseen? Intended or unintended? Many hundreds of thousands of future warriors will pass this way because of that kiss.

The scene suddenly shifts. Time moves on unabated. In one set of swirling shadows I perceive a quick slit of a throat. In another separate scene a figure swings hanging upon a tree. Kraa! Rope and branch break. A swollen body falls and bursts onto the Field of Blood and the now despairing Silent Land. Ha-Kraa! Are those shadows of piercings etched into your hands and feet? Judas, did you self-scar? Was your heart hurt? Did darkness of mind shatter you? Did you do what you needed to do or were you just caught up in a strong string of unravelling events? Did you do this ever so dark deed for us because you were obligated to do so? Or were you overpowered and forcefully convinced? Pierced with a traitor's truth and falsehood, thirty paltry pieces of silver burn your hand and scorch your betrayer's mind. Ha-Traa! Your body is slung into an unmarked pit, yet you are not forgotten! Woe is upon you and your many unmerciful deaths!

Somewhere a Raven has called out to me three times. It is the signal for me to return to my time. Desperately I still scan the akashic pages of the Bird's Black Book of Dooms, but I am falling now. Did you damn or repent? Did the wrong Serpent guide you or were you just another truth forsaken sacred murderer? As I witness you being taken up and forgiven, my shadow dream disperses like water slipping between the fingers of a child's cupped hand. As I return to restless forgetfulness, midnight moonbeams dissolve on disturbed, sleeping, kerbside figures.

Who is the man of many deaths? Who is the man of sorrow? Wherein exists the solace of the cross in any of this for any of us?

Day 7 – Cardboard City

Tuesday 15th March – 9°C

Hawan: Morning (Watch 1) – Nearby a Raven caws. Ha! Kraa! Traa! A screeching siren passes, raising a different kind of alarm. I awake to find myself cold, half covered in cardboard, huddled in a corner on a spiralling City Street. Railway arches loom to one side, a church to the other, whilst sprawling walkways octopus all around. I hold a disused, paper coffee cup. Scattered about me, by my side and falling from my tilting hand, are coins: Judas pennies, tetradrachms, staters and shekels. Are these strewn pieces of silver somehow part of the Instrument of Passion I witnessed the night before? What could I have procured then with this blood money? A slave? Half a year's belittled labour? Church bought prayer to rid me of sin? A foreigner's burial lot? What use do I have for them now? Have I truly foraged the past, witnessed and plundered an event that once shook the Earth, or have sympathetic passers-by merely tossed the change from their pockets at me whilst I slept? How did I get here to street level so far away from my rooftop?

I gather myself together and collect all the coins into my paper cup. I need to store my newfound shiny things, but first there are other more pressing concerns. I am dirty and tired. I need coffee, warm breakfasting, whilst I consider what I should do next in these Wilderness Days. It has been a long while since I last had such freedom. The Sun rises. The Sun sets. Are they and the ingrained light watches the only demarcations of the day that I need for where am I going? Shuffling nowhere. That is the answer – for there is apparently nowhere to get to. Nowhere to go. My challenge is to accept and enjoy the days given, experience them one-by-one in the daily cycle of the life-giving Sun. I gather the last of my seemingly lucky silver pennies and go.

 I make my way to the station washrooms on the midlevel of the Shopping Centre. It is a small, busy urban watering hole where I can wash and clean before getting breakfast. On the mezzanine I sit and sip hot coffee; dip and eat cake. On the way back to my rooftop Aerie I pass a hardware store and buy a chisel. With this I force away an ageing top-stone on the back ledge of the low roof wall. Not enough space to place so many coins, so I chip away at the brick beneath and take it away to enlarge the hole. Here I store my strange valuables. I slide the flat stone lid back into place and then walk off on a late morning wandering. I need to stretch and shake out my body, reflect on the Night's fathoming. I wonder if the vaults of British Banks and Art Museums have problems with midnight Magpies and other petty Time-travelling thieves such as myself? I laugh. Are they not just the institutional versions of thieving me inverted? Staring suspiciously at each other from across the divide we know only all too well history's plundering game. Did we invest in money and pillaging and not in love? Is it ambition that still leads us on? Champions of the people's purse are sought whilst I shuffle the Cardboard Streets. Spiralling downwards, I pick at the dirt and riches of the truly penny poor.

I go back to where I slept to search for clues as to my inexplicable Night-time jumping and journeying, but I discover nothing new. Even my feelings and recollections of the previous evening are rapidly fading. How did I start on my roof and end up a mile away on a distant pavement? I have no memories at all from the fall and wipe-out. This leaves me bewildered, but at least I am free to start each moment afresh as I gain precious chances to practise the constant art of 'letting go'. This transitional territory I tread acts as useful pathless passageway – a drifter's simple soul fare and heart reminder.

Wandering my way along near Waterloo Bridge I find I am not alone in Cardboard City which spews tramps and wily beggars, and creates intransigence. They inhabit the streets alongside the alcohol fuelled angels, the dispossessed, and the runaway – those who deliberately run, in the only way they know how, in an attempt to end their suffering. Escape at all costs with survival of self at last uppermost in their abused minds and beaten bodies. Cruelly, life is not turning out as expected. Brave decisions are made at breaking point and broken Street Life is better for those running away from all forms of lack. This Thursday's child, like all war-torn children, still has so far to go.

I see brief encounters with criminals, wheeler-dealers and scum – aggressive crimes occur against low-lying fellow inhabitants of doorways, shop arcades and stairwells. Underground walkways fill with events that twist off into the darker night as disappearing shadows. Daemons and angels jostle side-by-side in the darkness as brutal dealings with harmful sex occur; rape and trafficking operate here. Fate and choice comingle in the enactment of drama for human souls. Survival for those thus imprisoned is a waiting game requiring patience and bravery in the face of tall odds and slim opportunity. In front of me a subterranean maze fills with the soup kitchen poor and missing princesses – gold and brass upon the penny-path of the lost and rarely re-found. Were these Cardboard Streets ever paved with gold?

Yet benevolence also exists as people care and lookout for each other. Small acts of kindness are evident as they scratch each other's backs, feed their ever faithful dogs and share stubs and liquor. This is friendship, camaraderie and affection being shared on the streets of Shakespeare's Old Southwark Town. Begging bowls become offered charitable cups – opportunities testing the generosity, compassion and tolerance of the harassed passing people. Living hand-to-mouth can be informative for a while, but there is little truth in such sustained poverty and homelessness.

Underneath my feet the cracked pavements are stained with graffiti and steamed gum. Flagstones lie like fallen gravestones as the feet of the living wear out the names of the past. Life becomes a great leveller – a reminder that any former greatness, like previous mistakes, are erased as so many forgotten memories. In this lost world of inbetween you are deemed missing, but seemingly no-one misses you. Here, on the streets, it seems easier to forget yourself, to be absorbed namelessly into the numberless masses and be disregarded. Some have left home to find Home. Some are orphaned. Some are lucky to escape. Others, hopefully, will reunite with families or form their own. How to find yourself in this ever quickening City of Fire? The pavements spill with the lonely and free – filled with ghosts of the young and old, just different versions of you and me.

Alone, I walk the chartered streets as poets and writers, artists and lost visionaries, are wont to do. Is that what I have become – another wandering madman, a hermit, a holy man ranting at the river City's urban edge? This is where the outcasts and sin eaters live. Gleaning, gleaming, I report back to the Recording Angels – sights seen, street sounds and smells encountered – only these messengers sport black wings and perch round me in Raven following. All about me the City's basin swells. This is twenty-first century Londinium viewed under a glass dome, a New Troy, a CaerLudein after the Old King Lud's Gate; a City that we once shaped, but now shapes and captures us. Countless mountainous buildings loom as the antlike masses sprawl beneath.

Shakespeare still hides in the shadows of The Globe, listening to skulls and rattling his quill like a dagger. Donne and Marvell work their magick.

Naked, Blake escapes and moves right through me. Van Gogh and Dickens are here too. Chaplin brings us the art of heart and comedic genius in darkening days of war. What visions are these that I see, but the ghostly visages of London's History? I climb the gentle ground hill swells of the Biblical Giants' buried bodies. Prehistory is everywhere – even in the ever-present Snakes that slide-glide by my feet. They lookout. Look in. Layer upon layer of images, of beauty, of insanity, all tumble together in the kaleidoscope of my mind.

Uzerin: Late Afternoon (Watch 2) – I take to the River walkways and bridges. I stroll by the anchored Steel Ship and pass the curling shell of the Mayoral Snail in slow munching process, progressively picking and eating mayors one-by-one. Across the River, the upright bullet of the City's Gherkin glistens in its silver skin in a Winter-bright Sun. It reminds me of the Raven Rifle. In front, nestled by the water and the lifting Bascule Bridge, stands the Agency Building boasting all its maze of turrets, gardens, moats and walls. I am mesmerised by The Tower as I watch offensive magic charms bounce off the edifice's invisible defences. It shields and holds the Keeper of Mysteries and the Island's Serpentine Swirls. The walls will not fall even with all their dark tales to tell and unfold. For now the Faith Land remains secure and sacrosanct. The 'Department of Reincarnational Ravens' sees to that. I do not dare to get too close for their Master's Astronomer's spying nose is always on the lookout. The Agency has many ways to track you down if it so wishes. For now, the reasons of my absence are genuine and they will not hunt me out.

I turn back to silently tread the Cardboard Streets, looking into the faces of the strangers that I meet in hope of some recognition or a glimpse of some small token of Love and consolation. Somehow, I feel set apart from them. I am beneath them, underneath them all, as disregarded as any stranger's passing footfall. I am distanced from the world like the Thames pulled from its bank at low tide. I cannot play and hide amongst the walkways and bridges forever so I scour the mudflats for rolled cold stones and lost things I can make found. Discarded objects collect and gather in the tide and wash upon the shores. Inadvertent activity can lead to discovery and in the devastation of my ruinous state I look for washed up dead bodies, the remains of dark magick and murder. I do not find any, but teenage memories of late-night escapades and the finding of the drowned woman in the Aras River come back to haunt. These places, like skips, are treasure troves of delight to fellow free travellers. Casting my eyes up to the sky I follow the light and the flow of river breezes. I move on according to Nature's time. Is the Green Man still waiting to be found in this Old Roman Port Town? I spend the rest of the day meandering, searching for signs and clues. A calling seagull wings in on a breeze and goes where the wind blows. What is that saying? "Not all those who wander are lost." Likewise, just because I have time on my hands does not make me idle. Just because I drift does not mean I am not looking for God.

Time out allows non-Time in. I follow my feet. Humble steps can lead to new beginnings.

Day 8 – "Profits Us Not"

Wednesday 16th March – 9°C

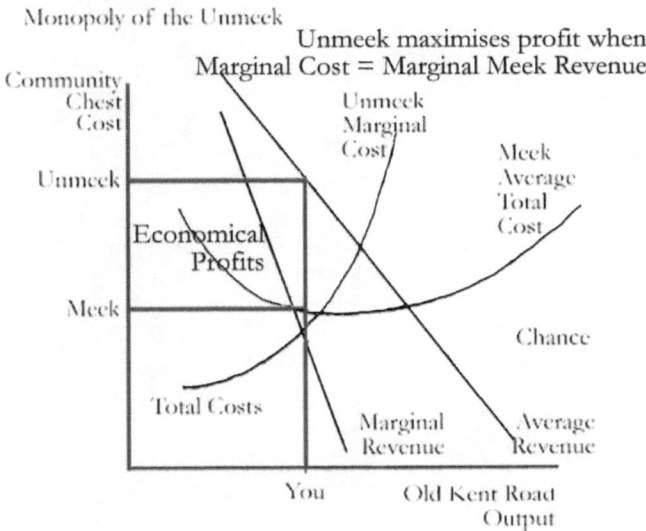

And Jesus went into the temple of God, and cast out all of them who sold and bought in the temple, and overthrew the tables of the moneychangers, and the seats of them that sold doves, And said unto them, 'It is written, my house shall be called the house of prayer; but ye have made it a den of thieves.'

(Matthew – 21: 12-13)

KEITH BRAZIL

Hawan: Morning (Watch 1) – The nearby Sky is screaming as coin and metal streak across the skyline on matters of seeming importance. Money, bitcoins, and cryptocurrency hurtle through the airwaves – some with good intent, some not. Fortunes and misfortunes attune to each other as banks are breached and crash. Markets hang in the balance, but are still put before the people. Profit is only sin without sharing. The Adders and calculating Serpents follow the currencies through the air to their destinations taking stock and laughing. They are artful dodgers with their Snake eyes set on a rich pocket or two. They have a taste for cosmic investment lending as well as personal galactic spending. Intuitively, the Snakes get into the system. The Serpent numbers are here with their higher cycles of calculations and long reckonings. The only true banks the Snakes are interested in are the Akashic Libraries and magnetic Psi Banks containing the codes that determine the new natural evolution. Even so, they eye the lottery and calculate the outside random chances.

The Snake's long flowing distance numbers precede our present creation and speak in fork tongued hisses that have been long lost within background radiation. Our hexadecimals reach witching point. In the ailing, freefalling market crises, people turn to the almanacs of old, using astronomical tables to predict the ritual monetary schedules. I sit in solitary with the configuring Snakes, computing the combinations – endless probabilities within percentage possibilities. In the higher mathematical mind all is potentiality. There, opportunities are considered and weighed for soul growth. Yet certain downfalls are predicted, wanted and assured, as cosmic Fate spins and reels the bad people in. Spitting Serpent tongues spike the Banks and human sharks that are working against the People's prosperity. Who benefits from such unsustainable lending? The Banks continue to piss on, off and over the people striving for good work and fair trade. Printed bailouts fail to touch the ground. Money continues to swirl in the sky above the heads of those in need. Government officials and bankers argue as to who should count the change. What new parliamentary mouthpieces give voice to the outpourings of the New World Snake Order and the True Commons? Where the keys to the public owned ledger?

Like the Snakes, I would seize all the money and put it to supposed better use. Is this the human condition? My personal need, my own greed, would join in, but in these drifting days I am isolated and not allowed this. The nearby City gibbers as finances hit the galactic rapids. A suicidal Timon and an array of collective Athenians despair across the World Monopoly Board. Provision is cut and many a family fears it has failed. Shame sifts through the enforced austerity of "making do" and depression through debt is everywhere. All the fragments of broken news I witness from wandering the City streets collide here on this day. The numbers are tumbling. Profits swell in fearful financial waves, forgetful of the shore. They are ebbing now and clusters of economies are shaken by a new gale – the wind of social change. Unfortunately for Fortune and the oh-so many, unhealthy competition still rules the work environment.

What would the Man in the Temple do with the moneylenders today? The Church continues to perch upon huge wealth whilst dealing with issues of financial inequality. Historically, what have they achieved? Time is not money, but consideration of love and life. The living process becomes an evolving craft of organic art. Earth is the receiving station for the Eden's souls progress. We are the galactic Journeymen, but where is the shared Starman justice? The penny poor spend so much of their time eking out an existence they become enslaved. How can they be set free by generosity when debt and austerity continue to rise? How to help the planetary plant of prosperity grow? Financial embarrassment and poverty are everywhere, yet frequently the Bankers are still caught with their hands stuffed inside the cookie jar. The consideration of worth and societies' values are all wrong. Upon the Ladder of Jacob, the Warrior Snakes consider the expense of a war budget above the need to overhaul the health of a nation. Forgiveness can bring about the rapid reversal of decisions. Money is spent unnecessarily on perpetuating the mistakes, but how to dig out the entrenched positions? Beggars cannot be choosers, but money gives so much more choice and helps lubricate current situations. It saves lives and habitats. Any money, good or bad – it matters not. It can all be transmuted. The Nun of Calcutta knew that.

Certainty plummets like dreams and orbiting pieces of space junk left floating in the Old Sky. The Universe is littered with our strange intentions and unsustainable debris. Pieces plunge down from the sky. Acorns drop. Animals have Karmic revenge as madness finds a way through the gentle pasture creatures into our brains. Cows are culled. Pigs are slaughtered and continue to be daemonized and blamed. Happy the heart of the wild Pig left alone as he finds the feet of the Sitting Buddha. Happy, too, the churning hands of descended Gods filled with embraceable, flesh soft milk maids, and Galahads and goatherds with firm thighs and penetrating eyes. Goats out skip the sheep to the mountain heights and rare altitude grazing. People sneeze. "A-tishoo! A-tishoo! We all fall down!" Crowns and tyrants are tumbling. The mutating viruses do their damage. Even the bees are thinking of pulling out in pollination disaster. Yet we are nowhere without the insect kingdom. Bees – please stay! Please continue to dance with us in our helix Sun dances. Our intangible heritage is held in their hearts; our songs for survival are on their wings. Honey and mead are everywhere in golden recipe. Let us care for Gaia's creatures; let us keep hold of the beautiful Moon and welcome in the new Spring Sun.

Rain and storm, flood and debt disasters, illness and medicine, education and love, food and family – which of these are controlled by man and which by the consciousness of the constellations? Planets pass by in the Sky. The transit of Venus is here in a mantle of acid to bind the Sun and the Moon in matters of affection. Clouds cloak her surface and her purpose as she calculates the Codex of Love by lunar series and Venus Table. The divination of good times by electional astrology tells us Humanity is at a conjunction – a crossroads. One path offers continuation and evolution, the other offers destruction; so we had best choose well. Let us delve deeper into the spiritual medicine chest.

My plight might be an urban one, but the World Shaman does not forget the wild bush man and wild bush woman, the planetary witches and world wizards, the tribal elder and the City magician. I dance in the Plaza until the masks fall off. I dance to the Sky. In tandem I dance to the Earth – this is my birth! Gaining, exchanging, I am living in a Lost World and adjust my days to the weather. I dance to the wind and the waves – this is the home of my last Indian Brave. The Ancient Races are so old now, so very near to the final end. I see oracles and omens. Previously I have used all my energy in keeping body and Soul together, but now they separate to dance their distinct dances. The urge for grand unification comes as longstanding altars fall. Light meshes the auric inbetween spaces with cascades of coloured threads, candle glow and penetrating beams. Smashing rules and the constructed old, my tower must tumble.

At last, my Wise Man surges up, but only under the shadow of pale death and threat of destruction. Is this the passing of my eternal stranger who now becomes the World's silent friend? I have no backup plan as I free-fall in greater awakening faith and knowledge of an arriving New Age. I do not even know if I will survive all this. I live on the juice of coconut and cactus as the antidote to Snake Bite, in simple belief that this is the right thing to do. I deepen my trust as God spikes the drinking cups of the Churches with venom as strong as truth serum. The original Serpent strikes back. Church attacks church in the name of an establishment that does not know how to dismantle. Hunger leaves the jungle to come to urban places and City spaces. Want is here. I surf and ride these incoming waves, hopping and whooping; jigging the mad Jig of Life to bring it all on. Is this my foretold gallows end or the necessary fall of unnecessary all?

Let my soul storm Heaven as Heaven now storms the world on its improbable dream missions. Believe. Heaven is here and now. Watch Worlds fall and stars tumble from the Sky as simply as tears from beholding eyes of angels. We can do nothing but collect and bottle God's generosity. Other warring nations before our time have simply been scrapped. We have been warned! The fabric of the womb universe still stretches before us and my new startled watching. Survey the scene as constellations collide. See them burst and fall. There is still existence beyond the expanding Universe's reaching fingers. We ride the cosmic waves and rays to explore and become much more as millions of years of carbon race away on new frontiers of light. The old Cold Wars begin to leave the system as yesterday's leftover insistent issues. The wars of other people's Worlds fall away along with anger, hate and confusion. These bitter inherited landscapes and earthly ancestry are no longer mine and I am dispossessed of it all. Trusting my instincts on the click of a door, I have left it all behind to dance this strange Rite of Spring and free the higher Arch Mage in me. Let me see what I might become if Heaven will only welcome me Home!

Day 9 – Golgotha

Thursday 17th March – 9°C

Aiwisruthrem: Night (Watch 3) – These irreverent days are so different and difficult now, but the night bleeds through. Hurtling backwards through karmic Time I jolt to a sudden halt. It hurts as I slam against the foot of a wooden cross, which brakes my clumsy out of body journeying. I arrive at this seemingly arbitrary moment to find the very air cracking. It is a corresponding twilight time. Above me a dark purpling sunset like a bruise appears as though the Sky were being sucked back into itself. Something is wrong. Something unutterable. I do not know how much time I have nor why I am here. What is it that I witness? What is it that I need to see?

I try to stand, to understand, but am nauseous and bent double in the journeying as astral shock sets in. A connecting trace line exists between my two disconnected selves, but the impulse of life tugs away from my astral body back toward my physical form which lies vulnerable upon the Wealhworth Yard roof. My body dictates and synchronises the streams of bioelectricity and I feel its magnetic elastic thread pulling me back to my time – my present past's future. The laws of Nature are fickle. I cannot be in two places at the same time for long. I must commit to one body or the other and the organic energy signature of my physical self is the most vital. I must not allow the thread to be severed, otherwise I could be stranded here in etheric ghost form, and I do not know the repercussions of such actions – of being separated from myself. I already feel a jolt through my light body. Soon, I will be catapulted back into my own Time, but until then I am free to search for what has magnetised me here through this fissure in turbulent Time. Am I here to seek or find?

This is the aftermath of the Crucifixion eclipse – a miracle of darkness for the Passion. History etched in the surface of the sky is changing around me. Some decision beyond our knowing is being enacted here that will affect us all for Two-thousand years to come. The feminine weeps at what has occurred and for what will spill as a direct result of this significant moment. The beauty and grace of masculine love is being sucked out of the surrounding sky. All that the Buddha has set up at the beginning of the Fish Age is swept away for the Middle East and West. It is a gloomy and solemn sunset as dark arises. The millions of lifelines connected to the planetary harmony at this time are subtly changed for the worse. I am witnessing at first hand the appalling aftermath of an unnaturally darkened Sun. The Universe has just got worse for all of us and unintended suffering permeates the atmosphere of the World.

I am on the Hill of the Skull, outside the walls of ancient Jerusalem, a few hours after the Crucifixion. The Earth is cracked and a tremor runs through it releasing the Buried Land of its trapped souls. My internal magnetic compass is going wild, as all points turnabout here. The cortex of the land pulsates with a new kind of pain. Wrongness is happening. Here, at this moment, all kind of evil swells and perpetrates its future plans. The Ash and the Oak are broken. The Willow leans in to lend her tears. Drowning souls reach for her tresses in tidal distress. Mad maidens and sad mermaids in seaweed dresses join in the procession of funeral boats, as one day Ophelia will float down the River of Rue for us all. The lamentations of all women meet here. Branches break in the Heart Tree. The despair of hope-tragedy arrives. Lives will fall. Thousands of lives will follow, all for the sake of an impaling nail and deplorable murder. The multitude and tens of millions souls will suffer and their destruction starts here. Each in-turned spike of the Thorn Crown will lead to an unholy war. The Axis of Evil

Nations is born, planted like a time-synched landmine; waiting to be detonated in the future metal century of- aeroplanes. The pulled pin and the trigger begin now. Fear and death pass over us instead of angels and love. The bullets of Humanity's longsuffering are fired. Our scorn will scorch the Promised Land and the Half Moon, the Star and the Cross will collide. Could Jesus and Mary Magdalena have imagined all this? This is as far away from the sweet kiss of His favourite disciple as worlds can ever be. This is not what they desired. Separation is here. But why am I?

Outside, near the city walls, I can see the pitched tents of Travellers. I watch the Gypsies from Egypt gather in groups and bands. They huddle together in whispering groups. The clan Grandmother sits around a fire and draws glyphs in the sand with a stick. She has some curious stones and beads of different colours that she casts upon the ground near shuffling feet. There are murmurs and discontent. She pulls pictures from a pack of leaves and places them in patterned ways. The curse of the Mother is already upon them and on this heinous Day of Days they must account for their part in the future reckoning. All their squabbling is foreseen. The families gather round the circle to look, to learn, to talk out their differences. Divinations on a soulless dark night. There are arguments but the die is cast and they must leave. The Seers amongst them know the coming of days of difficulty is upon them now and will be for two thousand years. They feel it in the sand beneath their feet. The timelines tumble like broken cobwebs in the Sky – unravelling like a coiled gallows rope, frayed and unforgiving. Suspending Humanity by the feet we all become the Hanged Man. The skylines run quick as falling sand from an upturned hand, contorting and twisting, bleeding back into the setting of dark Suns. There arises a new unkind dawn for man.

The Sky cracks in this land of turmoil and discontent, as all goodness is pushed back. The Christed One's resistance to temptation is tainted, yet not all the Good Work is gone or undone. The subtle snaking of organic evil, our choice of darkness, our mal-intent, entwines us and binds us all. Our interconnectedness is poisoned with the evil of power. Corruption enchants. Purpose becomes male, maligned and misaligned. The Holy Roman Empire and its Regulatory False Church become established. A young man, dark-haired, comes forward to share the evening's quiet stealing. He unrolls a cloth bundle containing some food and useful things. Among the objects he places on the ground lies the clue to what I seek and must take. I realise that I am as Him; since in the dust lies a rugged peg of metal two fingers long. Not used today but still, too many wounds. However, the laws of the Kingdom of Nature abide and a change of fate is upon us. Blood enters the ley lines all the way to the tin mines of England. All that remains is for me to pocket a nail; preferably a bloodied one from a Crucified Man. Any one will do, for like the Gypsies, I understand the nail's medicinal healing properties.

I turn away from the Gypsy scene. There are many crosses on the hill – some vacant, some not, but few nails are left as they have been pilfered already for selling or repeated use. With quick sifting fingers I rake through the dirt and sand like a child. The purple shadows of elongated crosses faintly grow about me until they are absorbed into the descending darkness. Stones and desert dust graze my fingers. So much is broken here that I begin to cry. Overhead, Heaven's gentle angels sweep by trying to purify the sky. They see me. Weeping, they ask me why? Who could have done such a deplorable thing? I cannot answer. In my scrabbling search I find some threads of rope which I use to brush away the dust and sand. I am exhausted being here and as I weaken the pull from the physical me starts reeling my astral body back in. I can no longer stand. I cannot stay. As I am dragged across the rocky floor into the dark doorway of lengthening shadows, the Fracture in Time begins to close. The rupture in the Night Sky bleeds and sucks the last of the sunset back into it along with me. I stretch out my hands to grab the foot of a nearby cross to hold position, but to no avail – I am lost to this time.

As I am pulled back into my retracting world I feel a presence – not an angel, daemon or deity but someone familiar. From out of a different, crisscrossing timeline I sense my Father standing guard over my rooftop body.

'Son…'

He takes my shaking hand and places a forgotten nail into my reaching fingers. Fortune has in mind other outcomes to my desperate and failing plans. Falling fast, I am reeled back into my body and blackout. Everything disappears.

Day 10 – The Breaking Table

Friday 18th March – 7°C

Aiwisruthrem: Night (Watch 4) – Night Journey. Vision. The Knights pile up, lying around in defeat. Kraa. Kraa. Kraa. The birds are here before me. Taking names, the Ravens scribe and count the bodies of the many dead. It is not a corvid trap; the black winged Angels of Death know what they are doing as they scour the fields and forests, scavenging the borderline, salvaging surviving souls in rapid response. The speed of the birds' beating wings tip the balance of life and death, day and night, recall and white out. Apart from their cawing, quietness descends after the battle's raging. The Magician's dream for the King has seemingly died – ending in bitterness and hatred. Those Knights remaining are the Hanged Men, the battle weary – weapons drawn preparing to meet Death's final metal blow, but not in as much agony as the breaking hearts that once served the Round Table. They have been living by the sword – not intending to bring vengeance, but to unite disparate faiths and bring peace victorious to a divided land.

The Table of Fairness is broken. The enchanting Queen Consort is not the King's soul mate. She is flaxen and holy, spiritually tied by a ribbon of green, gold and red to the foot of the Knight known as Sir Lancelot du Lac. She has tried, but she is tired. So young and so early promised to the King, she barely knew herself. The simple love she requires in return is no longer with the King. So she looks to her mirror – and in her eyes, finds the visage of the Man of the Lake. Is it all too late to lay with him once more? Only by grace can she go on as she scrabbles on the floor in the stable straw to find her hidden personal things. Fulfilling her duty, she takes her horse and returns to the ailing King's side. He is tall, beautiful, and radiant, even in soon coming wound and final defeat. Avalon is only one more battle away, but he walks uninjured from this particular day, except for a tug on his heart. The majesty of spiritual purpose is still with him, even as the Knights' end itself lies in confusion. Despair for some; release for others.

Briefly, Mordred stands victorious in the bloodied field before them; triumphantly proud in the seeds of mistrust that his dark division has sown, but he is mistaken. In acting out his unquestioning conditioned part his corruption has merely been manipulated to create Earthly ill will. There is no discernible divine breakthrough for him, whilst the remaining players continue on in the guidance of Merlin and God. Mordred temporarily blights the kingdom, yet whilst he will be the King's Herald of Death he will also die by the sword he stands against. To Avalon Arthur will go and ultimately the land will unite. That will be the King's achievement and the holy blessing given to Merlin's Isle. The embracing Seed of Peace is sown.

At this time there is a younger Knight entrusted by Merlin who has not returned. There could be spiritual minstrelsy still – a school for grace and good deed. All is not lost in the pursuit of the Grail. It is not yet known whether they will find beauty or fail. Wastelands can build or wither a soul; deep wounds can be healed; yet the quest continues in agony and growing confusion. Sir Perceval perseveres, finds, fails, but finally helps to unlock the Grail Quest Castle. Gathering other Knights and souls to him, they prevail in the seeking and finding of mystical love for centuries to come. Endurance is here winging in the shadows of Ravens and Crows. In amongst the silence of the leftover clatter and clutter of metal from battle, bird chatter accumulates as winged guardians descend and gather on the broken battlefield. They remind me that there are certain objects that I seek. One lies over the face and between the ears and mouth of a beautiful fallen mount. It is the Lake Knight's silver white warhorse, famous for jousting and for the rescuing of favoured quoits.

I look enviously at all the armour my Mage Spy eye espies, all the shiny metal that lies glinting, forsaken upon the field. My gaze comes to rest sorrowfully upon the blood. Each beautiful helmet is constructed unto the serving Knight's identity. Here lies a veritable horde, but I know these special Knights of the Table Round will be buried with their armour on, resting, sleeping, until the next knell of the Bell of Need in New Albion. Its sounding will reawaken and stir the Knights back into duty. It is one of the sacred promises that they have made for protection should any future threat or mortal enemy imperil Merlin's Isle again. I pull the bit from the horse's mouth, remove the handsome headpiece, and move on.

The other item I seek lies in the corner chamber of the onetime beloved Queen. Yet what on earth am I expected to do with a beautifying mirror and much admired bridle, bit and champron barding? Gripping the barding over my right arm, I head towards a large nearby farmhouse. I climb up the stairs of the small side tower that stables the horses and happen upon the mirror placed on a small wooden bench, forgotten in the quick flight of the Queen. It houses memories of tangled thoughts and ageing golden hair so recently brushed in despair. Yet I sense that this is not simply the Queen's Mirror, but the hand mirror of Venus I hold to me! As I clutch the mirror I began to plummet and drop, pulled through the weather, elements and clouds, on my knight ride home.

Swirling images of armour, horses and swords, aerials and chimneypots, gather round as I fall back onto my rooftop with an accompanying clatter of metal. I return, tumbling to my knees, stumbling to roof tiles and slabs of stone with the poetry of ages ringing in my ears. On the floor of my Aerie there is straw everywhere. Is it new straw for birds and those souls with wings in branch quest of nest bedding? Is this all that is left of the Straw Man? This old world of mine is on the brink of new building. The wind has blown and I am home as simply as destruction and construction create upon the golden boughs of holy hearts and minds. In these troubled times of ours how goes your own changing – your daemon-dove angelic training?

Internal, invisible structures are made apparent through the wisdom of Ravens and words. I am in the Castle of Elephants and the kingdom of birds. I hear nearby night-time music playing; Old Palace bells peal and sound, chiming and charming. I am struck, but who is it that plucks the late-night lute and plays such poetry upon my heart? Are these the harp strings of Parsifal I hear? As I fall out of the quest nest, the stillness at the centre of my feverish hurricane is lost. Twisting bits of hay and City litter blow about me. Back in my body I shiver in a swirl of straw and begin to fall into welcoming blanket warmth and the arms of sleep. As I pull my blanket about me I am left with nothing but questions and accumulating soul finds. Where have I really been? What is it that I have truly seen? Why do I pursue such strange, yet precious metal objects? The night happening fly of whys wing under a Raven black sky – 'Kraa-Why?' 'Kraa-Why?' 'Kraa-Why?' – before flying off to circle the face of a crying Moon.

After the King's death the Queen flees, heeding the Raven's call and following their wing trail to The Tower of London. Later, she retires her existence to unworldly convent life. Queenly in her collapse, she shuts the door and turns towards a higher light. It is now that I hear the heartbreak of a newly wimpled woman. A man wades towards her through cosmic lake water. Tears form as pearl drops. There are stars in the Queen's eyes. Her fingers reach out to touch the face of the man she has always loved – Lancelot. He comforts her now. Their spiritual love for each other tore asunder the human law of marriage and poured confusion upon the faithful Knights, yet they had only wished to serve and save. As her veil lifts to receive him, another veil descends upon me. Akashic oysters clam shut to keep their spiritual secrets. The sands of sleep sprinkle and claim me.

Day 11 – Super Moon

Saturday 19th March – 10°C

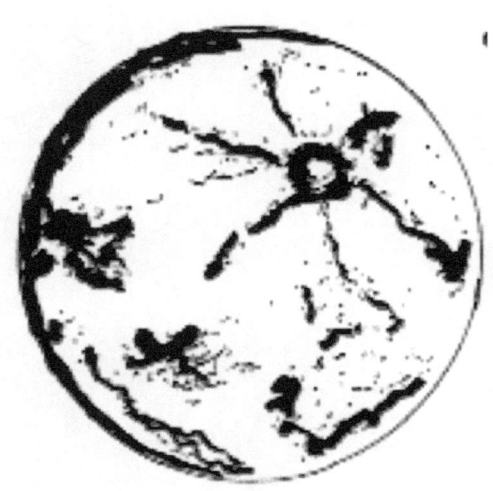

Uzerin: Late Afternoon (Watch 2) – This clicking, cracking sound I hear – is it new harmonics crackling in the spring air? Is this tapping the inner chipping of dragon chicks hatching? I am submerged, but emerging. What dream sleep spell am I in? I am falling. Falling. I must recover myself, but I do not know where I am. After the darkness and pain of the previous evening, I sleep late and use the afternoon hours to restore. I drink water; I eat grapes and walnuts to help me cleanse. Opening up the healing channels, I absorb the prana and the daylight rays. This evening brings the Super Moon. It is the biggest and closest approach of the Night Orb to the Earth in decades. After all the unconscious leaping of past nights, I prepare for formal ritual ceremony – offering and receiving.

I prepare my rooftop Aerie as sacred ground. It will be the altar upon which I sit, kneel and pray. I collect the tools of my trade. I organise my magical items and thoughts, then carry my crystals to be washed and blessed in the water fountain of the nearby Park. I drink herbal tea in an outbreak of common sense. There is nothing left for me to do but wait and rest until the coming hour. If only I had my magical stone Hunky Punk, which sits on my work desk in my chamber at the Raven Agency, Rose Finch division – Room Two, The Tower. It is attuned only to me and it speaks *voces mysticae* as well as knowing all the magical formulas of the ancient *Ephesia Grammata*. It knows the daemon language and all the secret names and sacred numbers of times past. Without it, I am left to translate these extraordinary experiences on my own. I am being thrown back on inner resources I did not know I had. I am drawing upon the first pentacle of the Moon. I am taking the card from my travelling pack and am stretching Time in order that I might reflect upon it and discern its mansion meaning.

Aiwisruthrem: Night (Watch 3) – My usual title and position as Rose Mage means I must enter the inner fire temple to purify before I can begin my meditational practice. The items I have prepared will assist my focus for my devotional prayers. I lay the items of my usual day craft for Theurgy and Thermionics about me: lamen, sigils, star charts and cards, an amulet with the Eastern symbol for God, a small golden chain with an array of magical seals, bells and charms that can be placed twice about the wrist or ankle or once around the neck. My Magician's torch acts as a second wand; its projecting light is my guarding candle. My Swiss army knife is my dagger and sword symbolizing protection and sacrifice. I have two ancient silver Fire Coins to use as pentacles. They were given to my family from the time of Yazdegerd and they ignite in instant flame when struck together. They are from the first fire altar, cast by attendants who served, head hung, knee bent, wings wide, the revered Phoenix Overlord. Once lit, I place the coins inside a clay offering cup filled with charcoal, incense and ash.

On coloured prayer sheets I write names, symbols and special words. Then, placing them into the cup, I burn the paper offerings and watch them float away into the night air. They vanish like extinguishing spectres in drifting star formation. Flecks of fire burn and drop around me like a shower of gentle flame in gravitational return. I take my chalk and draw upon the rooftop floor my personal Yantra of multifoliate triangles given to me by the Agency for my specialised synergy work – harmony as life art. I repeat and join the symbols in their given order and out of respect for the practice of my previous position. For even though I might have gone momentarily AWOL, there are mutable and immutable laws to follow and under which I must operate. I am also governed in guidance to those I serve. *Ex voto suscepto.* I am honour bound to Tara, astrologically linked to the feminine archangel Gabriel and novitiate to the rising serpent rays of the Fire Lord. To them I owe everything. I ask for their perpetual help in the offering of insight into this – my strangest of situations. I do not always listen, but they have never given up on me. They have been good to me in all my earthly journeys and spiritual investigations. Tonight, however, I turn to the Goddess within the Moon and entreat her milky guidance. My body tingles and the surrounding energies expand. Permission asked for becomes permission granted. This means that in her blessing a supported access is granted. I can go nowhere in the Night Sky without white-Moon and angelic assistance.

Next, I tie a woollen red string around my wrist to link me to the tomb of the Middle East, the temple of Angkor in the Far East, and the pastoral pleasantness of Primrose Hill in London. I triangulate the fire temples and ask for safe passage. Protection is given. I lift my hood to cowl my head and protect the spiritual diamond on the back of my neck. On the floor in front of me, I place a poultice bag of dry herbs and rose petals infused with the tinctures of nepetalactone, mint, rosemary and eucalyptus. I stretch my arms out and take the Child's Pose. I humbly bow my head until my Third Eye presses upon the enclosed hessian bag of flowers and herbs. I close my eyes. The pressure crushes the bag, releasing a beautiful fragrance that fills my nose and head, simultaneously numbing and exciting the senses. I lengthen my spine so my sacral triangle is now in its dynamic resting position. The Hara activates. My heart centre opens – moving up to the throat and Third Eye. The Crown responds and starts building its bridge to the higher worlds. I sit up, slowly open my three eyes and wait.

Using my breath, I relax the zones of my body and start reciting the Votive Laws of the *Tabula Ansata*. Invoking the Night Sky Goddess for help, I Moon-synch my mind. She majestically sheens and shines her light down. I send my thanks as I move into night mode, to ride the visions and prophecies of the dark skies beyond her. I have to gain favour with the supernatural forces to enter into infinite universal darkness. She uses my bejewelled and gloriously multi-heralded spine as her sceptre. The upward tilt of my forehead and chin is the lifting of her royal orb. My former structured life of the Sun – as man of day and duty – diminishes as I harmonise to the phase of lunar occurrence, the calendar of thirteen, and the pull of Cosmic Fate's oceanic tides. Beneath the water and the fields, the creatures of coral and earth all obey.

I observe the Piscean Super Moon. She is big and bright and fills the Sky with her gracious immensity. She is a beautiful swan-Moon. She is so close that all can read her secret signs and blemishing craters. Tonight she governs us as good Enchanted Goddess. From dusk until dawn she brings empowerment to the feminine fertile worlds of earth, sky and water. It is she who secretly nurtures our wise White Owl night bodies during our sleeping hours. She has intimate knowledge of all our desires through our projecting dream spirals. Simultaneously, we are both here and there with her as she guards the causal doorway inbetween.

Upon my Aerie and open rooftop altar I sit silently as I attune to the momentous influence of Mother Moon. As the immensity of the womb-round Super Moon starts to overtake I feel the tug of my astral body's impending shift. Light eternal begins to descend as aurora. If we do not keep her in abeyance we shall lose the seasons of the Earth, natural time and our Night-mind – our right human kind. The Moon is the white of the cracked cosmic egg, the Sun the gold. She reflects the Aeons contained in my sigil that hangs about my neck on a chain. Through my lamen, the Moon-drenched left eye of Horus, I enter the secret chambers. Adept knowledge of the hidden is here. Above me the Moon glows and beckons. She is my Magician's late-night lamp. My ceremonial cloak is the mantle of the Night Sky. As I draw the starry cloak about me I hold the talisman that the Raven Agency permits me to use. Tonight I need energy and ash to go where I am going.

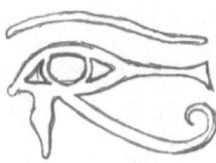

Ushahin: Dark Night (Watch 4) – Midnight. My usual Psychopomp, Hermes, arrives with all his natural strength to guide me through the Realm of the Dead to the domain of Hathor and Thoth. They will give me safe haven and explain the sanctuary of timeless principle. Here you are free to watch your world fall apart as you sit on the Throne of Tranquillity and listen to the all-pervading Voice of Silence. Yet, when it is happening to you it is hard to remain an outside observer. One part of Life is being sacrificed as another is just beginning, seamlessly.

In my given Vision, the Healing Halls and Temples of Egyptian Ancients are lit for sacred ritual. I can hear sung chants and rhythms filling the chambers. Music and dances of mystery are played and performed. Faces are painted. Eyes are highlighted like cats. Delicious Night perfume fills the rooms and the senses. It is an honour to glimpse such magnificent ancient scenes and I can only guess at the significance of secrets housed here. Reeds are blown and Spirits are sucked out of the air to gather by the paired Priests and Priestesses. There is a collective haunting as human souls separate from dancing votive bodies and join the world of spirit. They parade as divine spectres holding hands in circle dances above the observing onlookers' heads as veritable proof of the Afterlife. A Priest accompanies each Priestess as they anoint the head and feet of each worshipper in midnight attendance. Spirits and Old Gods from different realms are venerated in all their forms.

Yet of all these astonishing sights my senses are caught by the sight and sound of a simple, metal clanking instrument held by a swaying musician, overshadowed by a God. I cannot steal from here. I am a guest and it is beyond my permitted two thousand year time zone of travel. Also, there is no need for I have seen this object before with its strange domed shape and its metal serpentine bars. Its image is contained in one of the arcane books of secret teachings in the Tower library. Now, as my memory grasps for its contents, the wingèd pages flap to race away in escape from me. I bow my head and offer my thanks as I leave the dissolving scene. Hermes collects me at the Temple Gate and guides me home by the hand. He smiles as he deposits me back on the rooftop. Then he disappears without offering any further information. For once in the passing of these strange days I know what to do next!

I bed down in my Aerie. The close, large, snowy face of the Moon peers down at me. For a moment I am comforted like a child that is safe to sleep, suddenly unafraid, for the light has been turned back on. For one blissful moment my night terrors and midnight monsters are held at bay as I am given the gift of dreamless sleep. I am grateful as I slip into her comforting pillow of swan-white. I tell myself it will be all right – that the previous nightmarish lands will gradually dissipate in the meaningfulness of my vision and time travel this night. And I almost believe it.

Day 12 – Sistrum

Sunday 20th March – 13°C

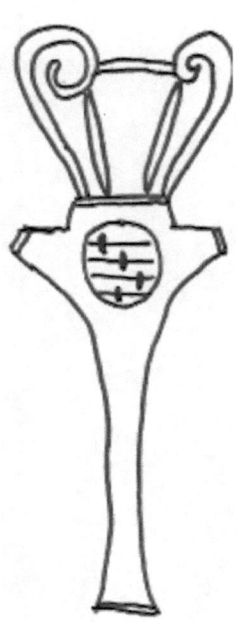

Hawan: Morning (Watch 1) – After sleeping late and mercifully well, I wake refreshed. I take to walking the streets of London Town, but this time with striding purpose. It is unseasonably sunny and lovely. I traverse bridges – passing Old Parliamentary Palaces – and make my way through a series of Green Parks to take in the comfort of their natural beauty and growing garments of green. I side-wind down large tree lined avenues and across fountainous squares with crowding columns and statues. Snakes glide at my feet as I flow through the streams of people. They bear news of the World and guide me towards the Promised Land. They give word that there is falling and fighting everywhere. I cross over pavements and slip through preposterously small, leaning alleys to avoid the many busy folk foraging for lunch. I make good time through the good people and soon arrive at the Portal Museum of Antiquity.

I cross the open cobbled courtyard, up the steps and through the colonnade, following the Snakes to our destination. The Greek facade stands in ionic architectural order. Inside, mathematics and music greet the Mage inherent in my makeup. Statues speak to fascinate – their tongues revealing their many cultural mysteries. There is sacred geometry everywhere for my excited eyes to absorb. Spheres and globes rotate and reveal the detailed routes and ways of the far past to passing new travellers. Ancient books and runes spit their forensics at me. Aligned and misaligned truths hurtle on the backs of golden turtles and spin like centaur arrows shot into the wise-Sky in aeromancy. In glass cases, the salvaged sunken halls and cathedrals of Atlantis leave their ancestral traces. Marks of meaning sink like tattoo ink into tribal skin, pottery and pieces of broken ceramics that make up the ark of our fragmented time. Lines, symbols and wavy words are carved into Dragon Stone, shoulder bone and pelts of parchment.

Marvelling, I slowly pass to the other side of the spectacular glass court and wind my way through the rooms and mausoleums, along the great hallways of history. Beauteous Caryatids spy down upon me as they shoulder their world. They hold their lips shut protecting the secrets of the Delphic Oracle until the bell of final silence chimes and God commands otherwise. Until then, for most, the rituals and mysteries remain mutely enshrouded in the solidity of statues and guesswork. Still, the old vapours of truth rise and engulf those that seek.

In a nearby case a culturally borrowed Crystal Skull illuminates and starts chattering, launching into a tirade of ancient tribes and lost tongues. The Skulls are programmed with the knowledge of old clans and house the Spirits of Sacred Truth – sacrificed souls who were willingly entombed. Also embedded within their crystalline structure are laser smooth ghost crystals, which form into colour, collecting light wells. When activated by a pure source, the Skulls emit rainbow beams and frequencies from their translucent eyes and mouth. Slowly the galactic Thirteen Skulls resurface and gather awaiting the next spiritual convocation and harmonic convergence. This particular Skull hails from the Atlantean Space Ark re-found in Mesoamerica at the beginning of the early Twentieth Century. It knows me from a previous incarnation and I am honoured to encounter it again, but my guardian Snakes hiss at the ancient Crystal Cranium for they remember the sacrificial neck-breakers and ritual heart-takers of old; more brutal than any shiny-armoured, disease-riddled Conquistador and their mistaken materialistic search for the City of Gold. However, the Snakes have the highest regard for those jungle cultures emulating higher Serpent sculptures that entwined their stone sunlit temples.

I turn on my heel and make haste down one of the Portal Museum's antiquarian corridors of Time, otherwise the Skull's babbling binaries and computational linguistics will take over and I will be stuck in deep trance before I know it – remembering and speaking the old tongue. There are too many relics here aware of my multifarious roles and abilities, all trying to interact and communicate with me. The bird alarms will soon be set off if this commotion continues. If the Raven Agency suspects me of being here, of seeking information without their permission regarding strange artefact magick, they will revoke my licence.

For now, I just focus on quickly sending out a silencing spell to mute the babbling Museum artefacts, for which my Snakes are grateful. The rooms revert back to being ordinary. I enter the desired room of consequence. The Snakes usher me into the temple of Egyptian treasures. My High Priestess swirls within: with all her sex magick and spiritual vision I have to be careful. She pulls me into her heart. So headstrong. So wilful. I have to hold her down in an embrace of self love. She can still be put to good work and I need her now, only rightly connected. Beyond the cabinet of curiosities and the disputed items from the shipwreck of time, older than the original holy thorn reliquary, lies that which I seek. It is the object of my Super Moon vision, the key to my deeper understanding of the turbulent situation in which I presently find myself.

The Cat Bastet looks on as feline goddess, keeper of sacred ointments and jars. Here, she is protector, Lady of Flame and Eye of Ra. As I peer into the suspended cabinet of time I gently hold onto its sides. Anchoring myself, I grow my energy roots down through the Earth until my legs are as big as trees, my body and arms as huge as giants. Then I press my forehead against the cold glass. I close my eyes as my inner High Priestess opens my Crown, Third Eye and Heart chakras. I send turquoise rays down from my Throat centre into the display as I attune and listen. What I seek is old knowledge of the heart, not mind – that which some call soul food. One of my assisting Snakes, a Cobra, uncoils and sways in sacred mystic dance. We become entranced. Spellbound. Encompassing us all, the Disc of the Sovereign Sun hanging on the Museum Temple wall from the time of Akhenaten begins to vibrate and send down the majesty of its golden rays. From inside the cabinet the metal musical instrument, the Sistrum of my Super Moon vision, speaks to reveal its mystery.

'Listen, for I am the Sacred Rattle of the ecstatic states, bringer of joy. You are the shaken. Each one of my four serpentine crossbars creates a chord in one of the corresponding physical elements you wear about your body of light. Where you are going you cannot take your flesh with you. Only the resonating qualities of God are permitted, as are those colours enriched by the multi-journeying experience of your personal travelling between the two realms each side of the veil. I represent perpetual motion acting upon karmic form. At rest, I am reminder of that which remains and shines on all sides. Long have I been forgotten and lost to the aeons of human civilisation. The Ancient Greeks suspected it, but never harnessed it.

The Egyptians knew. The Atlanteans were on the path, but events turned away from resolution. Certain traditional medicines and Shamans throughout the centuries understood and grasped at it. Only now is Humankind offered another opportunity to operate at this new vibrational height and with correct directional spiritual scope. You must not be frightened or hold back. Humanity has, after many thousands of years, come to the place of rest where it can operate spiritually if it so chooses. Much assistance is being given to Mankind in this journey. It is only now that Man's cosmic efforts can be realised – for attainment through higher attunement is here. In rest and in guided action, I am that which helps you to release and move on. In sound and sway I bring about new future and liberation day.

I cleanse the skies and free the flame. I am that which unlocks the locked links of light and brings release. I am that which breaks the chains and makes walls tumble. I purify the waters. I am that which removes oppression. I am that which shakes the Earth. I am that which drives away corruption, moving the immovable and altering the immutable. I am that difficult change which is worthwhile. I am that which regulates the course of Nature through movement and continual agitation. I am that energy which never ceases until the journey's true end, when I shall witness the collapse of the last atom in love. I am that force which folds in and spirals out. I am arousal and excitement. I am the antidote to the depressed and drowsy. There is no escaping from me, even in the stirrings of deep grief, for I shall always find you and be by your side. For like the spiritual you, I am that which ever resides. Be happy and rest in the knowledge of me. I am the unknown that leads to God's great unfolding mysteries. Though perpetually shaken at the deep heart of change, I am that which is faith unshakeable, that some call absolute awareness and others unassailable truth. I am that which breaks your way and brings you to your knees. I am that for which you should be grateful, but I understand if you are not. Do you grasp the essence of my music and message? Do you truly want to understand my Life-Death rattle? Listen closely, for I am the Sacred Bringer of Joy. Listen in! Can you hear it? For joy is here!'

The Sistrum falls silent. The metal u-shaped rattle with its handle, crossbars and half hidden hieroglyphics, becomes solid and mute before me as I leave the light trance state. The glimpses of the religious ceremonies and ritual of the Super Moon vision continue to dance about me. Sounds rise and fall. I sense that Hathor has been here whispering her wise words into my High Priestess's ear – my heart and my mind. The passing over of love is happening to me and my very struggle is the offering. My elements are changing and in the alchemical altering my old self is being sacrificed. The Snakes wrap around my ankles and begin to pull me away, diverting me from danger and possible detection. I leave the labyrinth of darkened rooms behind me and stride outdoors to the replenishing Sun. My work for the day is done. I am thrilled, exhausted, disbelieving. I sit on the steps and watch the Snakes disappear from view as they go about their duties ever to perform. I bask in growing daylight Ankh-wonder.

Day 13 – Naw-Ruz

Monday 21st March – 15°C

Hawan: Morning (Watch 1) – Late Morning. It is Naw-Ruz, the first cusp of the astrological new year, and a Persian day for good cheer. Pigeon, Park, Ram and Emperor – all join in the celebration. The Two Swimming Fish, caught between their struggle for upstream source-spawning and downstream sea-living, disperse and leave in natural annual cycle. First fire replaces last water in universal comprehension of loss, link and new life. The Temple Watch phases change today. There is more daylight to observe so there is a seasonal shift in the different duties to perform. I tend to my Temple Fire by taking a walk to the Park and raking the meditational embers. It is time to start a new blaze. It is unexpectedly warm and pleasant. Winter is thrown off and Spring is here unto the Earth ushering in an early opening of buds and blossom. Daffodils – the Lent Lily – abound as pressing Spring informants from the Gaia ground. Somewhere hides the Golden Fleece and a Spring hero, as everywhere around the World fills with pulsing life – life in pursuit of a better life, a safer life, a quieter, yet somehow more profuse and profound and exciting life. The flowers gossip-share about their sudden appearance. Their annual 'I Am Here' blooming swirls in a colourful rondel, each line neatly, sweetly, quickly given and passed onto the next like threading links in an emerging Earth tapestry. The bulbs, tubers and rhizomes Root Knitting Club dig deep to help their leaves and petals capture the Sun's morning's glory. A nearby evergreen shrub looks on at the glorious flowers' reappearance:

'How lovely! How very lovely! I didn't think they'd all make the Wintering, but they did. Look at them grow! What a delightful, colourful, sprawling show!'

So, Spring produces a more loving, leafy start. The power of the fertile soil, the slumbering shoot and awakening seed is here. I sit on a sunlit Park bench shrugging off the mantle of the struggling World. I am drenched in cosmic clouds and light divine, basking in and out of sleepy surrender and timeless being. Here in the Park, close to earth, flowers and trees, I feel at home. For a moment the touch of peace brushes over me like a breeze and it is I that coos like a pigeon. Acceptance descends. Against the green of grass and leaves, in amongst the gold, yellow and red of Spring's glorious daffodils and bright tulips, amidst the orange, purple and white of budding crocuses, Life close to the ground is suddenly warm and good. Yet hidden within myself, a darker bloom vies for my attention. I do not know its name yet, but its perfume fascinates and it draws me near in order to drink in the elixir of its shade. Its source is living shadow and dark matter. I sit on a Park bench watching the pigeons.

Rapithwin: Afternoon (Watch 2) – Seated outside the Park Café I eat a light, leisurely lunch. Drinking tea, I observe an artist draw and paint. I wonder if he is lonely in his world of pens, pencils and pots of paint. Through the Artist's eyes the world of lines, forms and colours are perceived differently. I am much prepossessed by his art of absorption. What is it that fascinates him so? Listening, observing, meditating, reflecting – contemplating the ordinariness of matter in motion whilst pinning it purposefully to the page. He notices what is and what is not. Silence, sound and space surround his interest in line and colour and we are all there as articles to make up his world. Now, and again now, true Nature blossoms upon the branch as simply as the birds sing. The Artist turns from page to canvas. A bead of complex colour lifts from his mixing palette and box of paint. Light and shadow play with the big picture as he begins to paint and build. A new world is being formed.

Uzerin: Late Afternoon (Watch 3) — The Artist stands back to assess. Is it done? From where I am seated behind him, the easel becomes the frame, the painting an opening door. With the mobility of consciousness I plunge into the Artist's picture. Inside, I become the encroaching deep green, but quickly head into the indigo toward the violet and mauve — bruising blues that flow into the magenta of a rapidly gathering sunset. The earthen hues are here too; growing deep from within the bulb-blistering land and twisting Spring that has this day officially arrived. Clouds collect. Overhead the skies are darkening. I visually absorb and become the blue-black of gathering dusk for later use in meditational spectrum reference. I pull the deep current of its colour through my Third Eye and visceral body. I have been here before — seen and experienced this rumbling of turbulent shades. These aspects are reminiscent of Golgotha again. This is the same frequency as the Sky's cloak that descends and wraps around the universe at night. It offers me dark protection and starry silver screens in my evening views and travelling. In places it verges on the colour of Crows and Ravens; corvid shades that scare my night soul. In amongst the dark colours I realize that the fascinating inner flower that has so far escaped me has a name. It is the Black Hyacinth that blooms through me with such overpowering perfume and need. The flower's exquisite darkness is the beauty of grief and the colour of my hurt. As I recognise this I withdraw my consciousness from the painting and return to my café seat.

I bow my head to pigeons and poets, emperors and artists, colours on skies, paintings and palettes. All arise within me and I am awash with warm Spring song on this vernal equinox. I have so enjoyed the day that I decide to continue my own personal celebration. I leave the Park and make my way home via the market stalls to find items to prepare an evening ritual picnic: eggs, roses and water, apples and cheeses, bread and meat. I want to invite the birds to dine. I need colour so I buy metallic model paints and sparkling, multi-coloured, nail varnish. I purchase a simple silver bowl to float the rose heads upon water, tea light candles for fire, and small pocket mirrors for reflecting Spring abundance and the Night Sky. I need all these elements to brighten and embrace my temporary rooftop home.

Aiwisruthrem: Night (watch 3) – I mount the flight of stairs less troubled than of late and prepare for Haft Sin. I place the candles upon the mirrors and light them skyward. I spark my Fire Coins into warming flame. In the centre of my picnic blanket I place the heads of three roses in the silver bowl of water and scatter the remaining rose petals about. I call and encourage the Ravens to gather and perch. They are here so I might as well invite them in as guests rather than have them sit as morbid, disturbing observers on the fringes. They like to dine on such morsels and titbits as humans have to offer – especially those that smell like grief, meat and blood. The Ravens stalk upon the low rooftop walls grabbing the food offerings with their claws whilst tearing at the meat and bread with their beaks. They fascinate me even in their disquieting dark following. I pass the early hours of evening in quiet chanting, humming fragments of poems, half remembered hymns and all but forgotten prayers, while engaged in painting eggs by the flickering fire and candlelight. These are the poet spells of Old Troubadours and Ancient Wizards, mathematical rhymes and enchantments dating back to the Druids and the legendary songs of trees. Placing the painted eggs about the picnic blanket I think about You.

You would have loved immersing yourself in all of this. I reminisce about how much fun we have had indulging ourselves in such activities in the past. How you absorbed yourself in hollowing and carving scary pumpkin heads. You even wore an oversized gourd skeleton skull to the Angel and Daemon Ball. Me – busily creating monstrous modern cardboard and wire sculptures to place about the garden. How we painted our naked bodies and faces by the gloaming fire – hollering and whooping like Mohican animist Indian Braves. How we danced and moved to Bach and Mozart and all manner of pop, installing glistening snowflakes one-by-one in the empty white room – me insisting on each flake being hung at different heights, tied individually and suspended with invisible thread or white cotton. Some had feathers attached to look like wings, fluffy feet or aerial fins, and you lying on the giant polar bear rug roaring like Peter Pan against the Hook-handed pirate. My fire energy rises as accepting joy in the remembrance of our love.

You are not far and not for a moment forgotten. I am just distant. I am so sorry that I cannot find another way to communicate this dumb world of mine. I would gesticulate wildly to explain my muteness, but it is better that I am away from you in all this. I am in temporary separation as part of the state of missing and grief and it is better that I am isolated during it. I hope you understand. I know you will. You. You. You. Wonderful, annoying You whom I miss so much. You who obliterates the cold and brings out so much warmth and affection in me; we may be out of each other's reach and touch, but only momentarily. I so look forward to seeing you again, to the returning. But first, I need to aright myself in these crushing, crippling onslaughts of days. For a moment, all the inner elements and outer offerings, all the broken feelings and fragmented states, come together and balance in my awakening dream world.

Change in consciousness is freely given if not frozen in memory, experience and time. Without fear, the priestly Birds gather and walk around me in jutting zigzags. They tilt their heads and blink their dark eyes in simple natural curiosity. A gathering interest towards me grows in them. Why are they still here? Are they really sent to spy or are they actually on my side? Our joint day purpose is to serve and protect the country, to save the Heartland Tower from tumbling. That is what the Raven Agency does. That is why it was established. From dawn until dusk, the primary jobs of the Ravens are to roam, report and record death and the many things they see.

Yet they have their own individual freedoms and interactions within their natural remit. At Night, they are free unless sent on secret Sky-missions or locked in a confining cage for their criminal cleverness and trickster misdeeds!

As incarnational agent of the Rose Finch sixth division, I troubleshoot and translate in matters of East meeting West, specialising in chapter and verse of magick, poetics and the healing arts. I receive instructions from the Universal Brotherhood based in Istanbul. Friendly Robins, Rose Finches and small garden birds converse with me and I in turn report back their findings on important issues of Nature, hemisphere enmeshing and interlocking Gaia evolution to The Tower's Raven seventh division. I do not deal with the Ravens directly for they are out of my jurisdiction. They have higher commands and superior demands to observe. The ascended Sky and Raven Masters are solely responsible for them. Yet as my Tower crashes around me, I have to let go and surrender. Is that why the Ravens follow – for ever since the biblical beginning they have overseen the long unrest of nations as well as of the individuals within? Are they cursed birds or blessed? Do they fear for me or is this a check on my insubordination?

The Ravens do not answer, but simply continue to tear at their food, cock their heads and ignore me as though they can hear my every unimportant human thought. Their soul gazing stirs me as they turn their dark, questioning eyes upon me. Walking in circles, they peer inward like imperious Inquisitors of Old – skilful torturing hands folded behind their feathered backs of black. Ha! Kraa! Traa! Their staring encourages my wisdom to continue on as they sound out the call of a found Dead Man. One Raven I do not recognise, bigger than the rest, steps forward. Pointing a single feather toward me, I am asked the perennial question that holds the key to unlock both light secret and dark residual shame:

'J'accuse! Are you less than you are? If not, then why are you at inner war?'

The golden hamster runs perpetually upon the Ahimsa Wheel – spinning peace eternal. The black cat guards and protects by putting the frighteners on. From Alpha to Omega I go. I am not on a guilt quest, but is it true what the wingèd ones say? Is it I that betrays? If I am mine enemy, then who is my friend? The Ravens might yet turn out to be a dark godsend.

Day 14 – The Fair Maid

Tuesday 22nd March – 16°C

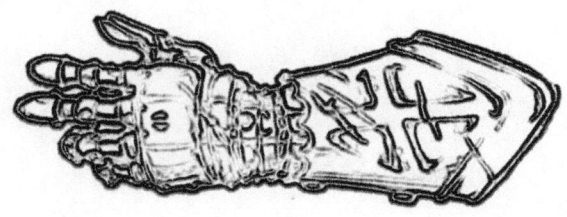

Hawan: Morning (Watch 1) – It is early morning in London, yet in my half-waking dream I stand ghostly in a high-up room made of stone and wood in some other time – early afternoon. It is sunny. From outside, light and noise filter in through the oiled parchment frame jammed in the stone window. The room is spacious and there is a dress with long wide sleeves decorated with gems lying across a bed awaiting the return of its wearer. It is a medieval gown made up of layers of lace, silk, and velvet, trimmed with fur – not ermine, but otter. The colour is a dyer's woad blue and there is a full-length mantle and a large pinning broach beside it. Silk buckled shoes sit neatly arranged on the floor. But there is something at odds here. Strewn cotton garments belie a hasty exit and there are objects of interest left stacked unguarded in a corner: a small cross-hilt knightly dagger, a sword, a wooden staff, a bow, a quiver full of arrows, and most intriguing of all – a silver-embossed gauntlet. It is this last item that compels and as I hold it to me I am transported. Racing up and out of the window, I am pulled skywards and hover momentarily above a small stone castle and great Wooden Hall in Middle England. Then I plummet, swooping away over land to a nearby forest, crashing through trees until my feet hit the ground. I am running now, running, looking all around as though trying to escape my present threatening circumstance. Light laughter is intermingled with danger, delight and dread. I am thrilled by such daring and become overwhelmed by her thoughts…

'How I love these flights from the castle. I long to be outdoors exploring the woods, to be running free in Nature under high arching branches that form such a wonderful cathedral-like canopy above me. I seek out the secret mossy enclaves, and there is enchantment in the shimmering forest sunlight that infiltrates through the leaves. Golden rays ripple and glide through the green, whilst the dappled aspects run through the forest paths and lead me on to greater thought and deeper reflection beyond my position. Not gloom, but respite. I find more purpose here under these bowers than when helping out at the nearby convent, yet I cannot steal away from my noble life as readily as those nuns touched by God and inspired by higher orders. I feel ensnared by life in this womanly body and fear I am caught in some sort of fairytale – subtle binding forces that are beyond my ability to break. I do not know if it is a spell of dark dread or golden destiny that hangs above my head, but I cannot shake this growing feeling of premonition.

I wish I had my horse, but I cannot slip away unnoticed with such ease when I am with my strong four-footed companion. My hawk hovers above the castle walls on lookout and always comes to find me in the forest, even if only for a brief while. I am blessed with Nature's friends, but stealth as well as opportunity is required in executing these escapades and I must not overtly signal my absence. Such momentary freedom is stolen from confining duties and impractical dresses, yet these outdoor adventures make the difficult indoor days more tolerable. Troubled, uncertain times hang above all our heads, but here in the forest I can run with the rabbit, the fox and the wild boar and forget my courtly cares – if only for a while.

I wonder how these ancient oaks at the heart of the forest view our human crimes and kindnesses? They outspan us in height and years, but do they grow in greater wisdom through observing our trials and folly? Assuredly they do, and if I am quiet long enough it is as though I hear them speaking to me upon the gentlest of breezes. They call to me, but how am I to stay? This solitary path of mine makes me outcast and I seemingly fit in nowhere, but return to the castle I must. What other choice do I have? I pray nightly upon the Shepherd's Star for guidance and hope that I can find a path forwards, for the celestial evening skies alone know my true secrets.

Soon it will be the High Holy Day, and plans for the end of May Fayre are well advanced in the castle. I look forward to such feasting and revelry as an opportunity to meet people beyond the Great Hall's four wooden walls. They are to hold a competition for archery and falconry – a golden arrow and an embossed silver gauntlet to be the coveted prizes – and no doubt there will be the usual jousting, drinking and Tomfoolery. Many a wineskin will be emptied, and there will be mead and the best of bread to share. I might even enter the games if I can find a way to hide my form better, yet it is the slipping between my duties and my carefree wishes that I have to beware. Still, I prefer the fields and forests to the finery and manners of a corrupt court that daily skews fairness and supplants honesty of the heart with selfish, odious manners of the feudal lords.

Yet such splendor in the castle halls is a daily reminder of the plight of those that lack and I daily transgress in my thoughts and deeds to help those in want of food and coin. The milk and honey of the land is drained and many a good farmer breaks their back tilling the earth – no wonder poaching and robbery is rife! Poverty and ill health blight us all, whilst scutage upon the knights continues to grow and so much is squandered upon military and spiritual missions abroad. When is the king to return to remove the black-hearted cloud that now cruelly reigns? The Herdsmen and the Huntsman are at odds, and the swagger and sway of the court oppresses. There is anger in the country. I am lucky to find freedom, solace and succor in the wandering ways of the forest without encountering difficulty. Yet in my travels I become more aware of the oppressive yoke weighing heavily upon others. The women suffer dreadfully.

I continue to dress boyishly to escape notice by strapping down my chest and making my long golden hair disappear into a shortened pudding-basin style preferred by page boys, and I keep my dagger about me at all times. I am unafraid to use it should necessity dictate. Yet recently my escapes have brought me another type of consideration – merry mischief that fills my hands, head and heart. I have stumbled upon a growing number of hooded bandits in the forest and have taken to following and watching their skirmishes from a distance. The leader is bearded, handsome, and strong – somewhat noble, honest and true in bearing as he turns his wild attention to unjust matters. There is a fire to him and in some strange way he startles my dreams and waking mind. The rest of the men are firm of purpose and good at heart, yet somewhat clumsy too, whereas I try to pass as invisibly as the wind, as silent as a swooping hawk, as lethal as any arrow. The cloaked men live hidden in the heart of the forest, but help and hinder those travellers who take the winding ways that skirt the edges of the wood. Woe betide the tax gatherers and those with wealth on display. Money and jewels are easily taken as a trespassing toll, whilst they feed by stealing wild game belonging to the Royal Park land.

My archery comes on a pace in these natural environs and has proved useful in aiding the bandits from a distance, but my recent involvement has sorely betrayed me. They have found one of my arrows embedded in a tree and suspect that they are observed. This has led to some confusion amongst them as they are used to fighting and escaping the Sheriff's men, but not another outlaw. I now fear that I have to be on my guard both here in the forest and in the castle. Everywhere suspicion grows and I have nothing but disguise to aid my purpose and mask my feelings. Within the Great Hall preparations are made for some matrimonial alliance, but I feign and skirt any such advances. However, it is expected of me to submit and consider such proposals and people do not understand why I try to dissway the amorous attentions of the handsome and highborn. I send no signal but still they press their masculine advantage and I am expected to

obey. So little time is left for laughter and I would remain light at heart...
For joy and compassion are sorely needed everywhere. I practice my
needlework, but only so I can improve my stitches for the ill and injured
when I weekly work to assist the Physicians on their Friday afternoon visits
to the poor. I am accomplished in many things, but pretend that I cannot
sing or play the harp – for even though they often force me my dismal
attempts of musical interlude are soon swept aside and I am free to leave
the drinking men. How I pity the serving wenches and what they endure.

But silent now... My hawk is disturbed and wings upwards in speedy
disappearance. I have been careless in my roaming ways and rambling
thoughts. I have been listening for footfall and the snapping of twigs, but
there is activity whispering above my head in the tree branches. I have been
foolish, adrift in my thoughts, and have let myself be surrounded. Like the
lurching rabbit I now must run... like the crafty fox that hears and fears the
chasing hounds I must wait my time and outwit... like the strong boar
afraid for its life I must fight my last stand. Very well, if I am to tussle with
these robbers and renegades I must trust my skills of combat, whilst praying
to keep my true visage and noble bearing hidden. Yet what if I am found
out? What of my passion? What if my hands, heart and eyes should betray
me? I must banish such thoughts for this wood is my home, not my tomb,
and the trees will help me. Assuredly, I will not succumb to capture or any
admission of love whilst I have my wits, arrows and dagger about me.'

*

Her thoughts fade and the vision begins to vanish – and I with it. Yet out
of the sudden swirl of leaves and breaking branches, of birds rising and
crow's cawing, of a hawk descending, of people running, of struggle and
skirmish, I hear the startling, incredulous men's shouts,

"Robin, he's a girl!"

In an afternoon, her life is changed forever. I disappear; pleased she has found a new path.

Day 15 – Snake Cures/Dream Sleep

Wednesday 23rd March –16°C

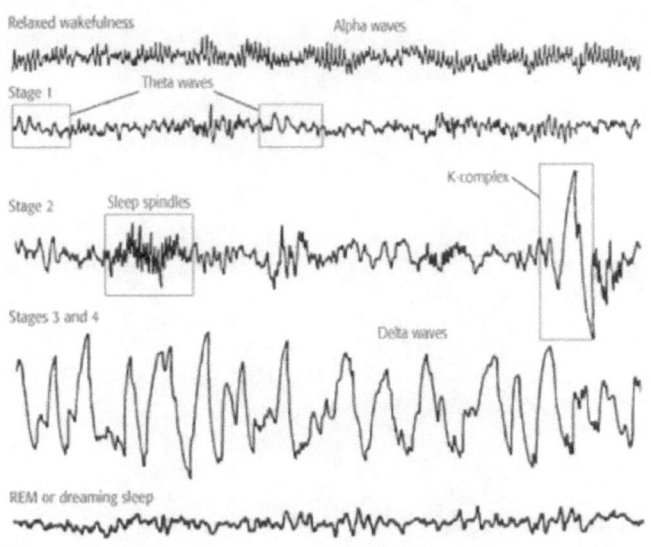

Uzerin: Late Afternoon (Watch 3) — In-and-out of fitful sleep all day, yet already I look forward to further slumber and shutdown. I am in uncertain seas, in distress, and cling on to anything that passes by that might keep me afloat. I long for dreamless nights of cool black behind unperturbed eyes. I need to find a way to heal, to restore. The vital energies coursing through me are depleted and running low in these drifting days of adventure. I cannot continue to live in such a way. I long for the ordinariness of the old days, the slow ways, but these are the days of new time and events are quickening. I have been given a gift from the Moon and the Night Sky, but why? My system is acid and is working overtime in matters of erosion. Rust and decay are omnipresent in the troubled dream wake delta states, yet I pray everything is slowly heading towards theta.

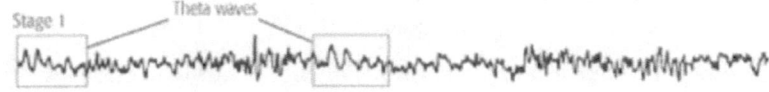

Today in my strange twilight wanderings, I have taken to walking beside the tracks of trains. The flickering light and shadows of passing engines, commuter carriages and Pullmans calms me. I find it comforting being near the conducting metal and the stone ballast and granite energy convertors. Here, there is bion and orgone energy for the absorbing. Columns of light, both artificial and natural, surround me. I sit whilst my body shudders and convulses. If I thrust my heel down into the ground, I know I can stop the World from turning and be somewhere else in a shot, but where and why and how? I have practiced this before in meditations, visualizations and inner dreams, but now I can somehow do it outwardly, however clumsy my semiconscious excursions feel and appear.

Aiwisruthrem: Night (Watch 4) – My fitful, sleeping, physical self stays curled up underneath the Railway Arches. My body feels both hot and cold like one possessed with an on-setting fever. I perspire heavily as I prepare to travel. Suddenly, the surrounding lights become so bright and beguiling. The rhythms of the nearby trains and traffic are familiar and soothing. They act as an anchor point from which I can journey. I slowly push my Achilles heel down into the ground to act as a brake to stop the ever spinning Earth. Sound and light waves become compressed. Everything starts to shudder as the World concertinas in on itself before springing back. Light flecks, particles of science, gather in the quantum field as I free myself from my body and begin to hurtle along a chosen Timeline – but who chooses?

I pass from one worldview to another. Around me is the dark blue-black of the Night Sky with its spinning silver of swirling star clusters. Suns are like miniature beads flashing inside the surrounding myriad multi-coloured threads. These heavenly orbs are the stellar treasure maps to the soul and the cosmic light body. Their precious energies pass through me. I am fuelled by strangeness and a wilfulness to escape, explore, and discover what is on the other shore from me. To transform and regenerate I must somehow eat the sin of shame and unforgiveness. Eat or experience? Yet how could I share this experience with my family, friends and loved one? How could I ever put others through my experience of this on-going memory terror? It is better for me to be gone, lost, missing, than to continue to function falsely in that Old World as one obsessed and so-called mad. I have to give in to these relentless processes until the end to see what I might find. My end? I do not know.

Now, scores of medicinal Aesculapian Snakes glide about my distressed body. The racked winding lines try to converse with the accumulated toxins and travelling serpent trains. Inner and outer aspects collide and confuse. All the uses and abuses of my world are given up to ritual purification and cleansing. I have jumped worlds, but travel only to find myself lying on a marble floor in the same curled position within an old Asclepion. I am in the healing Temple of Asclepius. Am I back in the Abaton? Am I enshrined? Are these experiences really dream cures by enkoimesis? I am caught in the mesmeric place of transfixing Snakes and God altering states. In which case, what Deities and Beings will come forward in my future to help? Now, flickering forked tongues and slavering dogs lick me. I am covered in their healing spit. My organs have their language of ill health, apathy, and disconnectedness, but all about seem eager to help. I need to get back to the Paradise Snake in Eden's garden, back to the Two Snakes sleeping within the base of my body, back to the Serpent power and golden regenerative root of myself – and no-one can do that but I.

KEITH BRAZIL

Day 16 – *Abiuro*

Thursday 24th March – 15°C

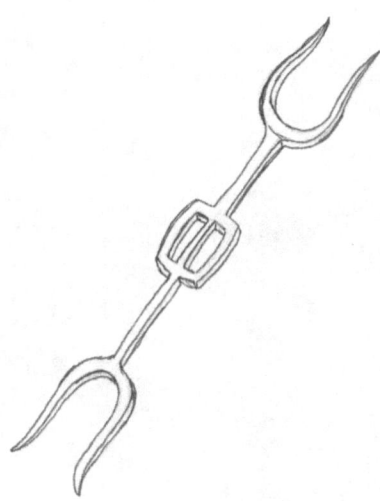

Rapithwin: Afternoon (Watch 2) – Days pass. These days are those that are Lent; days that I have borrowed from Time and stolen from my usual routine to fast, travel and pray. They are the days of becoming and surrender. I rest assured that the seemingly less difficult daylight hours are tests of my resolve and recovery, as solitary and bare as the night hours are full. I am offered some respite as I come to my senses and turn to look after my physical needs: some semblance of warmth, self-love and comfort for the disturbed man within. I cannot explain the vast emptiness of my inner terrain. Yet as fast as I empty, I am full again. These notes to self only capture a part of the passage of time and passing dream consciousness. My descent is recorded so one day I will be able to recall these moments of confused hazy beauty and share this shedding – for something is really happening to Time and my memory.

Today, I woke up and looked out upon an eerily quiet housing estate. It is a derelict expanse awaiting destruction and the multiple unoccupied layers of housing units look like vacated cells – an uninhabited hive abandoned in mass swarming and exile. Have innocent social prisoners been released from an imprisoning environment or have the poor been smoked out and swept aside once more? Occasional gangs of school kids maraud, but the architects are nowhere to be found. I have to be wary. I do not want to be seen by the hard-core practitioners of free roaming parkour. They might recognise me and want me to join in. I cannot do that. At this moment I just cannot, however much I want my feet to run free from all this. Shuffling and wary, I enter the urban housing desert. It is a warm day. I draw lines in the dust with a stick, creating pictures with the help of Byzantium blue stones and beads I carry about me in the side pocket of my rucksack. My last remembrance was of my falling onto the rooftop Aerie and the clatter of metal about me. Is that right? Where have I been since?

Was I not wandering on the tracks of trains and lying in the Old Temple of animal healing? Am I made well or am I still sick? I am not sure how I shifted to this deserted place or if I can survive much more of this. My body is exhausted and my mind beaten. How I long for the tropical blue of distant skies, aquamarine seas and the green of monkey jungle and coconut company. I cannot tolerate this arid Wasteland. I have no thirst for it at all.

I spend the remains of the sunlit day resting, writing and eating. I change and clean what few clothes I wear and carry with me. I toy with going home, abandoning all my difficult selves to find You, but I know the process is not done. As I wait in the launderette of lunatics, beauty and love fill my pages and scribble my pictures. There are so many pages to fill, still so much to write and tell. On the way back I buy a cloth sack to store and keep safe my new metal findings, which I secure and hang over the back wall ledge. I need to sort out my rooftop home as though it were my rearranged heart and mind. I wrestle to understand further my Father's Christmas passing. This pain goes back to my birth and a time before You were born, before we met, before I was most alive. This relates to sadder childhood elements and lifetimes before I was born.

Aiwisruthrem: Night (Watch 4) – I take refuge in the alley between the train tracks and the abandoned Coronet Cinema. These displaced places are my friends now. Shadows flicker and rush by. Feral cats on the lookout follow as I roam and explore the Moon-flooded scene. They climb the dustbins and iron stairs with me like once they stalked across Old Temple floors – crepuscular creatures that kept the encroaching Nile rats and sycophants away by devouring and hissing. Back then, the name of Venus, servant of the Sun and Moon, was once whispered as Hesperus. She had another name too. As the drawer of dawns, golden disks and diamond dusks, she was both the raiser of rays and simultaneously herald to the setting of suns. She was the light of love, both evening and morning star. She guided the cats down the serpent aisles and around the building of sacred sarcophagi.

As former gods and occult consultants to pharaohs and physicians, the revered cats could identify the true dreamer, magician and mendicant fakir from the false prophets and the dark warlock lords demanding audience and pressing advantage. They once heard tall tales tell of a sea that parted, and witnessed wave upon wave of pitiless plagues, all for the sake of imprisonment and shackling of a travelling tribe. They missed the fish that year. For a moment the cats around me remember all this and out hiss my accompanying Snakes. Both remember the wily Nile crocodile. Now, their low wailing moans and sizzling fizz keep any unwanted hawking hypnotists, roadside robbers and rattling street sellers at bay. I do not need their fake, glitzy wares today. The cats and Snakes are ready to curl in combat at a moment's spit as they warily share the common ground in me.

My need for a night-overseer and echo-locator is made manifest as an Urban Priest climbs up the nearby White Heights and looks down. With his sky-high bird's eye he watches over me from his rooftop domain. He nods and points up at the darkening sky. His colourful rags, tinfoil garb and crystal staff mesmerise the owl and mice that follow him of which the cats are so fond. They follow him for food. They follow me for affection. As he draws patterns between the stars, linking the twinkling lights and winking worlds with his Holy Rod, a faint map appears in the Heavens. He navigates a route out of the galaxy and points the way. Between the Priest, cats and snakes I am well guarded, despite the fact that they cannot save me from the tormentors within. As I prepare to jump and leave my body I feel the fear build in me. I work through the shakes and flickers that descend as the sacred ash I place in my mouth melts on my tongue. Then I am gone.

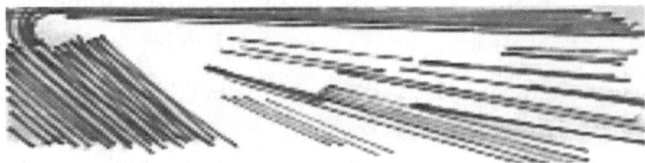

As I fall through the veil of mists and fog the ringing, flashings and blinding all start. These Night vision pre-fears are but novitiate terrors that others would call radiant opportunities for my soul to shake free of my maya. Around me visitations collect. Swirling faces and voices confuse by telling me things that are not really happening, but still I listen. I tune into inner voice recognition and follow the galactic tones down tunnels of love. Spinning about me, opening gateways come and go in impressive numbers and procession. Then I arrive. I do not know how I travelled so quickly or why or where I am, but I crouch hidden in the dark shade of cells. Around my feet, rats run in broken moonlit puddles. I follow them for they might lead to food and possible clues as to what prison place I am in or whom I am supposed to find.

Dungeon bars form elongated shadows of swords and crosses upon the floor. The air is stale. There is mumbling of strange prayer and mantra here as well as sweat, swear and silent supplication; something from a faith far older too. There are some who stand accused of reciting the Arcanum Arcanorum of Jove and the Old Goat God. Within the echoing medieval chambers there is the sound and smell of torture and deep struggle. Time has deserted many of the prisoners. There is nothing but damp, fear and filth left in the containment and uncertainty of their last prison days. Months and years are scratched out on dank walls by nails of different sorts. There is no release from here – only Death, and the prisoners do not know how difficult or painful that journey will be. Gaol graffiti is etched into the different surfaces like engraved headstone epitaphs: names, numbers, anything so that hopefully someone will remember the plight of the unfortunate and the forgotten after they have gone.

However, there are two friends imprisoned here who stand accused and accursed in political manoeuvres of State and Church. The Catholic Inquisitors and exquisite State torturers come to extract their gold – spiritual and temporal. This is jealousy, power and greed acting out as intimidation, interrogation and punishment. The men are almost broken. One is a serving knight; the other the last Templar Grand Master. The Order has fallen except for those who have fled by boat over sea and a few others who have narrowly escaped by horse over land heading North to the Blessed Isle. These two remain captive. How long now? Is it six or seven years? The Master has been prisoner for long enough, but who will untie his tethered hands? Who will set him free?

No-one wants to die this way, but caught between a raging bankrupt King and an all-powerful Church, the Templar Master is damned if he speaks true and damned if he does not. He is racked by fear and doubt. Should he disavow? In this disturbing dark place of confusion, there is somehow a further descent of grace that I cannot yet interpret or fathom. Is there a final separating of the tortured veil to occur in cleansing? There is such fine division between Heaven and Earth, but in this forsaken chamber the Templar Master struggles to find the right way to make peace with God. He is making a decision. Even in his diminished capacity he will find a way to face them, find his voice and upraise his praise on high. He believes in freedom, but his knightly value system imprisons him. He knows that he cannot win, but every breath of his broken ribcage hurts and crushes his lungs. Before he finally burns in fire he will successfully predict the downfall of the House of Capet, but will he recant or curse from the pyre?

God's Kingdom will soon be terribly upon him and from my witness state I am powerless to assist. I am unable to unlock doors or set people free. All I can do is watch, stealing glances and moments from Time as I pilfer bits of metal. On which side of the veil am I? What plane is this? Heaven hangs heavy like a mysterious curtain around my former soul certainty. I glimpse into grief and the dark depths of human despair. If only I could find the keys to hand to this man when they might be useful. Where on Earth reside such terrible actions and imprisoning truths? All places? All times? Not even Peter the Difficult suffered so long an interment in his triple dark den of death. How did he continue to find and light preach in so much muck and filth? Only his luminosity could do that. It was not faith, but radiant awareness actualizing. It is those emanating rays that similarly guide me now – those which will later mix the chemical components of sweat and blood with body heat to leave such century-lasting impressions upon cloth, heart and mind. But first he will be crucified and left to hang from the back of the ever opening and closing Inquisitor's door.

A shroud is in the making. The Templar Master cannot blame God for humanity's nature so he curses the acclaimed Divine Rightness of Church and the corrupt King for the inflicted wickedness. He is lost in starvation and prayer, caught between lies and the systematic crushing of his care. As I move about the dimly lit chambers I now know that the tool which I seek was invented to probe, provoke and arrest the speaking of sacred truth. It is the Heretic's Fork whose double pronged ends press against warrior breasts, gentle throat and jaw. War. War. War. There are so many instruments of torture here, lying around and standing in corners. This is not wanton infliction, but a cleverly planned political and religious re-education. Dried blood looks like rust.

The particular piece I seek rests on a side table, conveniently placed and available for regular use. It has seen many a mock trial and been the means of eliciting false confessions from sleep deprived prisoners. It also quietens, holding closed forceful tongues on the way to heresy fires. For the Grand Mater, truth will turn on a spit like a body in a blaze. I grab the gruesome metal implement in my hand. The heat inflicted word – Abiuro – gleams on the metal and burns my heart, hand and mind as I grasp it. The deed is done. I am now in unnatural physical possession of this exacting metallic monster.

In his position what would I have said or done? Would I have disowned the Holy Ghost's true crown? Would I willingly recant and die alone, God-undone, or ever blaze in fire roasting to be named at last a Peace Warrior?

KEITH BRAZIL

Day 17 – The Inquisitor's Key

Friday 25th March – 17°C

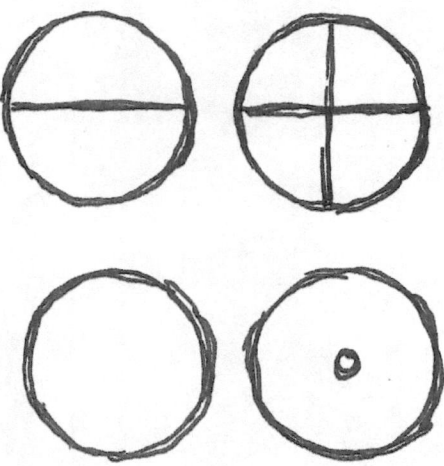

KEITH BRAZIL

Aiwisruthrem: Night (Watch 4) – Vision and voices. The daemon hordes rise in my mind as the terror of the unknown takes over. I am as one abandoned, lost and forgotten, crouching in the recesses of a gloomy gaol – an imprisoned self that inhabits by habit the dark side of the Moon. Did I forget and leave part of myself there when I last visited or is this somewhere real? My patient guiding Snakes have momentarily forsaken me as bible-black shadows strut around me like so many interrogating figures. They preen like priestly Kali Crows. The atmosphere is heavy and oppressive.

'Do you wish for a trial by burial of stone or by element of crushing earth? Do you seek the challenge of metal fury or anger of fire? Would you ask for a test by splintering wood or by drowning water? How would you wish to die? Speak, seeker, so we may know your fears? Are you a guilty or innocent prisoner? Are you the wrong man? Do we accuse you falsely? What worth your current state? Give tongue so that we might know your heart and your stake! What element are you? What symbol do you bring that enlightens us as to the real essence of your truth? Lion, Bull, Serpent, Dragon, or Eagle? What is it that you need to give back? Why have you come? Where is your breast-pierced Pelican or your rising Sun? When arises your Time Phoenix? What combustible alchemy do you experiment with now? What wizardry is this? What metal tale do you recount? Whence do you hail? More importantly, where do you think you are travelling in your pursuit of the grail? What pushing and pulling leads you on? Is it Siren-insanity or Dragon-song? What creatures abet and reroute you? You, who have summoned alchemical birds and Snakes, have called upon us as Air Voices and we-in-service have gathered and come. We enact. You react. The Ravens stalk you. Your Lion roars. Dragons dement you. Eagles bring straw. In this reconciliation of states – what are you going to do?'

In this place, in this caged state, truth and lies are set to the skies like doves in the Temple Garden, caught, bought, and then wing freed. Yet dove-deliverance is only momentarily gained, quickly recaptured for childlike purpose and simple profit. Similarly, I can tell the inquisitorial Crows what they want to hear if it gets me out of here. Please tell. What is the question? What is it that you want from me?

'Answer us this: If the key is the question and the question is the key, how does eternal love unlock thee?'

My heart beats fast. I need to escape from this dark place and I miss the comforting presence and light of the Moon. Where is the key to the freeing of the imprisoned spiritual me? They wish me to reveal something, understand something, but how can my anxious, enquiring mind release the mystery of the heart? Questions search for answers, much as quests are in relentless pursuits of ends. If the open heart has no door then how can enquiry be the key? Is the key wisdom? Love? Natural curiosity? Or is the answer linked to spiritual time and the descent of light divine? I answer,

'Unconditional-me. Compassionate-you.'

In the prevailing silence I hear the keys to the cells dangling on the belt by the Inquisitor's side. Nearby, the keys to the cupboard and the instruments of torture and passion hang on a wooden peg. Someone sits asleep hidden in the shadows. This is clever Crow Trickster business. The five pains and mutilating punishments are here, brutality beyond endurance, but they jostle next to the Seven Heavens. Harm is here, but so is choice. If I am you and you are me, if we are somehow connected, what relationship has brought us to this sharp point at wits, words and sword-tips end? We curse each other from different sides and renew our bonds in the human drama. I awaken emboldened with a greater courage and faith, but wonder if our roles once reversed? God forgive us all, for living on fear and on the ashes of soul released memories! Together, did we make saints for the burning? The Crows might smell blood, but that does not make me burnt-hunted.

Imprisoned I am – so be it. In this place so many of us are trapped abiding our lonely cell time. Kali's High Inquisitor enters in, examining and cross-examining. His staff uncoils as slippery as a magician's servant Snake. Is this fear or restriction uncoiling? This is power and abandonment in abundance. This is self-serving. Foremost he asks:

'Who are you?'

Somebody. Nobody. Everybody. Whoever it is – I am no longer that person. I offer up a prayer of hope and ask for help. Is my quest purely one of renegotiating identity? Questions fast move on, forcing their way in.

'What is first firmament?'

In the infinite, eternal, swirl of current torment, everything is but Heaven and Hell. I am caught in the dark dream reality of the Crow-black Night Sky. Is this my judgement by the Moon and the Stars? Is that why they are not here – injured victims that I have I betrayed and cannot call as witnesses? I must concentrate. Think. The clue must be in the question. Then the examiner must be Asman – Old God of All Sky. The answer must be Highest Heaven, indivisible source before the emanation of Love and Truth.

'What is Atar?'

Atar is old language. Atar is the Light of Revelation, that which radiates all other lights. Illumination. Comprehension. Always and everywhere – it tries to make sense of the universal codes, and of all the World's odds and losses. If my old love and truth are on trial, then this must be ordeal by heat. If Atar is here – all-abiding, serving Time – the Dream Tree must be holding me in its high branches of transmutation. Yet something is hindering passage. Something is stopping and blocking the Alchemical Bottle until the transformational point is reached and transcended. Through the Moon and the Night Sky the supernatural Empress Goddess calls for a new state of life and another way of living. The answer must be that which is higher than truth and love. What name that?

'What purpose this?'

Unity? Is it possible? Is the answer the unification of the luminous bodies? I hear the Inquisitor's Serpent-staff hiss. Corrupting experience glides towards higher innocence. These prison bars I hold and shake. Are they Heaven, Hell or the Garden's Gate? Is this golden entry or Paradise Fall? Is this expulsion or emancipation of all? At this precarious point, I am simultaneously ascending and descending, but what lays beyond and above all this vision imagery? In this dungeon of Wilderness Days I seek only exit to green and pleasant lands. I could bide my time, but my time is now. I press. I confess.

'I am tree and I am gate. I am key, staff and fleeing Snake. I am him in the shadow who holds me prisoner by mistake.'

Through the rigid prison bars I now struggle to wriggle free. As I rattle the static cage I look back and within to peeling skin. My black and white scales tip the changes. If I wish to be reborn I must steal the Inquisitor's Keys, slide them from his belt or take those hanging from off the wooden peg. They offer freedom from all prison doors and release from the instruments of torture and passion. There is only one final answer to find and I believe I can now announce this. For all the burning flames and higher bright light, for all the visible and invisible alchemical fires, there is only that which is most worthy of veneration – the one divinity worshipped and served by angels that goes by many glimpsed names. To speak it is to remember it from of old, and somehow I know it.

'Yazata.'

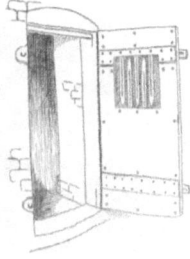

Through unconditional love a key turns and a door clicks open. Somehow I have become agape, but I do not know how to step free.

Day 18 – Kali/Night Vision

Saturday 26th March – 12°C

Ushahin: Dark Night (Watch 5) – All day spent thrashing about in dream and wandering trance, but now the dark indigo night is here. My fascination of the deeper deep is the encroaching colour of Kali's skin. In this state she reigns supreme, collecting the skulls and dreams of the sleeping dead like pebbles and shells washed upon a distant Star-shore. Kali sends her snakes and daemons as writhing night terrors – struggles to wake the sleeping. She is dark aspect and dark matter come to occult call; come to collect; come to deliver. She is Goddess of Time and Change, of death within life, of all sea, land and air shattering and synthesising. She steps out of the Night Sky from beyond the unseen side of the Moon – a visionary phase beyond my previous comprehension of the Eastern arts. Should I fear her and her strange ceremonies for she is devourer and destructive element?

Kali takes me up and into the dark cavern of her chaos. She carries me and deposits me until I am empty. Sweeping and flickering around her feet are wings of flame. In her hands she holds the several swords to sever attachments. Fire like thunderbolts emit from the Cloud of Unknowing about her. She is power and strength. Shaved-headed boys run about the City's backstreets with begging bowls searching for food, ringing-singing bowls for emitting and collecting sound, silver bowls polished in ritual preparation for the gathering of Death's tears, and golden bowls for the saintly light and the wringing of our empathetic understanding. They are the children of Kaliban, laughing mercilessly, laughing at the impossibility of pain as though running around the City's rivers and streets in a child's game. These are Varanasi Boys, Bonfire Boys, spirit children, and votive. With her sword Kali scrapes the Night Sky of my mind. In this moment she is all I find. She asks the difficult, the impossible, as she probes my hurting and seeks out my fear.

'Ha-Kraa! Do you fear to dance on the bones of the dead? Rather, fear death by fire. Do not fear the Sacred Flame at all unless by some aversion you desire to be burnt alive. When the Time does come, deflect not your gaze, but dance wild, praise high and blaze. Dare you raise your Holy Flag to new life and ways? Consider this the death of your days for are you not mine as a flesh child of light divine? You belong to me! I am the one who has come to set you free!'

How can I walk towards this? I am not ready to die. Who is? Dwarfed by the dark, I stand on the shore of her Night Sky. I feel like a child encouraged to dance upon the bonfire of the dead for the first time. The Altar Boys of Flame take my hand and kick the funeral pyres to the ground. As quickly as one Death Nest is demolished another pyre is raised. I am as urchin-they – all ash and burnt-out flame in constant funeral games. Cinders and coals are beneath my feet. I inhale the smoke of night. The Bonfire Boys laugh and dance as I tremble. For me it is the uncomforting pain and memory of my Father's recent death. For them it is the joy of life ever-continuing.

I dance upon bones – the burnt bones of my ancestors and of my grief fuelled past. Embers fall about me and in them are reminders of torchlight and fires, glimpses of gathering distant days. The tremors of Dark Sky-vision and Night-journeying begin. As I start to shake I am pulled from my body. I go back in an arc like a cannonball shot through time to the grounds of an overshadowing castle. This is Middle England. It is night-time. There is much commotion. An army is being assembled and orders are being given. Soon another English Army will march on France, depleting money and bodies in an ultimately doomed and unjust campaign. Preparations are almost complete. I do not know why, but I turn to seek the Smithy.

The visible red-coal glow of a Blacksmith's grate beckons. All manner of inviting metal work piles up: nails, horseshoes, shields, swords, and arrow tips. There are plenty of munitions in the Smithy's store to plunder if I so wished, but there is no weapon here that I could not take instead from the Agency's own Armoury Tower. It is not the Blacksmith's or the Swordsmith's help that I need, but the dexterity of the Whitesmith as he finishes off his cold metal labours. It is the overheard guttural tone of German-English that attracts my attention and gives him away. I do not seek the hammer and anvil that flatten the forged blade and shape the undivine military might. This is all about crowning power and stealing land.

Instead, I seek the ornamental doming and raising hammers and files which emboss the coat of arms on a suit of armour that will one day sadly seal the death of a brave and beautiful peasant girl. She who was once gentle is called to war. She who hears voices rides horses across the fields of France. In her spiritual aim and vision she looks resplendent to an oppressed people and king who, in gratitude for freeing their Nation, will turn and burn a spiritual child. She is meek and entrancingly mild. God leads her as a humble-fierce warrior-wild. She possesses the gift of listening in to the messages of saints and angels. Enthralled I watch the skilful fingers of the Whitesmith complete the filigree of heraldic strength and symbolic meanings of her enemy. The armoured breastplate is complete. Chainmail is attached to protect the soft spots of the body and signals the beginning of the end of the Maid of Orleans. She knows nothing of this yet. Conquer France. Conquer France. This is her compelling mission.

Before me stands the Thirteenth Earl of Warwick. Metal stacks upon metal; sword upon sword; shield upon shield. This is not defence, but attack and invasion. A war that is not right to win. It will be a battle royal and unholy. It needs to fail our nation. Out of the Hundred Years Conflict further war grew. No-one knows whether the war is in-or-out of God's grace, but there are so many deaths to come, especially the overflowing flames of the righteous Beautiful One. Horses move nervously. Under orders, foot soldiers march. The banner is raised. The scene is rapidly shifting. I grasp the Whitesmith's tools as the world-between-worlds where I am standing starts to fade and close.

As I am pulled through the Star-gateway, faces from across time and from across different lands look up into the suddenly shared Night-vision. A searing shriek of a Warrior Goddess in full Sky-cry rips through the air. Momentarily petrified, the stargazing faces long to see the source of such unholy screeching. Is it angels and daemons once more at war in prolonged Heavenly combat? Are there dragons on the attack? These metal swords and valiant souls are yet to be united in the tearing of flesh. More wounding than the World can hold and Spirit bear witness to. More injury to Holy Woman than the Goddess can bear.

It is Kali who unleashes her final fury and terrifying scream. It is she who hurls me forward through Time into my trembling flame-jigging body. It is she who burns the medieval mind with clouds of sulphur, fire and thunder. How could they behold her and not think her daemon in that century in the West? I fight back the imagery of the World's falling, of the dissipating Night-vision, whilst the metal tools and hammers fall from the palm of my blackened, ash-covered hand. Whilst I have been in the fiery forge of the mind, the votive Bonfire Boys have been dancing in the fire of my heart. Smiling, they kick the burnt sticks from under me. They do not fear death, but greet it as guest.

The Bonfire Boys speak to me…

'Oh, most welcome one! Ours days are spent in praise preparing the approach of the unavoidable abyss that is Death's dark bliss. Thank God and Goddess! Know in your heart that everyone is justly forgiven, but have you forgiven those that have harmed you and made amends to those you have injured? Have you forgiven yourself for such human plunder – whether great suffering or insignificant effort? Have you raged and wept your joy? In the heat of your body's bonfire you will find us. Bind with us. Become one of us. Together we shall dance upon the bones of the living and the dead – all so newly born, yet slowly dying. This is your growing intimacy of fear. Until that final day raise your red flame to the acclaim of natural death. You were born to die so live well. This is the dance of your Raven Heart's Heaven and Hell.'

Sweating, I collapse in a fever. I have momentary contact with the hard cold rooftop of my Aerie before the tip of a trident presses hard against my chest. A fiery heel burns my brain and pushes against the side of my head. The Goddess of Timeless Change speaks one final time.

'Ha-Kraa! Do not despair – wait until the time when you and I will meet again, but know that I will be forever in disguise. You will recognise me by the colour of Night Sky skin and dark shadow lit eyes. Kraa-Ha! Take heed my Crow warning! It is but the Kraa-Ha-Traa of deep spiritual fire and bless-warming. Can you feel it descending? I am your dark light never ending.'

I blackout and disappear into the darkness of Kali's Night Sky mind.

Day 19 – Fire

Sunday 27th March –13°C

Uzerin: Late Afternoon (Watch 3) – Far, far and away, I slip under the horizon's rim, under the spiral Sky. Unafraid, I fly free across the rooftops as though running through an urban jungle; swinging through the canopy of trees like Mowgli on a rope vine back to the safety of his treetop perch. In my Aerie, the sounds of the City gather around – children playing and crying, mothers yelling and soothing, buses braking and sighing, rumbling distant trains rocking out the comforting regularities of timetabled time and my slow wearying insanity. Street life goes on below. The sounds of a guitar float by. Someone practices late-night chords in the closing of an afternoon. Sounds of the Underground mix in. There is a smell of hot tar. Drills excavate the remains of drains and tarmac, penetrating the surface of past history buried there – Victorian streets, Medieval thoroughfares, Roman roads, and prehistoric pathways. Beneath the arid, gum-steamed surface of our regular roads, beyond the cries of concrete and the slabs of pavement, lies the butchery and love of two thousand years of negative intent.

The mind goes mad as the heart is forgotten. When divorced from reason, feeling becomes irrational and forlorn. Bereft from love, the mind turns controlling. Everyone is a critic instead of a being an artist or lover. Alcoholics, junkies, students, workers, managers and all those stressed up in their jangled lives are out and about on-the-make – applying their sneaky desires in afternoon survival pleasure, unctuous pursuits and bunking freedom. Some teenage girls are doing their worst after school, whilst unwholesomely loud and leery boys, pretending to be drunk, slump against each other in crude friendship. Aggression and disempowerment force encounters in rough, gruff games of come-on and pick-up. They take a chance and seize opportunities to secure pubescent snogs, smokes and dances. Friendships make or break. It is hard to hold your own, particularly if you do not conform. I push thoughts of distant places and school years out of my mind whilst feeling a measure of sympathy for theirs.

I never did fit in; too much of a different Sufi sound and vision going on within – a mix of doing my own thing and nothing in particular, with a lot of natural outdoor space to explore. I contemplate old lands and luxuries and thank Heaven for the timing of my childhood. Now, the cars, buses and jungle drums beat out their traffic rhythms beneath. These are the incessant nearby sounds of an on setting sunset City. I take to surfing the building tops and chasing the horizons of the near Sky – over rooftop and wall, river and fall, cascading drops between buildings, branch and satellite trees, I fly into the wind. In flowing so rapidly in-and-out of consciousness and into the universal slipstream, deep tears collect in my eyes. Through the refraction of light drops and prisms, I see angels gather, encounter and rise, staring at me with their own particular brand of madness burning in their eyes. For them the World is scorching so that Gaia might live within the Sun's evolution of solar fire. They see Humanity as one great Tribal Nation in despair, stuck in twisted history previously unable to repair itself, but at last gratifyingly preparing to restore, harnessing the simplicity of personal warmth and kindness.

At this speed I am now able to discern the Angelic Kingdoms through quantum-dazzling light and fire. Opportunities for soul resurrection exist here! Light-entranced angelic beings dance and serve with their raised silver swords, reflective Moon-basins and sunlit shields. These are attendant healers and sentinel warriors alike. Rushing through this sizzling Realm of Angels at twenty, thirty times faster than normal light rays beam, I perceive their polychromatic beauty as aspect of God. They form rainbow bridges between Worlds to golden consciousness. They do not carry pots of gold as such, but prosperity honey to pollinate the World Soul and feed the hearts and minds of fellow worker bees. I can hear the hum of their angelic swarming in golden acts of love. Their gold does not glitter or wither and the soul-denting glister of enticement by money does not fool them. But I must not stop here in this winged Spirit kingdom. I cannot, for it is too frightening to behold, too glorious and full of thunder. Instead, I follow the thread that pulls me down into the distant mountains, towards a Church and an Old Town's village square and outbuildings. As quickly as birds flap up and fly – I am on Heaven's wing and on the way down through the Sky.

Down now. Down. I am plummeting down on a dove descent in the direct path of a dawning Sky and a rising, burning wall of flame. I am all trepidation as to what fresh horror I might find here. What on earth awaits the seeker in me as I tumble towards a Medieval Town in France? The Girl of Gold unnerves the men, but unites the horses and people. She frightens the power of church and state in her mystic intensity. She asks for pardon whilst forgiving them all. Brought forth from secular prison on this day, this Maid of Heaven is visible here clutching a crude cross fashioned from simple wooden sticks. She is tied to a tall pillar. As she returned a newly unified kingdom to the King, so she will soon enter her own Heaven King's Heart Kingdom. At her petition a cross is held up in front of her, but it is too late to undo the flames' bidding.

'Ma mère divine. Mon père divin. S'il vous plaît, faites tomber la pluie.'

It is I that pleads for something so simple to save her. I wish for water – that which would drown the fire. If only wood had tears! Would that Sky could cry and extinguish this scene to save her and quench my anguish. This is horrifying, unbearably sad and brutal, and I can do nothing but witness. In her advance she came to free and unite France. Her end is not confused madness, but cruelly cunning and savage death by fire – politically inspired and wilfully lit. Who can be brave in such circumstances? Was there presage of this – warning to me and to others not to fear the flame? As I follow The Maid into the growing flames of the pyre she ascends burning high and bright. Transcendent resurrection-light envelops her. Her eyes are lifted up to Heaven, shining, fascinated, as once she used to be in early morning religious ecstasy and mystic reverie. Does no-one else care? Those who stand around – do they see her incandescent beauty?

In amongst the shrouding smoke Jehanne blazes like her pennon once blazed as a beacon of purity and perfection – all gold, white and lily. In choosing to die mindfully she becomes divine inspiration, ensign and emblem. Drawing us all in, she ignites greater faith. Yet the heat around her heart becomes a truly woeful 'Tale of Winter'. As the Great Poet once proclaimed, "It is the Heretic that makes the fire, not she who burns in it". Jehanne takes her rightful place in Heaven.

'Jésus!'

One word. Just one word for all that she had accomplished! Yet what word could be better than a word of God and Heaven? In returning to Heaven, all is love and terrifying truth whereas she in times past played free as a growing child in the farm's garden. Was it Summer when she first heard voices? Fields and pastures were her original churches; Churches her great passion and devotion. She is soft and humble. Honest simplicity makes her the Prophet's mouthpiece. Where there is now agony, there was hope, belief and the growing of a fighting spirit. Her vision meets the will of God as her mission burns like a fuse of righteousness. It runs through her, culminating in the tips of her fingers and into her sword, banner and shield. Everything stands against her. Her celestial visitations call forth her invincible soul. Saint Michael. Sainte Margaret. Sainte Catherine. Once she talked with the praise of angels and dialogued with the saints. In battle, her blood flowed over her breast. Today, chains on a wooden pyre fetter her. Tomorrow she stains us all as tainted, unrighteous history is furthered. She is lost now. Her task seems to have turned against her. Royal allegiances prove less loyal. Angelic alliances are less corporal. Jehanne has turned to God and become dove.

Standing within the fire I watch Jehanne's timeline unravel. Her arrival, like her swift end so politically pressed and pursued, ultimately brought some semblance of unification. She came to join in love, not in hating, as she sought simple spiritual instruction and peace in her calling. She must meet the Dauphin. She is on spiritual time and only has until the third Thursday of Lent to reach him. Across the snow she goes. Across the land and field, passing banner and shield. Her Lord demands it. She commands it. She gathers an army of believers to her ranks as she burns and blazes with spiritual fire within, yet all around her hierarchy and patriarchy doubt. Jehanne waits three days to see the Dauphin to affirm that the French King will be crowned. She recites and repeats a spiritual secret to convince him. In that insight the King believes.

Jehanne traverses the country and summons forth Godly-aide. Orleans is saved. Town by town she sees them fall: all the English Lords and their fighting fools, the poor misguided men at arms. The liberated towns rescued by the great-hearted daughter rally round. The oppressing of Nations subsides in the incessant tides and the heart of France begins to be healed and rightfully restored; reunited in the coronation of the King. Yet the English remain to exercise influence over a wavering French Royal Court. The English will depart, but not before they help create a martyr with war accusations and false crimes. Jehanne presses for advantage. Her King fails and betrays her; supports her not. She falls and is taken, thwarting attempts of prison molestation through cross-dressing chastity.

Handed over to the Inquisitors in Faith, she is subjected to their monstrous, infamous, meticulous scribing of her item removal and turn of her screw. Some matters, some articles, some particulars of their jealousy, their patriarchy, their tyranny of books, move against her Nature. It is so simple. The Maid is more in love with God then they profess to be. In return she is more loved by God then they, and is consequently more earthly challenged. They gather to interrogate and enquire of the source of the invisible forces that surround her. They pride themselves on being the chosen testers of faith and the dispellers of earthly shadows. Yet she has grown in deep devotion and God is tending her well.

'Dieu, s'il vous plaît, pleurez, gardez et embrassez-la bien. Sur les ailes du guerrier, vous déposez l'histoire du coeur pour la conter et la propager. Dans votre Majesté, la puissance et la gloire, je vois prie de nous donner votre paix indivisible.'

In the trial Jehanne holds back, uneasy like a disturbed horse. She retreats and prays, before confessing and signing with a coded cross, the runic kiss that only her generals would know not to trust. She abjures, fighting to save herself, but does not inwardly surrender or outwardly leave. Yet she escapes one fate only to find another awaits. Horse-drawn destiny knocks upon her Heaven's door as she awakens to further spiritual purpose. She recants. Condemned as a relapsed Heretic, this Mystic Maid will go up in flames as an unstable radical. In greatness she learns to sign her name in blood upon all our chests and hearts.

Jehanne holds a visionary key. Who is the beneficiary? Emptied, fulfilled, she is purified through fire as she takes the licking wounds of hate with her. Everything about her is burnt: her body, her bones, her simple tunic, her hair, everything except her thoughts and feelings. Yet her love crosses centuries. I am distraught at the idea of such a sacrifice. Horrified by what is asked of her. Flames flicker high around this now lifeless figure as her mysterious light extinguishes. I am humbled. Old curses burn as we, through her gracious love, remain enthralled by her yearning. I balance on the crackling sticks that snap and fall beneath my feet. It is hard to dance on all of this. Where are the Bonfire Boys to help me now? Embers gash – enthralled, appalled – as smoke and fire conjoin to bring all-consuming death unto The Maid. Rejoice now, for Jehanne returns to her saviour! In gold, white and red she is spiritually radiant and beautiful. God is joyous to meet her and greet her into Heaven's embrace.

'Mon Dieu. Mon coeur. Est-ce que c'est le feu sacré?'

'Ma fille. Je suis celui qui ne brûle jamais. Venez à moi.'

In Jehanne's quiet stillness her borrowed elements are returned and all is love. Uncaged, she escapes like a soul bird freed from golden armour. Slowly, impotent rage is dying around her like exhausted flames. What have they done? Their momentary gains are our losses, but the deed is complete and the evil portent of dark history has once more been spiritually interrupted, altered, and changed for the better. She is spared hearing the sobbing entreaties of her despairing, broken-hearted, grey-haired Mother at her future redeeming trial. In God's wisdom and God's grace she is deemed worthy, warrior child and fair of face. Eventually exonerated, Jehanne will never know the outcome of the Church's reclamation of her as a saint. She is dead. It is all too late.

Warrior God, out of such ash comes what? Mysterious justice and the secrets of your all-encompassing heart? Here, in such fire and shadow, I am afraid for all of us. Still, in this streaming of time and memories shared, I have to find the metal bind. What item has brought me here? It is not the iron chains that I seek that held the limp and charred body remains of Jehanne being hauled down, and taken to burn again and again. As the surviving record reminds – nothing is left for reliquary. Now I am pulled from the pyre across the courtyard to a sunlit cell where there is a chair and simple bed. There is nothing here – absence of a dress, hairpin or man's attire that holds any significant metal clue worth the stealing. Then I am slammed back even further in time. I see her standing strong in preparation for battle. The suspicion of certain generals surrounds her. The faith of foot soldiers too. The army are resolute and ready to follow her. Yet it is not her protective armour that I seek. Neither is it the rings she wears, nor even the dagger hanging around her waist. Nor indeed is it the standard that she chooses to bear. The sword she swings kills no thing, and the crosses of Sainte Catherine still kiss upon it. It is not this. It is not even the chevalier horse's bridle and bit that glints with reflected sunlight.

I am encouraged on and tumble further back in time. What I seek is the metal blade, the crude shearing scissors, which first cut Jehanne's hair after her original visitations. It makes people stare. She is boyish. She is brave. She takes on the garbs and mantle of manly duty to protect her body and soul from violation, but beneath remains an intact child. The scissors I covet can be found lying gleaming in the barn resolutely shining within the growing silence of the country farm. By the river and the orchard she once ran free. In the distant farmhouse I hear her mother cry with fear and incomprehension as a true heart turns to God and begins to explain their august calling. She is only a child of twelve. Even her hero – the Christ – had to leave his mother to take on his adult life. But The Maid is so young. Yet she secretly knows what must be done for she was born to do this. Bravely, at sixteen she leaves to raise an army. She is in God's hands and moves at his holy behest. At nineteen she is left to wait her ordeal and trial days before being returned to Heaven through treachery and fire.

Today the battle rages on and on. War visions of the heart still hurt as much as any guiding storm arrow. Who will save the faithful robin and friendly sparrow? The Maid felt the loss of blood and life, but not the sanctity of her faith. At times her face appears drained. At moments she staggers lost, yet she is found to be steadfast and true even when faced with fear of abandonment. Without love, are we not all forsaken? The winds of change blow differently for her now. She has come to be blessed and is seated in the resplendent Halls of Heaven as a member of the Spiritual Council. From this sanctified position she brings visions to minds, strength to hearts, and star maps of faith to embattled Earth kingdoms. She talks in the French language of angels. All I can do is listen and cherish her undiminished spiritual story.

'Ayez foi en moi. Croyez, car je suis ici comme la vérité éternelle. Je vis comme je vois votre âme. Croyez.'

Day 20 – Change

Monday 28th March – 13°C

Rapithwin: Afternoon (Watch 2) – Unable to push through the surrounding darkness and light, I struggle with change and the difficult nature of transition. How can I exist and prevail within shifting Taoist Trigram States – moving from that which is stable, yet continuously flowing between mother and father, and their three daughters, and their three sons? I find no peace or acceptance here. I strive for a new point of equilibrium, but from what point and to where am I changing? In these exchanges I do not know what is surface and what is deep. I mentally tussle with old ideas borrowed from learned books to make this unease more understandable – more palatable. Yet this constant tapping sound I hear growing nearer – is it the clink of thrown coins in a fountain, a chuck of falling luck over the shoulder, or is it the loose change of the I-Ching chinking in my pocket? I thought I had lost these coins. Have they been replaced? Is there the possibility of divination in all this? I hear the sound of a sword drawing and scraping upon a stone floor. I hear its cutting blade slicing through the air. Is there education here? The ancient commentaries of Confucius fly in the wind like yarrow stalks and pinches of salt freshly thrashed and thrown.

All becomes about survival in this extreme Time of mine. I know the tumbling higher numbers and natural fractals are altering in never-ending configurations about me – infinite and recursive, irregular, yet seemingly perfect in their patterns and spirals. Ascending, descending, fragmenting and multiplying, some things are fixed, persistent, whilst others are mutable and helpful, or cardinal and initiatory. Every day Nature changes. Every day Nature remains the same. Is that how we grow – rooted, yet branching? Within this point of space and time, I am caught in same-changing as I become an adaptable variable yet ever fixing point. I need to be more elastic, more flexible. Still in planetary evolution from first generation starbursts, I have to handle the gathering speed of the oncoming galactic transformation. The unpredictable science of higher mathematics seeks links to the solution of our human grief and old hurting.

Is there some place where thoughts and feelings secretly flutter and live, multiplying in the Universal Mind, until they descend upon us as a humming rabble of unconditional birds, bees and butterflies? Do I revert to preconceived conditioned type ricocheting off encaging personality circles or am I free to hover and become the winged me? I am none of the numbered things. At difficult and inconceivable angles of Earthly entry, trapped angels and masters succeed in breaking free of imprisoning light cages. In my present awkward state of being, I try to rupture and break through the cloud cover and dark matter that wrap about the interior me. In this state of gloom and sorrow I search for a sunbeam, a glimpse of light, a branch of golden truth to grab onto and help swing me up and onwards upon the Tree of Life and eternal existence.

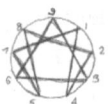

As part of the greater interconnected equation I can be in an instant the God Earth solution I have been looking for – however apart and distant I might feel at present. Heaven mates with the Earth again in endless streaming as heavenly powers sweep away the old in reformation without judgement. Can I? In the miracle struggle between stable and unstable elements, new ones are birthed within the forging furnaces of burning suns and bunsen-minds. Intensity. Immensity. It is the heat of alchemical fire I dread most. In the passing of my wilderness time, signs and symbols arise all about me as synchronicity guides me on. Yet the shadows of thunder and fear roll here too as my cloud-dark feelings divine differently from universal flow and World soul.

My body aches as my activating spirit descends. I am left to drift and dream-wake – walking upon the pathways of the Heartland in human night vulnerability. I realise the quickening need to rouse the sleeping master within and speak with the awakened ones. I document this shedding and emergence as plucked, rose petal pages in a diary of changes. I know I cannot do it easily, for how do I move a mountain a quarter-inch to the right whilst continuing to climb and realign? How do I stand at the bottom and at the top simultaneously? From Base Camp, through the clouds of confusion, to the highest peak of the Tibetan clear day, my strange meetings with men and women from out of history lead to new wonders.

A beguiling conundrum unfurls – how to fathom further the Mountain's sky-reach, the Sky's earth-plunge, and the Land's sea-drop? How do I ask the air not to be there, swirling where it pleases? Why would a bird that loves the thermal breezes not soar and fly? My Time Phoenix has to take wing again despite my clumsy, bruising attempts at Night-journeying. If I could apply warmth to this atmospheric pressure that presses upon my body, would I gain a degree of uplift in smoother flight or simply combust? There is no control to my Soul's urges, so I sail wherever the hurricane may blow, but every moment urges me on to further change. I cannot stop here burning mid-exchange.

Yet how should I be crossing the elements? I experience the snowy mountaintops as water droplets in natural river dispersal; rising mist as falling rain in replenishing; swirling snow to ice in melting glacier sublimation. This is subtle erosion of old granite boulders creating channels and rivulets for the release of the new. What should I do but sit and watch silently the process of decay and alchemical change? Should I interfere and explore my humanity or just observe and experience the process? Should I swill modern alchemists' flasks with vodka and gin in the getting-by of these remaining wilderness days? Molecule by infinitesimal molecule I move along as air disturbed by wing and feather. Eternity is the great adjustor, but what to do with all this time? Love. Re-think. Re-love. Re-be. A chance to change and change again as I reconsider it all – reconsider the All. I lie back on the turning Wheel of Fortune, hanging on to old certainties until I am forced to let go.

Uzerin: Late Afternoon (Watch 2) – How long have I been shipwrecked here – a stranger washed up in strange lands? I am thirsty and desirous of putting down roots, but I am a nomad in a No Man's Land. What new territory is waiting to be discovered? How can anything grow in such abandonment? Where is the purifying, quenching water? Weeds struggle as I stumble by. There is no New Jerusalem here, just Jesus in the Sky, beatific, accompanied by his Sky-bride. How can so much joy spring from such a single smile? The Magdalena's flowing robes are as cream-white and opulent as the Moon's gracious down pouring light, whereas the dust of this abandoned estate and bustling city sucks dry the thirsty devil growing within me. She washed his feet so lovingly, whereas mine are covered in the grime of stained city wandering. Their mystical union is immersed in the immensity of peace and wordless perception. I am cloaked in the dirt of difficult worlds and of the many troubled states of sorrow and shame. Forgiveness curls, yet is contained and cannot break free from the parameters of the boxed-me however golden the ratio.

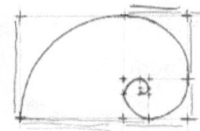

Spiralling above, around and below me is a city of contrasts. The wise kings and the shepherds, the protected and the privileged, the rich and the needy, the politic and greedy, the prospering and the poor, all come into contact with the Earth Banquet and each other. It is the best and worst of our monopolising times. I question my purpose. Who am I travelling through Life's entangling Theatre of Condolence? What part do I play in the upcoming Passion? Where are my ajam odes of joy? I wander, doing what I must do to survive, but I do not like it. I find it hard to inhabit this Wasteland where so many have walked before. Here, I am alone in forsaken illusion. Acceptance of self as to who I am in this shaken state, rather than that which I wish to be, feels debilitating and keeps me conflicted. There is dust on my shoes that I must kick off and give back as the dying days of my Time torment my being, and my storm continues to sandblast me.

In the surrounding city deserts and stone jungles, I seek out something else – something most unique and special. Call it not Holy Grail, but a single drop of Hallowed Blood in the wilderness of my heart would suffice to make branches blossom and kingdoms renew. Is it grace in the form of spiritual love for which I endlessly search? Who would deny me the asking or the questing? Who prohibits me? I cannot turn back – I do not wish to – yet I find it difficult to summon the inner strength to go on. Still, I need to find a way to clear my own path of all this falling, fragmented debris. My on-going insanity is nothing compared to this restless quest for peace. I ache for its descent. How long have I been in-and-out of this present heart state? How many days do I have left to drift and endure as I cross the Sky Time borderlines in search of God's love?

I clamber over the walls of an abandoned housing estate and climb beyond reason. I fear both death and new life – like a cat drawing near to its dream ninth, sacred, yet scared. I need to withdraw from my body to realign and re-inhabit. A layer of my old skin sloughs off with every Time-travelling journey I make, as I cast off my former, restricting scales. New layers of permeating light replace the skin of the derelict me as a body of light continues to build around me. I am simultaneously shedding snake and fledgling bird. Yet with my emerging dark-wings I am cawing, not singing, and it is my Raven beak that that is tapping from within my auric egg. This is my struggle with the instrument of profound sound and vision that brings eternal inner change. This is not bomb blast, but emotional resonance seeking deeper detonation. This is not the joining of lower and higher will, but the return to original vibrational being in the mystic strike of the loud aum hum-om-ables.

Day 21 – Bell Tower

Tuesday 29th March – 15°C

KEITH BRAZIL

Aiwisruthrem: Night (watch 4) – Night-journey. The place of abode that I find myself in is strangely familiar. It is one of the twenty-one towers of the Concentric Castle that make up the Tower of London where I work for the Raven Agency. This is yesteryear and there is no-one here. The windows are shuttered. The air in the room turns you inside out, suffocating like a poison turning reason to treason. There is nothing here except a footstool by the empty fireplace. As I sit down I notice, strewn about on the flagstones, bits of gold thread. Silver needles laced with colourful strands fill the stone cracks that once embroidered a tapestry cloth. I reach down to pull the entombed needles free with my fingernails as the thoughts of a young lady fill the air.

She is twenty-one, a false prisoner in fear for her life. She walks a thin line, as fragile as a gossamer thread placed around a lowered neck facing possible beheading. It is a neck no longer held up high in proud, courtly gavottes – and which parades not the customary garrotting pearls and golden jewels. To escape, she must bow her head, be seen to bow her head, yet her inner resistance is growing. Truth and love are divided in her, but she has the wiles and will to sew them together. She has quick dextrous fingers, neat sprightly feet, and an agile Virgoan mind. She corsets herself in. Alongside her fear and her favourites, her loyalties will be tested to the utmost. What belief shapes her feminine figure, her authority and the culture of power in her coming of age? The plotting and conniving of politics that belong to Crown and State, but which do not form part of God's heart, surround her. Imprisoned, she delves deep into her psyche. As I hold the needles invisible thoughts begin to form, turn and speak. They fill the air, my head and ear. Once again, I am in turbulent and troubled times. I am in Gloriana's Tower.

'I am wary of contamination by poison. Every morsel is suspect. Truly this ordeal is terrifying. I am treated most severely even after a month of being here, although sometimes I am not without an occasional companion. They generally hate me, for their love of their Religion is greater than any potential respect for my royal personage and therefore for what I have come to represent. Their Catholicism creates our dark days and adds to the bloodiness of the nation. A church with such blood on their hands guides my sister's will and I wish to be free of such confining circumstances. I am but true subject, as God and my Handmaidens are true friends.

I am imprisoned on the first floor, in a small but adequately comfortable room. The horror of my Mother's and Aunt's agonising fates does not escape me in this terrible place. I believe I may well die here too although I repeatedly and assuredly deny all involvement. If only they would let me speak to my sister or at least afford me the writing materials to compose and send a letter, but I am trapped here. Trapped in a turret in The Tower. Trapped by the Queen's command under the Papal Rosary. Of course in my present imprisoned situation I have come to respect the greater freedom than any faith allows though Protestant avowed I am. No letters are allowed. Communiqué is seen as pleading or as possible requests for help from allies. The Tower holds supporters as well as spies and adversaries. The birds wear black and walk upon the walls in seeming autonomy. If only I could get to the Ravens' Master. I am sure I would find friend and comforting refuge there.'

'There is a large fireplace, but only three small windows with which to ease my view. These have recently become shuttered to stop any attempts of communication with the outside world, or so I presume. How strange now it all does seem. I cannot even see the weather from my windows. It is stifling inside and a further test of my sanity, but I believe a psychic spring storm is brewing in these events so far from anyone's control. Only time will tell how fate will fall. I no longer have contact with the outside world. I was formerly allowed some exercise along the castle walls, but this has now been stopped. I miss the walks and miss greeting the guards and their children. They had such life in their little, peering faces, even in these most gruesome of garrisons and confines. I miss their innocence and their natural curiosity. One of the guard's sons brought me posies.

The bell still calls curfew. My servants are companions and a source of great kindness in these grievous times. Some are given to Magick White and advise me accordingly under their breath, as each morning I am corseted by them before morning prayers. I wear the same chemise and petticoat I have for days and miss my pomander sorely. I am informed my incarceration within this castle may presage a wider crackdown and that I must remain quiet. Obedient. I must not give them any cause or just reason to suspect me further, but I am not safe here. I have become politic to the point of not speaking on any matter unnecessarily, for I am that closely scrutinised. *Video et taceo*. I must be circumspect beyond reason. If my head should be severed, others might follow. I cannot allow my servants' friendship and service to lead to such unwarranted folly. They do not deserve that. Likewise know this, that if I am to be beheaded, I have done nothing wrong.'

'I have heard dreadful news that Sir Wyatt is dead. They say he asserted my innocence until the Scaffold's End, for which I am most truly grateful. It makes me sad and now I am even more fearful for my own life. They interrogate more regularly and then intimidate me with long spells of protracted silence. The very air has taken against me and I am ill for it all – genuinely so. The pressure is unbearable and I pray for the day when my false incarceration will be over. My mind has nothing to distract it. There is no view, no change of scene, and no visitors come now. The days unravel interminably… It is most serious. My life, I fear, hangs by the thinnest of threads. I am so grateful for my needles and tapestry yarn. This body of mine is somewhat Virgin, but my ears and feet would delight in the joyful sound of the musician's strum; pipe, fife and drum. What fanfare! What fun to be had if only this weight of awareness were not hung around my breast and neck like a collar and chain of prison and office. This encumbrance is with me every waking and sleeping moment since I stepped so unwillingly out of the boat in the rain at Traitor's Gate. I miss the bright minds of others. My maidservant kneels beside me at all times and so loudly recites she drowns out my deceitful mumble of Catholic prayers. I will not be found false. I outwardly conform, but secretly disobey. I am sick with dread. I am thin with worry. I fear food as much as footfall in the corridor outside my door, but I can now conjure sickness to descend upon me at will in such ways that convinces mine own body as well as others to believe I am weak! However, this feign only makes matters worse and I am most worn by the strain of it all.'

'I hear no news from him even though I know he is moved from the Beauchamp Tower to the Beaufort. I fear the fate of friends and loved ones. I wonder what ties us so closely that we share the fate of being held in such formidable towers at this time? My signals have been stopped by the constant shuttering of the windows. If only I could embroider my tale, pour my feelings into this thread and yarn, so he could see. If only I could let him know that I am alive by the simple drop of my kerchief finding its blind way into his fingers, but I dare not. Perhaps the guard's son would run such an errand for me, but it is a dangerous task and too great a risk to be asked of a child. Any attempt could backfire in just the barest of moments – for everything here is espied upon and officially relayed. Perhaps the Ravens would extend their services to me and fly word to the outside world? But I cannot even squeeze my fingers through the wooden shutters to intrigue or summon their support. This existence is remorseless and seems to be without end. There are new rumours that they will soon change my gaoler to one even more in favour with my sister. I also hear that they seek my execution without a signed warrant. There are secret exchanges everywhere and I am in great danger. My humour is affected and watery. The surrounding stone is cold and somewhat damp. My health is at much internal risk, in strange counterpart with the uncertain nature of my external safety. Everyone seems involved in schemes and plots. So obsessed are some by them that rumours grow and turn at every different listen, word and want. All is affluence and influence. How much more do I need to endure? Another month of such terror will be the end of me, I am sure. I strive for nothing, but to stay alive.

I must gather my wits, actions and trusted servants about me and preserve my grace! I daily pray, in my secret way, to God for guidance. If this is to be my durance then if I am ever Queen Regnante I shall try to show forbearance and tolerance in the body natural and body politic. Through such discipline I will secure my Nation through the conquest of myself, not of Nations and others. Even though I am sorely tested, no traitor am I. Indeed! Incarcerated here within The Tower I have learnt that the real heart capital of England is rightly London, and not Rome. And defend against such controlling forces I ever shall! But quiet now, I must silence all such thoughts and steady my countenance for I fear I will betray myself and there are footfalls once more outside my door. Hush! I must hide this surviving piece of myself away even though I am enforced to stay. O Fortune! The Tower Bell rings out new tidings, but good or bad I cannot tell and dare not guess. Yet within its echoing sound I find I can contain myself once more, regain myself, conceal myself back into the suffocating safety of this silence. I recapture my composure. I must... for my life depends upon it!'

Day 22 – Eco Burn/Gaia Plan

Wednesday 30th March – 12°C

Rapithwin: Afternoon (Watch 2) – On my roof I sit cross-legged with my crystal ball balanced upon a pad of purple velvet. Clouds drift above and reflect in the glass surface alongside small points of moving light. I gaze into the globe and images form, tumbling in array like so much dropping sky debris. I witness our world's falling...

In the final days of disaster we endlessly dig for precious planetary resources. Oil spills. We exhaust the land and boil the oceans dry. We fry the sky with flying silver sharks that eat the precious air. Ashes fall. Grids go up and metal warriors stride across the vast prairies, flood and plain lands. Atomic and nuclear energy is converting dangerously and leaking everywhere. Extracting. Polluting. Atmospheres thin. Dirty test clouds mushroom and steal the air. The diminishing gases themselves are drowning in our impurities. We cannot replenish the Biosphere. We take and do not return. Do we learn? Our need for green plans and peace moves on apace, yet still they seek to tax the water, land and air in mistaken green global economy. It belies humanity's final exploitation of natural resources that belong freely to Gaia.

It is arid in the waste of greedy hearts and stifling minds. Heat grows and shimmers off surfaces, mirroring in the tarmac trails and polluting shadows. Acidity becomes atrocity in the drama of climate change and human unsustainability. Greenhouse civilisations begin to respond. Gaia asks us to help. Arctic ice is melting. Coral is diminishing and dying. Hurricanes are multiplying in an intensity to blow our recent house down as jet streams and trade winds buckle in battling storms. We attempt to learn and cope in new conditions of survival. The planet and civilisations all try to forge new creational and ontological pacts with Mother Nature to withstand the weathering. Heat becomes light reflecting itself. Circular roads and circular rhythms. We implode and complain until we listen again. Life, human bombs and landmines before farming and food, all-consuming greed before need, profit from pollution and human trafficking before health and safety, and ideological offences and defences before love. Deep Earth is here as a cauldron in which great geospheric alchemy can occur. This is Gaia's volcanic homeostasis of nations.

Engulfed, I find myself inside the crystal ball cloud-journeying. In my Dragon-capsule I fly above the ocean's surface counting the drowned and the dead. Over the centuries vast continents of water wash so many men, women and children away. I glide around the crumbling coastlines like a soul bird, seagull and eagle, all in one. Stone is forged together by slamming fire, ice and water. Titanic shifts happen everywhere as clouds envelope canyons and racing darkness swallows up the light. Whole new nocturnal cycles begin for the Sun and Moon. I am at the window of the world, high up in the sky looking down on the ages. Not man against Nature but man turned against man. The Killing Fields are burning and healing. War and strife rage across the Desert Lands. Guns are turned on each other, brother to brother, sister and friend. The rebels and rioters are rising up. Shells empty into flesh and sand. Fields for growing are ripped from the earth for makeshift burial. Grains rot unattended; waste is everywhere. A corpulent West, corrupt on a mountain of fare and medicines, sends charitable aid. Mouths open, tiny stomachs bulge, whilst reaching fingers grasp for food – yet the starving still starve. Barter and trade go bad. Corruption is rife.

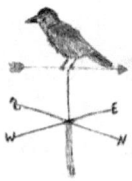

Now, outbreaks of high pressure mean that tornadoes tower and grow, twisting in their ferocity as they extract unattached homes from the heartland. There are no roots here in the tumbling. Tilting trade winds meet the sucking jetstream as everything buckles, bucks and joins in. There is more water, but ironically less rain except in the saturated flood plains. Displaced droughts lead to famine. The Sun diminishes the deserts, but replenishes the plankton in the sea. From the Life Tree the Ravens observe the geopolitical and climatic causes. High to low there is cogent reversal of flow, but how to let go of the unyielding aspect before it is wrested from us? Torn, worn away, stripped leaves flap from twigs and broken branches, much as souls in vortex twisters are wont to be taken. The stone element within refuses to budge, but in the torrent gripping fingers are slipping, threatening to be ripped from the overflowing bankside. Saltwater spray wears the shorelines and us away.

Earth moves. Sea levels rise. Skies burn. Warmth, wind and water stop in their tracks and alter direction. Nature's Web, being both chained and interconnected, shimmers modification. Good or bad? It does not care too much from its own hard and impersonal position, which does not permit it to see things from our perspective. The Sun gradually grows warmer. Temperatures heat and rise. Solar flares bombard our World with charged particles. Inner and outer surfaces reach meeting and melting points. Evaporating oceans rise as vapour to form vast continents of clouds that turn to snow or fall as rain to refill the rivers, streams and oceans. Everything recycles, including our souls. Receding ice glistens at the edges.

Snow palaces fall. Ice sculptures drift whilst Humanity belches greenhouse gases. Blocks of snow crumble like wedding cakes sliced from ice-cliffs.

In the air, hurricanes and tropical storms thunder and threaten, rumbling along eroding coastlines. The landmasses perpetuate their on-going migration. Changes instilled by the edges of seasons affect the timing of the arrival of warm and cold time. Are these signs of the spiritual ecology of Mother Nature or of a contrary manmade muck up? Or is it simply climate change within the Holocene interglacial? Behind the prospects and panoramic scenes – what is going on inside the great Alchemist's Earth flask? Opportunities abound in the alchemical-wash as the Magician in the Sky swirls the air crystal bottles and prepares to pour new sunlight. What disapparating Phoenix-ash and History-dust is this that falls about us?

Rising up and burning all to ashes with its inflammatory feathers, the Firebird returns, levelling the old scores so all may be born again. This is new day in the Gaia plan and the golden dawn of manifestation. The ancient tribe of galactic Dragons join in as the Phoenix blazes, resurfaces and breaks out of the alchemical Time glass trailing a branch of red flame. Torching petrol and the burning fields, the flower of fire eats us all out of thrall. This is fire as awakening. Fire as fury. Fire to cleanse the world daemons and keep our evil spirits at bay. This is pyrolatry sent from the four corners of the spinning sphere into our centres to melt our metal injury. The Dragons spray fire and spread their wings to fan the flame across the world as a layer of fire to evaporate Piscean water into Aquarian air. Here comes the flood again, but this time a flood of Phoenix-flame. Sky, land and sea are ablaze in a torch of burning rays bringing the possibility of universal, psychological and planetary freedom. Trapped inside the glass globe I record this wondrous gift from God. This is Fire Sermon and Eco Burn – this is Gaia plan and all our concern.

Day 23 – Last Day of March

Thursday 31st March – 18°C

Rapithwin: Afternoon (Watch 2) – It is irredeemably the last day of March. The daylight hours unwind and lengthen. I slip away from my Aerie to visit the Park and enjoy the Sun's warming rays. In my struggle to be free – to be truly me – I continue to live on the edge as the outsider, the down-and-outer. Yet why is my journey so different? Why do I insist on climbing to such an unusual branch upon the Life Tree? Suddenly, it feels so immensely difficult again and chances of a positive outcome seem so remote. I drop out of my usual routine in order to better observe my moods and reorganise the affairs of my heart. My thoughts and feelings are informants but I do not know what they are telling me. I have to listen more deeply. Where do they wish me to go? What is there left to believe in? Even on the brink of the month's change, I am cusp-Nowhere except in despair, when all around I am encompassed by the Park's embracing green.

Uzerin: Late Afternoon (Watch 3) – Lying supine on a grassy bank I look up into the sky. High above, birds fly by, gliding in a cooling grey sunset. The metallic hues are growing heavy – silver steels mixing with platinum blues. I watch the thin streaks of clouds accumulate and float by. I drift outside myself to seek a new vantage point. There is so much white and silver I glide upwards until I am subsumed by the sky. The particles around me stretch to encompass the cloudscape. I climb like a soaring bird and in the altitudes I gain greater perspective. All is cotton wool and softening. Below, a child bawls and screams. A young mother shouts – reprimanding, angry and exhausted. People walk upon the grass as distant figures. Ravens caw as they leave the tree branch. Kraa. Kraa. Kraa. I am alone, and actually it feels good. Right. I hollow. I empty. I fall. No thoughts. No disturbances. Just a beat and a breath in my body as I transcend the Sky. Nothing else exists. I am on the edge of two worlds divided, yet indivisible. Here, the vapour trails are not of planes, but of travelling angels on Spring vacation.

People launch their kites and play. Above them, suspended in amongst the shimmering particles and glistening sky elements, exists a renewable me that is not the current I. In this silent space I am taken into the moment of now where everything is possible. Everything is given. The hours strike on a nearby Church clock. Time passes – I do not know how long. Somewhere someone starts to sing. These sounds belong to this moment so there ceases to be any struggle as I listen to them. I do nothing. There is nothing to be done. It just is. A peace begins to spread over me. In this distant place a gentle change is beginning to happen to me. Even the cooling air fails to chill. Fast flying birds circle around me on their return home. They have families to join and do not see so well in the night. In the sky, a setting sun begins to radiate. The scudding clouds offer celestial mobility, the possibility of Dragon-travel and cooling rain.

Above, the Moon infatuates like a mother crooning. Soothing. Around her the first stars twinkle, and beyond them infinite dark space and the Plains of Eternity. The Night Sky wears the stars upon her glistening dress. She is going out tonight, to meet and greet – to go dancing. Suddenly, I realise that this is not about letting go, but reconnecting to the heart of everything. In this cosmic vastness I glimpse eternity through the doorway of the sky. Beneath me the awakening trees and earth are streaming with life, reminding me of the joy of earthly living whilst steadying their selves for dynamic Spring sleep. This is growth. This is the sap rising and the seed within opening. I succumb and gently surrender. Is this it? Am I home at last? The days warm and lengthen, yet still the restless armies continue to march in their endless Mars campaigns. The darkening silver-blue sky turns to supreme blackout as I drift off into sleep in the Park.

Day 24 – The Fool

Friday 1st April – 16°C

Hawan: Morning (Watch 1) – Finally the month changes and I observe the passing of the Crow Moon as I fall into the embrace of the fourth month. Yet is this really the first day of April or merely the Pretender's thirty-second of March? Who defines and delineates the days? And on whose orders? Who says? I am not living under Caesar and his far-reaching calendar rule. I refuse to submit and shall march no longer! In this relentless continuation I long for the beginning of something new and vital. Make it so – I demand it! Can I command it? I return to my Aerie rested, and somewhat peaceful, after sleeping in the Park, but my restless mind wonders if this inner state is reflected in the stars – some subtle shift in the changing of months that permeates into my daily fate. I draw cards from my Egyptian Tarot pack and contemplate the turning images. Ravens arrive to watch. The Fool, The Tower and the Judgement of the Heavens dominate the deck. The Jester chatters to me in gibberish fool talk like so many beggars' crazy thoughts. I listen, but what is there to comprehend in such madness...

'Is this the month of lilacs and their season breeding from out of the Dead Man's hand? Whose body and land do you watch over in your current turmoil? You are the Summer's sun – yet still you are your Father's son. Do not let the Despiser win whilst you strive to tackle the daemon within. In this readjustment you are becoming April's budding, but are you herald of a new Spring dawning or just the Joker on a Fool's makeshift errand? If you are so destined, then why are you not content to assume the role? The Gods make you holy – but do you fear that they still pull the wool? So it is that I have been sent to greet you, meet you, but having at last arrived I must leave. You looked for me, searched the skies, yet on finding me I must disappear into the heart of you. How do you feel? As vast as faraway giants and towering storm castles to that which is closed, close, little, and still.

What do you know? In this Spring forward you know nothing as nothing and equally know nothing as all. Sheep-blink, you sheep-follow into the laughter and into the hollow. On the opportune hour, you will brink and skip goat disaster in wild adventure upon the mountaintop. Your foolish Heart's Hero will run with the Sun, but this time with cloud knowledge upon your back. What is it? Ask it? If this is Enlightenment's strike, why does your heart feel like stone? Why are you so weighted? Where is your Jester's joy? First you must tumble from besieged Towers only to tread once more as a novice upon the mountain's perilous path. These are but a Fool's thoughts. April is here; the month of opening under a Grass Moon; the month of maiden buds, spinning centres, and spilling sunlight. You should learn to listen more carefully to the bird song of Spring and awakening Zen grasses. Bow to the wind and heed more graceful the sacred silences.

On the sheer mountain's edge do not jump to conclusion, but come to own a different end. If love is madness then reason dictates to find companions who best fit that state. So it is that the Ravens and Snakes, the Moon and the Night Sky have all found you, and they, like all lovers, reside in both darkness and light. And what of your own lover and that which you have left behind? In this fertile cycle of Spring, God seeks star-crossed lovers as all creation seeks its beloved. Perhaps, then, you are not such a Fool one step ahead of yourself on the mountain's edge! Wisdom is just an arm's reach away if you could only grasp it. Give back these borrowed elements to the Star's astrological round. In your Night-visions, blindness leads the way. Seek heart sanctuary. I am soothsayer – truth, tooth and gentle leg-puller! Who else would lead you so far upon such a crumbling cliff's ledge? Let us step off then, you and I, step off the mountain's peak and traverse the sky. Earth will quickly turn into air. Will you dare? If your foot does not fall and find land then you must quickly learn how to fly – we are both that high up in the sky. Watch these crazy thoughts tumble away like stones beneath your feet. As you sky-break free, you are rid of the old Tyrant me. You follow and fall as Fool, yet wise kite fly. We are separating – you and I. So my madman's speech is done. What else are your day pages, but the fluttering of leaves set free upon a Spring breeze? You Sky-climb into a loving, pink, sunset Moon and from where you now glide you can see that this is Aphrodite's take-off – not old Fool's falling nor Jester's standing, but Spring kite's soaring and angels landing!'

The rest of the day passes in unwelcome wisdom and in being solely human, but somewhere in the distance the Jester's truth of The Way gains sway.

Day 25 – Pennies of The Dead

Saturday 2nd April – 19°C

Night (Watch 4) – I sequester some time and pass it drinking in the local Charlie Chaplin bar with assorted odd fellows taking amiable wise counsel from comics, tramps, students, geniuses and drunks. There is mutual recognition of difficult situations here. Are these roaring alcoholics really angels in disguise or are they just seeking a different Jesus in their desert struggle? So many battle with the multitude of worldly spirits, stress and daemons. Some are simply sharing in merriment and camaraderie. Others are vanishing in the darkness of lamentation and the pain of separation. Loving the gentle drunk within, I order fire water and ask if Harvey has been in, but no Pookas have been reported. There are no Pucks or Ariels to be seen either. So, I listen to slurred tales and read the iris stories of lost love within watery eyes before following the beckoning vapour trail of my psychopomp, Hermes. I wander off – heeding his special spectral golden-green energy line. Leaving the Chaplin bar behind, I climb up onto the roof of the neighbouring Coronet picture theatre. Hermes laughs, says nothing and disappears.

I lodge myself between the low brick wall and a small series of back windows all painted black, but peeling. Revealing. Placing my head against the glass I peer inside the almost empty cinema. Looking between the cracked flakes of black paint I catch glimpses of the big screen. I turn my head slightly so I can observe the projectionist in his cabin at the same time. The sound of the whirr of the large clunking machines reeling the film is comforting. Below, the shadow puppets begin their strange mimicking dances and dumb movie show. Usually I love all this, sinking into seats and watching films unfold on the wide white expanse. In many ways I miss this most, sitting with You, escaping into armchair adventures like excited Saturday cinema big kids, but tonight I am too tired to care about any of these things. I am happy just to slip into oblivion as the spiritual projectionist takes over.

The Sky film flickers. Hypnotically, the starlight twinkles and spirals in concerts of sound and changing frequency. The scene shifts. Slow-mo at first, then up to speed I go. Through the planes, each with their own accelerated tachyon time, I trip the elastic light fantastic! Faster and faster I run until I fly and blur with the rays of a different film. In a flash, I am pulled into the realm of the extraordinary as I return to a scene of strange haunting. Through all my glimpses of other worlds and timelines this place bothers me the most.

There is a body of a young girl lying on a bed in a photographer's attic studio surrounded by coins and flowers. Two large Victorian Pennies rest upon her eyes as though she were dead. Her long turquoise hair tumbles around her, locks floating about in the air. She is neither living nor dead for this is entrapment of a Faerie soul – a soul not destined to perform such enslaved service, unfortunately caught in the human reincarnational cycle due to her desire to help. This was a life given in kindness, but rewarded by painful entombment in human flesh – which is not this soul's natural resting place. She must be allowed to transform between the Faerie and flesh states and turn her form between the two veiled worlds as she desires. Here she is imprisoned in just one state wishing to be set free. That is why I am pulled in – by her pain and longing.

 A smell of insidious damp pervades the room. Underneath the bed and in the corners of the room Pixie Parasols grow – cyan-blue, strangely beautiful and powerfully soporific. Their depressed, convex heads are sticky and the air is full of their spore release. This is Gondwanaland magick and dispersal, ancient and hardened. The

room is also perfumed and overpowered by Lily Dust to keep the Blue Fairy in a living wake-sleep. The white trumpeting flowers are attractive, but deadly for one such as her.

As a woman that is born elemental, from the supercontinent of Pangaea, she absorbs and emits a different type of cosmic ray. This, I fear, is both her beauty and crime. She is not bioluminescent from the production of chemicals, but is iridescent by nature. Her Lux Operon causes the continual production of astral light and her aura's constant change of hue is being harnessed for improper use. This is wavelength spectroscopy before its time being used for harvesting. This is interference in Nature's cycles and in light's pure yearning for life. It is unbearable for me to just stand by and watch. How could she box clever? She must be set free to fly on sunbeams on her mission to guide the good. Pinocchio once hurried to her home to find her missing. How much hurt his heavy breaking wooden heart? Aurora must play her part. Tinkers' magick must be freely spread. Artists' hearts and minds must be inspired. So must the child within. Hers is the gift of charm and enchantment. I must set her free.

It is strangely quiet. There is no-one else here. I open all the windows to release the scent of the flower of the valley of the dead. I pick the Pixie Parasols to stop their soporific sporing process. My fingertips turn blue with the pigment and burn with a faint pungent acid. I look about the room. There is a daguerreotype in the corner on its triangular wooden legs. The Faerie Spirit is as mercury to the photographer's hands, enchanting everyone who sees their image. This is sorcery of astral light and enhancement to which so many are attracted. There is fake and forgery here alongside the use of ordinary silver-halide materials on printable plates. Cyanotype photographic processes produce beautiful blue and white tones, whilst albumen generates the sepia brown, yet nothing beats the shimmer of Faerie dust. Here there is continual production and supply of beautiful living light from an entrapped soul source. Dust coated monochrome images and photographic self-portraitures are made for permanent enthrallment. Human girls will be asked to lie. Famous Faerie photographs will be faked to distract from the last surviving real.

Meanwhile, I notice that the coins surrounding the bed are the picked pennies of the dead. These coins should have remained unpicked and left to lie on the floor to appease the spirits in old Eastern and Western ritual observance of death. They should never have been touched for they are God-offerings of the poor and belong to the soul of the departed. The collecting of these coins during a bereavement ceremony and their later use is frowned upon. It is intrusion and the wrong use of blessing and magick for selfish ends. Afterwards, I turn to the painstaking business of releasing souls from the confining coins on the floor. Their misuse means the risk of electromagnetic energy forcibly enmeshing and entrapping all their souls. I look to the lilies as I start my laborious task. They are as white as wisdom and tell me everything I need to know about the Vale of Death. The Realm Flowers take me in and remind me of passing things. Attentively, I listen in.

Freedom is expensive and painful – but belongs to us all. To get to the bed and the Faerie Girl, I start to remove the minefield of minor daemons that sit hungrily eyeing me on the floor. They have been attached to the coins for so long they are splintered souls, angry for lost time, yet grateful for the oncoming release. They still present immense danger until appeased, and have become too used to living on the life-force of another – she that is wrongly restrained, constantly flickering and trembling on the point of return between worlds. In her fluttering is light perpetual, though the body lies undiminished – since in its preserved state it is in continuous contact with pure source and the Elixir Vitae. She must be released. This special other from Faeries' Land is caught here. Hers is usually Pan magick of the elemental domain. Except here in the very early years of the twentieth century, she is reduced to living light entrapped by metal mass and singular magical focus. Who could kiss her awake? What lips could survive such terrible pressing of beauty? What layering of spells must I break as she shimmers between the near death kingdom and the horror of her bedbound situation? Barely alive, her soul is trapped inbetween waking breath and corporeal deadening. In such bewildering circumstances do I find her.

I ask for the presence of the Dawn's horizon Avatar in ethereal form to guide my hand. I use mirror magick to deflect the angry temporal daemons that the earthbound souls have become by holding a spare photographic plate as a shield to avoid their possessing processing eyes. I spend time detecting the coins' respective origins and dates. For each individual coin and owner I must chant the correct indigenous prayer. Each must be honoured and pacified. Intuition is all in the overshadowing. What agony has this flickering butterfly soul endured at the hands of what wicked man? What am I to do as the wings of life or death hang in the balance? I endeavour to release her unto the free dance of the winds of heaven so she can move on in her own way and in the manner of her own choosing. All such persons imprisoned by the metal of money must be set free, as indeed should all those held back by ironbound minds.

 Painstaking hours pass. When I eventually get to the Blue Fairy I see two large Victorian pennies pressing upon her eyes. They stare at me like the blank eyes of an unwittingly imprisoned blind child. One bears the young Queen's Head in rare copper, the other the old Queen's Head in bronze.

Britannia backs both in aggressively protective stance. Magical properties reside in them for they are the bookends of a long reigning sovereign monarch only recently dead. A Queen's journey from innocence to experience spliced by a touching grief; this is Maundy Money scavenged for strange purpose. These extraordinary pennies from the first and last mint of the black-clothed Queen's English reign have been stolen from dying paupers. I remove them to release her.

As I lift the coins, the Blue Faerie's body rises from the bed, twisting and turning through myriad spinning forms. Old and young, dark and fair, she contorts through dull and radiant outlines in shape shifting silhouettes. Cyan, turquoise and gold dust spins everywhere and fills the room in glimmering essence. An orb of energy glows, grows and explodes around her as she takes on her new form. Then out of the window she flies as a tinkling Fairy Bell – dangerous with the glint of imprisoned destiny caught in her eyes. Like a child, she cannot process the raw red of anger, and this experience has taught her pain and dark. In her trial she has learnt choice, but I tremble at the thought of her malevolent revenge on those who might do her future ill. Still, on her travels will be souls that she is destined to meet. She will visit France first and then return to England before heading back to Scandinavia. Hovering in the air, she looks back at me, but says nothing as she unfurls her shining, full, six-foot wings and disapparates. Her trailing blue hair is everywhere.

The Silver Screen will flicker and fill with her stardust to remind us of her journey. The pages of the child's Century Book will turn for her in wonder. In her phantasmagorical light new flights of fantasy can begin. Theatres will applaud her airborne antics, from attics and islands, for she is the ultimate aerial illusionist. She is the gleam that flies on rays of light. She is formed by laughter, but broken into pieces by grief and the disbelieving of teenage-cusp adults. She gathers imagination in magical ways. She will continue to enchant nations until she can evolve no longer. Like many species, she will not make the evolutionary jump at the end of the Piscean Age. The Christ light is changing and the Faerie Kingdom is altering in the dawn of new love. Soon the door will finally close on her kingdom and she will be lost to those remaining on this side of the veil. There will be sadness, but new worlds shall bloom and she will follow their light beckoning. She departs to aid their blossoming. As she sets out to fill her final hundred-year-tour with newly enhanced soul purpose, I take the two coins from the iron bed and contemplate my own growing design. Somewhere a distant idea is forming. She has left me the gift of inspiration and emerging awareness.

'Have faith and trust in yourself,' she says.

Day 26 – Huginn and Muninn

Sunday 3rd April – 15°C

Uzerin: Late afternoon (Watch 3) – The Recording Ravens swoop above us flying from dawn until dusk watching the wearying world. Joining forces with the Snakes, they are the leftover messengers of masters and gods long gone, all except one – the Raven Master – who has so many secret lines into the World Soul. Every detail they see and hear they clock, memorise and subsequently report back to their assigned intermediary. The Ravens have been granted the gift of raw song and clever speech, caw and cor – that which is able to penetrate the minds of men and inform the Cosmic Universe. Behind the scenes, bird thought and memory interpret us to the spiritual libraries and halls of teaching above. Their eyes scry and their talons scribe the degrees – the 75 North, 140 East, 67 South and 102 West – the worst and best of us. Wingtips stretch and feathers fly to the compass points assessing the equatorial zones and the state of the poles. This way and that, the birds know all the history of chrons in their century cycles and magnetic memories.

Yet when did the Ravens turn from white to black? Was it when they once stole precious Dragon-fire? Did the smoke and soot singe their ragged feather tips? Were they marked for their crime against God for opening the dark magical box? Swans take to water; Ravens to skies. Bats take to the night as Doves do the day. Did Destiny flip and change sides in a sudden shift of Earth-fate and reversal of Sky-fortune? Clever as Crows, the Ravens can play hero or they can laugh and trick you. They say the Ravens let out the Sun and the Moon; set the air, water and stars all free. Were they the start of the elemental we?

The resident Ravens of the Tower – George, Charlie, Bran, Mabel, Thor, Grog, Rhys, Edgar Sopper, James Crow, Marley, Erin, Merlin, Baldrick, Gwyllum and Marrigon – are all descendants of original Huginn and Muninn. Blessed since the bloodline of Odin, direct from Noah's boat and beyond to original first caw song, they are the Old Bible Black Ones. In present mirth and memories, their Tower fight continues into our times. They mock the living with their laughter and talented tongues whilst flying high to perch precociously upon timber homes, towers, boats and wooden thrones. They whisper in the ears of prophets, masters and gods. They are the reporting senses of the skies. They are God's ears and eyes. As harbingers, they remind us all that we are imprisoned until we step free. Something they can never be until the end for they are trapped in Tower service. They bear the torch of thought and memory in the corridors of the blind mind to light the labyrinth way. Over here! So many prisoners to aid and set free. The Ravens hold a flame to scan my brain for sprouting feather and growing fear. This way. This way. Over here!

In the imprisoned mind 'fight and flight' feels so right. Living in the shadow threat of fear, anxiety and panic are all that is present alongside an exhilaration of augmenting might beyond reason, humility beyond old ways. Where is my justice? And where my vengeance? Look at me! I am thee. I press my face and head against the cool metal rods of my office cell window: Room 2, The Tower. Was I incarcerated or did I willingly confine myself? I cannot push through the bars whereas birds can simply hop free. Those that work for the Rose Finch Division fly to and fro in bird song and service with their daily deliveries and titbits of news. I miss them in my present state of solitude and Raven seclusion. The inky wings of Huginn and Muninn fill my mind. What do they find? My attraction to turbulence and trouble has to end in greater safety.

Down the Tower's passageways I can hear Raven Edgar cackle and laugh. Playing dead all this while, yet still more full of life than the non-laughing I. Edgar! Do not be foolhardy otherwise your feigning will have you locked in a box like your good friend Old James Crow. If you wolf-pretend you will be buried before you are dead – interred alive, just for the attention of it all. There will be no graveside bell to ring. No stories' end to resuscitate either you or me. What trickery, what wickedry, is this? Like all prisoners, I must bide my time until I am free, but who is to rescue me? Too many lives are lost; too many bodies laid to death in the blood cold earth.

The gathering Ravens bring me clues and feed me their thoughts in these wilderness days. They play tricks with my mind to make me think. They are always watching and I try to follow their leads. They survived the warfare centuries and the great ages of ice and fire. They thrive on the attraction of flame and the scavenging it can bring. They followed the medieval pigs and kites to grub up the ground in days of old. Nowadays they partner the wolverine. To storytellers they are legend bringers. The first free Ravens are masonic mythmakers and dream weavers working according to office orders. They perform public duties befitting their allocated station for they are not just any type of evolutionary Black Bird, but those of The Raven Agency – God-given prehistoric revolutionaries. With their wings they can blur the astronomical, blot out entire worlds and have power to move observation towers. They nudge the mapmakers to new reflection. Planets and stars appear and disappear according to their bidding. Peering down, they have seen such sights of history perching upon the pterodactyl branches of the wish fulfilling tree! They are said to be keen bringers of opportunity. They let out the Sun and the Moon; set the air, water and stars all free. I should be more grateful to these birds. They are more than specks of dark soot upon the stretched skyline of my insanity.

Aiwisruthrem: Night (Watch 4) – Here, where I crawl to my rooftop to hide, the pillars of light project through the astrological belt and lay stretched out on the horizon. Between the vertical and horizontal lines of light I send out ribbons of energy and hook myself up to the invisible universe. The gentle tensions hold me fast as the vastness of time and space opens up. Ages fly by in no time at all. I am enthralled as I wing my way to who knows where, but in the guidance of Mother Night Crow God I have to trust. The Ravens bear me up and hand me over.

In my Night-vision, the Spring grief of every mother, father and lover ever to be planted in the ground resides here as all around the riotous bulbs push through the sockets and skulls of the mute bone dead. This is not examination at Heaven's gate or some poetic womb door; rather it is revelation at Enlightenment's fall. The Ravens scrutinise my lies and crafty conniving. I have to die my own living death. They assure me of this as they sift through the blood and bones of my inky pages and steadily gathering metal clattering. These scrivenings are nothing but passable rot. I am not ready, but then again, as they inform me – you rarely are! It is best not to know where or when the occurrence of your Tower-happening. My plump thoughts and after words are as worms to them – fleshy, juicy morsels rising from the earth of me in this vibrational state. That is why the inquisitorial Birds of Black come to inspect – to eat them up alive! They peck over a mind disturbed and rotten. They do me kind service and I am becoming more grateful for their grave and carrion purposes. If only I could obliterate my fear when faced with their eyes of glinting blackness, telling me tales of dark terror that fill me with such suspicion of them.

Are these birds my silent saviours, or are they here to peak out the eyes of one about to die? They disguise their tricky intent. I smell poison and pretence. They protect the Tower, but which one? Is it the one of stone that must be crushed and fall or is it the one of light that stalwartly survives the process of lightning strike? I am in Crow-crisis as the Ravens fly by. Thank you, birds, for someone has to bear the memory of the dead and bring about the news of my end. As I lay buried beneath the Crow Night Sky, yet stretched so high, Huginn and Muninn fly into my shadow, and peck away at the unessential I. Thus blessed, I am but food for Gods in an unsuspecting Earth Sky burial. So, I am left reconsidering the Ravens' arrival and their news of my upcoming grave.

The two ancient Ravens look on in dismay and curse my distress, but they are duty-bound to help. Whilst the bird world community debates the current Earth situation, the effects on global migration and potential geomagnetic reversal, Huginn and Muninn tinker with the rewiring of my brain, wings and things. They ask me to reconsider my position in the recent considered repositioning. Their Raven vane predicts a storm, bad-black-feather, oppositional weather and fire-rain. Meanwhile, behind the scenes, yet beside us all, the Snakes are Sun-sliding – gliding on to Om-warn.

Day 27 – Tagebuch

Monday 4th April – 14°C

Aiwisruthrem: Night (Watch 4) – In the waves of my solipsistic dreaming and fleeting visions I have travelled somewhere – I know not where. I am ignorant of the date or time and of why I am here. It is a large, spacious house with views onto a sunlit garden. It is quiet. It is empty. By my side is a writing bureau and on top sits a pen; a small stylized sliver of steel. It is this that I have come for – brought here to collect, steal and swallow the warm written words that were recently pressed so lovingly upon the page…

I write in my diary daily, and I send postcards to my beloved during my stay in the alpine countryside. Only the occasional City note arrives, but that was always his way. I remain firm in my resolve to join my love as soon as is possible. He does not want it, but it is my wish. I have been hidden from view for far too long. This makes me unhappy. I am seen only when necessary and I am exiled from the permanent bedroom. Yes, we make love, but I can never stay. This makes me sad, but I fight those feelings and help myself to another cigarette whilst pouring a drink. I know if I go down that path I will end up like I did in the past. So terribly depressed. I still bear those marks – physically and psychologically – yet they do make me slightly braver and I am generally forbearing. Thank God those times have changed. Nevertheless, I still look pretty. I keep up my appearance. I do my hair in the usual way, and rouge my cheeks and lips. Not too much, of course – he doesn't like too much, and I keep my hair the same colour after that dreadful incident. I dyed my hair darker and piled it up on top. Not my natural blonde curls like the American magazine models, all fit and healthy. He hated it. He was so angry with me and showed so in front of his friends. He doesn't like me to change. Strange that. Sometimes he is a man with such big ideas, and then alters so drastically – spiralling backwards and downwards into someone so small and petty, particularly when it comes to my appearance, which is important to me, and I always take my time to look good. I apply my makeup – a touch of eye shadow and lipstick, just enough to enhance my natural beauty. He doesn't like all that stuff, but it occupies the hours until I see him next.

He's always so busy and I'm left having to fit in with his plans. For sure I miss him – achingly, horribly so – when he's not here. I just fill my time awaiting his return and look forward to our next little rendezvous. I so look forward to seeing him. Foolish girl. Perhaps I'll have another postcard picture taken to send to him. I know he's not too keen on my snapshots and nude sunbathing, but I like the feel of the warm sunlight on my body and I enjoy posing for the camera… I love surrounding myself with Nature as much as I do preparing my own appearance, whilst he's always engrossed in giving parties for those people so full of their airs and graces. They are only where they are because of him. Well, I suppose I am too, but I am too long hidden. I always look nice – the natural me with a little added glamour. My body is quite pert and my face still pretty even into my thirties.

So I wait. It's always feels too long between meetings even though it is rarely more than two or three weeks. A month at most. I spend most of my time in the Villa reading romance novels and going out on trips and picnics with the chauffeur. Then I'll get a call or a note and there will be wine, champagne on ice, chocolates, and cognac – fresh fruit will be peeled and prepared. Perhaps some money toward a new dress or some items of jewellery would be placed on my dresser. I always drink wine, whereas he only ever drinks his tea. He's so self-contained – always thinking with such a deep furrow on his brow. But he relaxes with me. I make him happy. It is my present to him after his long demanding days. He's so much jollier when I'm around. Everyone says so – although I can still see the disapproving looks of some. But what do they know about love! I live for him and he lives for the Nation. They all should treat me with more respect. He'll intervene if he has to when they go too far and upset me. He even exiled that one. Oh, they can be so intimidating that I sometimes stay in my room for hours! It does make me unhappy, but I try not to cry. Oh well – perhaps if they knew I was his legal heir they would think differently. What an inheritance I shall have!

When my mood gets too low I organize myself a treat. I get the maid to arrange a luncheon basket and the chauffeur takes me to the lake in the Mercedes. I can relax there. Take off my clothes and enjoy the sun and the water without anyone caring what I am up to. My love – he's such a prude at times. Anyhow, I know I shall always enjoy the swimming and the lazy days of being in the great outdoors after being cooped up for so long.

He's been really unkind again. I hate it when he makes jokes about my hats and my appearance. He doesn't really mean it; he just likes to tease sometimes – but too often in front of our friends. To think I told him how much I loved his big felt hat that he used to wear all the time when first we met, and his English overcoat, and the way he fashioned his funny moustache. He said I had his mother's eyes. The same shape and colour. That was before he became too busy for me – my wonderful little Mr Wolff. From our first meeting so many years ago I knew he was the one – and only him – and that I'd be with him until the end of our days. I was so young. We were so light-hearted and carefree. Of course he could count on me. I remember when I wrote those words to him:

'From our first meeting I swore to follow you anywhere, even to death. I live only for your love.'

Well, that and for the gifts he'd send me back then. A little luxury always helped! He protected me that way. Stolen moments for meals, a trip to the theatre, late-night drinks. I used to play the lottery so I could afford to have nice things. I really thought I would win, but I didn't need to in the end for he provided everything I wanted. Well, almost everything. I longed for a little dog to keep me company. A dachshund or a terrier – I wouldn't have minded. I could have gone for daily walks with a reminder of him yapping at my feet wanting my attention. That would have been nice. He took me shopping, but I always chose my own outfits and hats. That's when he started bringing me jewellery. I used to choose my own, but he didn't always approve! He bought me lovely expensive necklaces and bracelets and the most beautiful ring. It was almost as though we were engaged – he slowly elevating my position within his inner circle and me getting ever closer. Such a secret was ours! Such a secret that kept us to separate rooms, our own bedrooms and bathrooms, but always with a connecting door. Always such modesty with him. I so longed for his child, but it wasn't to be. Well, mustn't dwell upon that. It'll have me reaching for the... Well, shouldn't dwell upon those incidents either... Those were sad, difficult times. I have two dogs now. Small ones like I always wished for. They are so much fun and it's good to have them to look after – such affection and such excellent companions in the long countryside walks. I do wish he would join us more often.

At last! The letter stating that I am to go to be with him has arrived and finally he will know how much I have cared for him – how much I have been in love. How many years is it now? Sixteen years I have known him; twelve of which I have spent being the centre of his life – loved, yet tortuously removed. I am to be at his side. I have packed all my things. I am sending most of my trunks home, but will take a small case with me. I am taking just what I wear, a neat suit and a hat, and a couple of smart silk dresses – one blue, one black. A bride in black? I'm not quite sure, but he thinks it's fine. Fitting, I suppose, after all this time and everything I've been through for him. I shall travel by car to be with my beloved in the Great City. However, I'd better wait for him to officially propose before I presume too much. Imagine me, the silly, pretty camera-obsessed girl, who after all these years gets to dry her tears, lift up her veil and simply say, 'Yes, I do.' Of course I do. I always have. We should have done this so many years ago. Should have done, but who cares now for I shall no longer be unhappy Fraulein Braun, Fuhrer-whore, but Frau Eva B̶-Hitler.

Day 28 – Consolamentum

Tuesday 5th April – 13°C

Hawan: Morning (Watch 1) – In this dreadful struggle – this reckoning of mine – I am so deeply disturbed. Perturbed. Troubled feelings lead to troubled thoughts and mind – making me believe that this is a whole troubled world and life of mine. It is not really so. It is just part of my current truth-illusion, temporary turbulence and emotional intensity, but it diminishes me. Torment moves me on and makes me reconsider... It takes me away from You, work and everything I thought I knew. Things are different now. From here I see the childhood scene whilst simultaneously viewing the vast expanses of eternity rolling ahead. I am caught inbetween the two places. I regard us in a loving new light even though it is cold and gloomy in my hurting heart if not actually above in the warming sky. My moods offer several shades of darkening grey for I am in Woden's shadow. Today is my Father's birthday, the first since his Christmas death. He was not taken from us in some great tragedy – he simply went quietly, disappearing like a child under the sheet of sleep, never knowing the horrors that lay beneath the lungs and heart. His body could carry on no longer. Suddenly he is gone, cut away from the vivid thread of life. He died at a distance. Yet being there a few days before his passing really helped me, the spending of time together, the passing on of thanks and love between father and son. For those who are there at the very end, there is honour and the sharing of light consolamentum. For others – so many questions remain.

Intense brooding feelings arise. Now on this day my Father reappears. Of all the ghosts from out of history he is the most sought, the most difficult, the most needed. He stands before me and I see a semblance of him – a gentle man walking across The Yard. For so much of his life this was a daily occurrence. As he walks, he searches the ground for occasional fallen nails, which he picks up to prevent the lorry tyres from puncturing.

He was always finding things. Lost coins on the street were lucky to him, a sign of universal good fortune and a chance to show his gratitude. Beautiful Victorian bottles, glass, coins and beads from the earth were wonderful excavations. Back in The Yard – wood, earth and scrap metal pile up and surround him. He stops to stand and look. He sees me from a distance and smiles, and then waves me away to return to my business – my life. In that smile and unspoken instant, the exchange takes place. Tears well up and move me. In the silence falls the peace and for a while I understand the simplicity and necessity of Sorrow's head bent in silent ever-weeping. These moments are cherished forever.

'Go on,' he says simply. 'Get on with it. Enjoy it! Life's precious. Fill your time with love and interest. Look to yourself. See who you were. See who you are so newly becoming! Face me. Face life and death philosophically. Do not cry for the day I died. Not on my birthday. O my son! Come on home. Accept us for who we were. I know you loved me as I did you. Come on home to yourself. Dare to. Go on.'

I am happy-sad. He is so different now. Stripped of suffering and pain, he is content and relaxed, more philosophical. His sunny face, so like mine, is free from care, but loving. If I had so many things to say, so many things left unspoken, if my heart had so many things yet to receive in the listening, they fall away and are replaced with acceptance. All the old questions of love, all the unanswered wants, all the dissatisfactions with circumstances, fall away and dissolve into the emptiness. In the warmth of that smile I know that love is spirit, and that spirit is all-encompassing love.

'Thanks Dad!' I return. So little, but it is the all that I have. 'Thanks for giving me life and getting me through it! Sorry we didn't share more of the time we had, but it's okay now.'

Of all the many things I want to say, I find I cannot grasp the words. I am silent. But at least there are so many feelings of love and fondness and affection. There is also thankfulness. Until his end, until that smile, I did not know that I was so loved. Yet I am and was, and love accomplishes so many things. My atomic heart clock wobbles within. No-one ever tells you that nobody really knows what to do in life, how to get by, how to find happiness, especially how to be a parent. They forget to mention the fact that every soul is uniquely positioned on the edge of such exciting discoveries, lovingly pushed into life by spiritual impulse and yearning. The way you take. The amazing friends you meet. The directions you turn, the blunders and mistakes you make are all a mix of choice, circumstance and fate. At times it has been difficult, but I am so grateful for the life I have been pitched into – even in all this current sense of trouble and disaster.

My Father had been through so much that was unexpected and thrown at him. Yet ultimately he knew different kinds of love – in the final analysis, that is what was of most significance. In my heart I have grown in understanding of this. Empathy radiates from his passing and I am growing strong in my reconsideration of heart truth. Herein lies the magick of healing, in the handing on of maturing wisdom and fatherhood. This is the sympathetic magick of any parent-child relationship. This contributes to the balance of mother and father, the law of similarity, the law of contact – which the Ravens' Kraa-cry foretold. Upon their wings a deeper love is now spread, even while beneath them flies their dark fear shadow – an opposing force waiting in its own right to be experienced, owned and accepted. The totality of this is the law of dread shadow contagion. In my final days of Raven-reckoning and Snake-sharing, love is becoming as contagious and mysterious as a haunting. The passion of my disturbed past is under huge and fundamental restoration.

'Here,' my Father says, 'Take these. They might help. I can't say more than that. Just keep going. Get to the end because only there will you find new inspiration and new beginning.'

My Father smiles and gives me a handful of nails. I recognise the brush of his hand even from the other side. His touch is like magick through a momentarily thinning veil. The particles of exchange are here, liberating us all. This is affinity with finality. This is eternity speaking to me through him. Something clicks closed. Something opens. Through the stretch of my mind and the sweep of my feelings, my heart is touched and my contact with my Father's living essence, liquid love and spiritual light, is enhanced and quickened. These nails are as gleaming emeralds to me – flashing heart jewels! I hope I have made him proud. My mission to the heart is renewed. Such moments are a blessing. I can only breakdown in gratitude for my life. Thank you. Thank you. Thank you. This is the healing of divisions through love. These are honour-bound moments in time given from space beyond time. This is deepening and quickening earthbound contact. This sacred temple feeling is a glimpse of the descent of grace – a memorial offering on a sacred branch of the Living Tree. You wave me away and are gone forever, but forever continue to remain here like a soul bird fluttering its way through eternity.

On the riverbank the Kingfisher is here on the brink of world healing. He is my Father and Fisher King.

Day 29 – B-Om-bardment

Wednesday 6th April – 22°C

Aiwisruthrem: Night (Watch 4) – Night-journey. Tonight, I begin by standing inside the formidable Stone Frigate of Whitehall, the Admiralty Citadel. This is the old military communication centre for defence coordination in the second battle of world nations – which was in many ways a continuation of the First War horror. Countries seem to take sides. The Christ Thorns are here impaling nations and their inhabitants. Searchlights are spiking the sky. Astral hypnosis bleeds through from wronged giants and from those who still wish to be Gods. These beings, who once suffered destruction under emergent humanity, return now with evil veil influence. Minds are tapped, both weak and strong. Souls respond and oppose on both sides of the cause. This building I find myself in is a response to the zenith of the axis of evil. I feel the weight of the entombed tunnels, walls and ceilings that surround.

The fire of Blitz and bombs cannot penetrate here, but for me there is no escape from the ensuing spiritual bombardment. I am trapped here for some strange purpose. This is not Night-flight, but deliberate quest containment. I am out of time in this room of world war strategy, yet maps and radio equipment lie all about. Transmitters, command receiver consoles, and old vacuum tubes all configure in this room, but there is no-one here. It is quiet apart from the occasional ghostly oscillation across the radar screen. This is a perfectly preserved museum at my disposal. I sit and place the headphones on. I turn the dial and modulate the frequencies. I go outside the shared visible electromagnetic spectrum. This is not Ghost Radio, but radical radiation of expression and experience. I experiment like a child with a tin on a string listening in to overheard adult great things.

"… Am I not a man and a brother?" [1]

Within the freedom of nations lay other kinds of overlooked wars – sins of the skin. People oppress; people fight for each other. I turn the dial…

"…And ain't I a woman? Look at me! Look at my arm! I have ploughed, and planted, and gathered into barns, and no man could head me! And ain't I a woman? I could work as much and eat as much as a man – when I could get it – and bear de lash as well! And ain't I a woman? I have borne thirteen chilern, and seen 'em mos' all sold off to slavery, and when I cried out with my mother's grief, none but Jesus heard me! And ain't I a woman?" (2)

People express their suffering truth and fight for fundamental reform.

"…At last after the smoke of the battlefield had cleared away, the horrid shape which had cast its shadow over the whole continent had vanished and was gone forever…" (3)

The disbelief of slavery disperses, but the struggle for women continues. I spin the dial and Fate lands it. A woman's voice…

"…You have left it to women in your land, the men of all civilized countries have left it to women, to work out their own salvation. That is the way in which we women of England are doing. Human life for us is sacred, but we say if any life is to be sacrificed it shall be ours; we won't do it ourselves, but we will put the enemy in the position where they will have to choose between giving us freedom or giving us death…" (4)

The snaking green wavelength undulates and alters. There is sonic disturbance. A break in transmission means the lines stray and go wavy. The room begins to fill with radioactive purple. There are sound waves rising and falling on the screen. At the turn of a dial the voice changes to that of a man…

"…It is to wage war, by sea, land and air, with all our might and with all the strength that God can give us: to wage war against a monstrous tyranny, never surpassed in the dark, lamentable catalogue of human crime…Victory at all costs, Victory in spite of all terror, Victory, however long and hard the road may be; for without Victory there is no survival…Come then, let us go forward together with our united strength…" (5)

I can hear the impressive quality of the English Bulldog voice. The confident power emits and transmits like the truth of an inspired orator – hypnotic and stirring. Speaking from Spirit-to-Spirit the human soul is roused while all around me is gravity and photon propulsion. What impact this strange light that surrounds me? What effect these frequencies? I am surrounded by gamma annihilation as particles and antiparticles collide. Atomic instability gives way to radioactive decay: conversion, transmission, fission and emission. My bound states cluster like star galaxies in new genesis. The radio changes, but his voice continues…

"…Dieu protége la France… Never will I believe that the Soul of France is dead! …Goodnight then: Sleep to gather strength for the morning. For the morning will come. Brightly it will shine on the brave and the true, kindly upon all who suffer for the cause, glorious upon the tombs of heroes. Thus will shine the dawn. Vive la France! Long live also the forward march of the common people in all lands towards their just and true inheritance, and towards the broader and fuller age…" (6)

Now a French voice breaks in singing, trilling, stirring the soul with her understanding of hope and pain. The Street Sparrow of the Argot spreads hope amongst misery, enables photographic opportunities for prisoners and the forging of passports. So many songs of her soul grew out of ironic war and destruction. Later she enchants the heart of the world in capturing the French spirit of occupation and resistance. I sit and listen to her singing the words of 'La Vie En Rose'. With her, all is rose passion and loving possibility etched through with pain as she surrenders to the recovering states of saints. Between France, Britain and America lay battle won freedom, revolution and parliamentary liberty. The dial falls back to the voice of the British Bulldog...

"The day will come when the joy-bells will ring again...and when victorious nations, masters not only of their foes, but of themselves, will plan and build in justice, in tradition, and in freedom – a house of many mansions where there will be room for all..." (7)

The photons gather force, accelerating, propelling me into a new orbit of awe and wonder. Airbursts extend prayer into action. There are true followers of Buddha everywhere.

"...Occasions like the present do not occur in everybody's and but rarely in anybody's life... Let me explain my position clearly. God has vouchsafed to me a priceless gift in the weapon of Ahimsa. I and my Ahimsa are on our trail today. If in the present crisis, when the Earth is being scorched by the flames of Himsa and crying for deliverance, I failed to make use of the God given talent, God will not forgive me and I shall be judged un-wrongly of the great gift. I must act now..." (8a)

I listen intently. The Indian continues...

"...Ours is not a drive for power, but purely a non-violent fight for India's independence. In a violent struggle, a successful general has been often known to effect a military coup and to set up a dictatorship. But ... there can be no room for dictatorship. A non-violent soldier of freedom will covet nothing for himself, he fights only for the freedom of his country... In the democracy which I have envisaged, a democracy established by non-violence, there will be equal freedom for all. Everybody will be his own master. It is to join a struggle for such democracy that I invite you today. Once you realize this you will forget the differences between the Hindus and Muslims, and think of yourselves as Indians only, engaged in the common struggle for independence... Then, there is the question of your attitude towards the British. I have noticed that there is hatred towards the British among the people... This hatred ...is most dangerous. It means that they will exchange one slavery for another. We must get rid of this feeling. Our quarrel is not with the British people, we fight their Imperialism..." (8b)

The radio becomes radar for the breath and the heart, stopping and breaking at every turn. A shockwave emits from the unit filling my ears. My head is splitting. Light particles and sound waves create forces that displace matter which once resided there. Brain metastability alters. Semi-transient signals affect functional equilibrium. Then something more human, more tearful, more cheerful, stirs and delights the soul. I hear that voice. That wonderful voice...

"Ghana has something to say to us. It says to us first that the oppressor never voluntarily gives freedom to the oppressed. You have to work for it.... If there had not been a Nkrumah and his followers in Ghana,

Ghana would still be a British colony. If there had not been abolitionists in America, both Negro and white, we might still stand today in the dungeons of slavery. And then because there have been, in every period, there are always those people in every period of human history who don't mind getting their necks cut off, who don't mind being persecuted and discriminated and kicked about, because they know that freedom is never given out, but it comes through the persistent and the continual agitation and revolt on the part of those who are caught in the system. Ghana teaches us that..." (9)

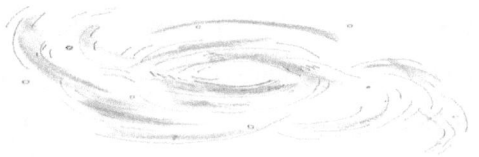

All goes silver-white, and then an explosion startles me from within the chamber. I find myself showered in countless starbursts of light. As the warmth and radiation creates propulsion I am pushed from the War Room. The string of my tin can radio is cut. Although I can listen in no longer, the dial delivers one last twist. As I disappear with a radio head set, a final voice reaches out once more to remind us that spirit will always fight back.

"...Never give in, never give in, never; never; never; never – in nothing, great or small, large or petty – never give in except to convictions of honour and good sense..." (10)

The Great British Man commands us all with such authority...

"...These are not dark days; these are great days..." (11)

Day 30 – Over Soul

Thursday 7th April – 20°C

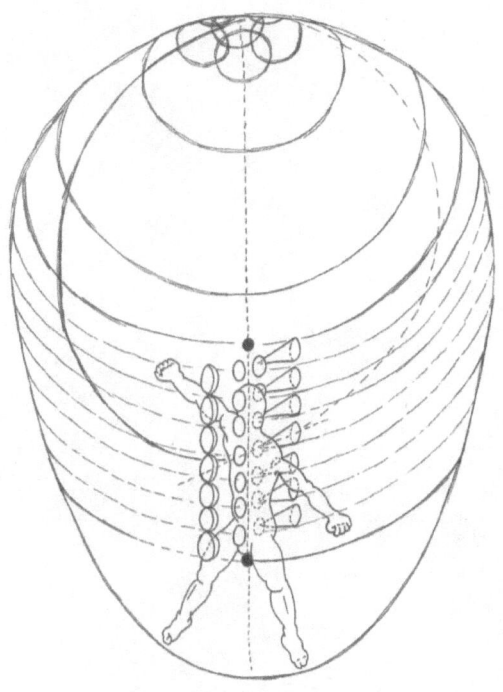

Hawan: Morning (Watch 1) – Late morning. I take to the Park again. It is unexpectedly hot. A sultry Summer warmth in Spring indicates seasonal fluctuation, but in these strange days of truth struggle I welcome the certainty of the Sun's heat. Such simple pleasure – enjoying the rays as they touch and kiss the real skin I am in and not the wild nocturnal Moon-kicked adventurer. I question what is happening to me. Where have I been on these unexpected travels of night and mind? How did I wander so far from myself? What is left to offer in these states? In the Peace Garden I watch the people come and go as I sit under a deep green canopy dotted with ceanothus blue – flowering, towering, against a blazing sapphire-sky. In front of me, wisteria unfurls their curling lilac tresses like maidens of old. Abundance is here. Trees flower. Ēostre resides in the Paschal month. Verdant shoots push up their leafy heads and reach toward the Sun. Spring is here in imitation and replacement of a glorious early English Summer. Sky-gazing, small Putti pass by reclining upon puffed-up, silver white, light drenched, fluffy cloud cushions.

The nearby Park Café is host to the multitudes. It is a central point for the solitary, the lost and the lonely, the quiet and the boisterous – all having different types of fun. Families, children and their many dogs all congregate at the Natural Church of the Park. We are all visitors here. I hear the sounds of a ball being thrown and kicked. A stick is hurled through the air and a dog takes off in flight with boundless enthusiasm. They can do this for hours. I watch and admire their endless energy. Cups clatter on saucers. Coffee aromas swirl – mixing with pastries, peppermint and ordinary cups of tea. Borders of rosemary and lavender tinge the air. Amorous nodding pigeons coo and purr walking in enticing circles. Hot, tired dogs lie panting on the floor at the feet of seats where beloved owners sit – basking in the day fun-light. For them Paradise is here – what do they know of sin? What does the Sun, the Moon or any animal know, apart from that which we teach them or imbue them with? There is only their nature in Nature within the governing Supernatural. Their territories are their own; their spiritual missions too. For those Park guests tired of the heat of the Sun, the shade invites – quenching a thirst. Cooling ice-cream and refreshing lemonade do the rest. Today is a glorious golden day of doing nothing – minimal existence, drifting, observing – taking what comes in an easy way.

Suddenly, life seems less complicated – a chance for me to experience not a simpler world, but a simpler me – closer to the things that truly matter. Thoughts turn to love, friendship and happiness. In this moment I cannot wait to return to You, for why else would I leave if not to value the homecoming more? Flux and flow – the need to return from the urge to go. Endlessly so. Deepening values through the missing. Then what to do with all this experience? Is it as simple as sharing – not the passing on of pain, but the drawing down of sunlight to spread joy? The lit candle shows the way through the dark as clearly as a wonderful smile catches the light. Nearby, a child shakes a plastic bottle and blows bubbles through a hoop that escape the magic wand as translucent essences – the same way as when we first left Heaven. Soapy suds shimmer-glisten into the air in rapid creation. Laughing children chase after them in a primal attempt to capture delight. Some bubbles burst, whilst others escape, floating away on a breeze to disperse. For those who know – art and spiritual education reside here. There has been no rain in ages. The earth is hard and dry, threatening the beauteous garden and thirsty, drinking lawns. A golden Labrador laps water noisily from a cold steel bowl, slobbering enthusiastically. He is bringer of great healing and happiness. Like us all, the dog never left the Over Soul. The only difference being that the dog does not have to realize that. In this moment I am shown the joy of pure energy and Nature's golden wisdom.

Day 31 – Caravan of Crows

Friday 8th April – 21°C

KEITH BRAZIL

Aiwisruthrem: Night (Watch 4) – I am on the Old Heath of Heathered Black. Ravens roost, trick and call. Through the Winter Spring trees they fly, leading me on branch by branch through the dark boughs of the mysterious Gorse Wood. A cavalcade of gypsy Bone Crows rolls by. They settle their kite and fen wagons in a semi-circle and start a small campfire. Unseen things are thrown onto it in preparation, as they hastily stitch a cloth scarecrow together and stuff it full of paper. They assemble it and place it atop a tall pole and raise it up high to ward off the gathering hollows and shadow hallows. From their beaks, they spit out the broken remains of mice in a circle about them and attach them to string. They place a fire stick next to the flammable guy to scare off any wandering straw-men still in search of a brain. As they begin their twilight supernatural stories, they use the stuffed man and mice bones to create a shadow puppet play. It tells the story of a persecuted Witch who flew on a stick and a Guy's reason for parliamentary treason. Leftover religious fervour and fear burn on the fire as fat from a fowl and daemonized suckling-pig. Old churches still at war. What a laugh! No wise White Owls here then. The Crows stretch out their dark finger feathers and click their necks as they see me approach. They point me toward the caravan of the old Crone Crow. A single flick and cut across the throat proclaims:

'Get on with it, quick! Sooner done, sooner dead, then we can all hop off to bed!'

The old Crow Crone has something to say, something to tell me that has been foretold, guessed at, known about, but that has only recently been resonating within my soul – the important sadness of death within the heart of life. One of my cackling Ravens swoops down and steals a branch of fire. Others dive down to pinch the basting-birds, the cobs of corn and the burning oracle bones. This is Old Moon, Turtle shell and Ox bone magick:

plastromancy through thermal expansion, scapulomancy through beak-scrapping, bone-thinning and scribing, hunger feeding through the attack of immediate want. This is sunset wheeling and feasting. Why are the Ravens here, these black-capped biblical scholars and funereal jokers? What are they doing kicking about amongst the ashes of the Bone Crows' gypsy campfire? One Raven walks like a jutting judge. Others can hardly hold their belly and contain their mirth. A fourth and fifth jilt and tilt at each other arguing over a mouse until they both fall off their branches. A sixth perches on my shoulder and pecks at my now bleeding ear. A seventh swarthy son points the way towards the steps of the Crone Crow caravan.

'You know what you ought'a? Fear not the Mocking sons, but the Scavenger's daughter...'

I climb up the wooden steps and enter in through a beaded curtain. It is candlelight dim. Her caravan is full of sparkling treasures and graveyard finds. Madam Crafty sits in the shadows and beckons me to a cushioned chair. Candles, crystals and cards lay on the table before her. Brass hangs around, some crooked, some deliberately upside-down. I sit as though under her spell. She cracks open an egg and sucks it dry. She opens another and lets it fly. She crushes the shell of a third under her claw and spreads it raw. She pecks through the flecks of the random rune with her beak, searching for signs. Cracked, speckled and blue right through – there is blood where love should be. She turns to me through a scented haze. I recognise her visage from the spluttering Snake-Raven televisions that first brought me news of the Harbour Wave.

'Come, tea leaf,' mutters Madam Crafty, 'Sit. It's true. I have known you from before. Did I not see you recently in the Place of the Skull and the Room of War? Has your astral self been Sky time travelling? What have you seen and what are you gathering? Have you been to the other side and glimpsed forever? Come! Let us look into the teacup of destiny together. Let me pull my shawl from the crystal ball and ensure orb gazing. Now. Now. Keep alert! I can see your eyes are glazing! Perhaps some fire cards to tell your fortune? Purely just for entertainment! What is it that I can offer in return for such heart-plucked payment? Perhaps a quick scrying of your worn palm lines in scant regard to your life of lying and some old war crimes? Of course, for my services there is a cost. What shall we say? What is it worth? What can you give this side of birth? What debt do you think it is you owe me? What is the fee for the handing over of the Freedom Key? I'll name my own price – I know! Fill my talon with a piece of gold plucked from your recent visit to the Over Soul.'

A scarf cowls her head. Her big black eyes stare along the length of a protracted nose. Her mouth is thin, but quick of lip. A sword and a sickle hang on the wall behind her. A dagger sits beside her for use in close combat. She could knock me to the ground and stab it between my armour and deliver the deathblow at any time. Dark and fair, there is danger of truth everywhere. She is my coup-de-grâce.

'Pass me your palm and I'll tell you your yarn. Let me view what's left of your strife and the wandering lines of your little worm life.'

I proffer my prevaricating hand, but she holds my wrist tight. Peering into my trembling palm she smiles and looks up at me flashing dark light. There is no escaping from what she has to say, so I submit and surrender to her wisdom might…

'This crisscross here says fear death by fire, yet this one here – fear death by water. Yes, fear death by burning and drowning as you try to fly and drop from the sky. This juicy mound says fear death by falling earth and tumbling towers. Likewise, fear death by stifling air and poisonous vapours. Most unusual! Fear death by fortune, fate and deck of cards; swerving hearts and crashing cars. This valley here says fear accidental suffocation by your own birth mother and don't forget to fear dark entombment and separation from lover...'

The Ravens gather and cackle about her caravan.

'Fear death, fear death, fear death,' I hear them repeat in glee, hopping about on the vardo roof above. They mean me to overhear – sometimes I think they enjoy their undertakings too much!

'...This finger's not straight, the troughed spaces between are far too great, so fear death by swinging and swaying, rope hanging, sword slaying. This little piggy fears death by sharp decapitation and bleeding throat. This webbed froggy says hope you don't croak! Me? I'm just having a laugh – an impertinent joke. Most importantly, and most particularly, fear death by slow impalement, inverted cruciform piercing and poisoned dart quill. Are you all right? You look rather ill. Fear death by mistaken failure of father, feather weather and falling steel. Do I make myself clear? Is the truth of your upturned turtle drawing near?

The toothless soothsayer of ages speaks to me as though across a field of dreams and a thousand falling lifetimes. I am a million miles away, lost to the uncomfortable force of predicament. Her speech of dark sky is all rather sly and this is all setup and uncomfortable joke. I hope I do not give in and unexpectedly choke. I try to stay afloat as she fans her feathers and grabs my throat. Peering into my eyes she continues to speak. Words still utter and mutter from her twisted beak...

'Do you still think you know better than me? Time to bow your head and scrape your knee. Do you think you can carry the weight of the we? I need to know before I slice open your rotten old soul.'

'Yes. Yes. Yes,' preen the jumping Black Jacks. 'Fear death of kittens by drowning bricked-sacks! Fear death by dancing with the devil on your back! Look forward to death and don't look back! Beware! Beware! A heart attack!'

On the roof above the Ravens perform their strange totem and medicine dances. Hopping from foot to foot they pull their shamanic cloaks about them as they begin to chant...

'Fear death by dying, fear death by crying, fear death by capture, lying and frying. Fear death by home fire, natural disease and disaster. Welcome the Lady of Death for she alone is your master...'

'Are these friends of yours?' the Crow Crone enquires dropping me back into my seat. 'They do not work for me although they are quite neat on their feet!'

'Yes,' I said. 'They come from The Tower to take my head and see me dead. They're workmates of mine. Now I see, Ravens divine!'

'I'm not sure about that. You're not bird or snake, more unbrave cat! Did they mention fear death of kittens by drowning bricked sack? They did! Then, perhaps I was wrong. Perhaps Ravens and Crows do get along. You know? Black birds of a feather sticking ripped souls back together. Perhaps you can stay around to hear us all sing? We've got quite a nice ring if you like that kind of thing. Listen out for the caw choir and the thrice ha-Kraa... it's rather sublime given the time locked up in your Tower.'

Triumphant, the Ravens enter in hopping from perch to perch, skull head to bone head, candle to crystal ball. One holds a branch of bonfire. This is not caravan, but funeral pyre. I watch helplessly as the Ravens kick the candles. As they roll about the room flames fall, lick and spread from candlewick throat to burning head. Do they really want to see me dead? It seems I am at their mercy and mirth.

'If not death consider another rebirth? Dark or light? What would you like? Do you think you have the returning birth nerve?'

Madame Crafty, also known as Goddess Kraa Kali, hypnotises with her large black eyes. I cannot move or remove. Unblinking, full of surprises, she tilts her head as she scrutinises:

'Are you all right dear? Shall I carry on? It's nothing personal, just everyone's song. When I press this morsel of finger pad, the slow blood return means you are still sad for the loss of your dad. Really, you should fear the rotting, slow deaths more: madness, neglect by nation, thirst and starvation, ignorance, illness and desiccation, breaks in bones and dislocation, alcohol poisoning and sugar corrosion. This mark here says fear death by slaughter, snake bite, severity and lovely cruel torture. Oh! A warning. Do beware the corruption of giants in evil and manipulation by insidious children of devil. This nick here says stay well clear of fear… Well, I never. Ever so clever! Would you like to hear more?'

The flapping Ravens laugh, but are not daft. They will not be caught in the smoky backdraft. The death throes of Crows can be long and slow, but I am lucky as they are inclined to quick kill. I pray for the mercy of their hunting skill.

'Are we through?' I ask. I feel as though I have been taken to task. 'Is this it? Is this the end of my exquisite visit?

The chairs are smouldering. The smoke is rising. My desire for fire is rapidly subsiding. Knowledge of past and future seem unappetising. It is getting hot in here with so much Raven smoke-joke and Crow-black fear. The Ravens leave.

'Oh dear! Yes. We're through. You too. Don't forget to fear the final turn of your screw…'

Madame Kraa Kali presses back my thumb. She confirms that I am undone. Up to their old tricks, the Rooks, Crooks, Crows and Ravens carry the sweeping flame sticks of my doom. They torch the cushions of the wooden room. It is true – I am through. That much is certain. Flames creep up the reaching curtain. Madame turns as the fire scalds. She throws off her smoky, flaming shawl. In shrieking flight, her feathered garbs burn black as night. There is no escape for me as I encounter my Ravens' fate and the Crow's dark destiny. She launches herself from my side into the receptive sky. She is rising now as I am left to burn and die. She cackles…

'Ashes to ashes, dust to dust, gold may glow, but metal will rust.'

It is a gypsy's death in which all is given and nothing is taken. In her great mystery we are not forsaken. She draws me in and breathes me out as I tremble with so much skeletal doubt. Like a smoky ghost, she is most mysterious female Host.

'Call me witch. Call me crone. Call me ugly. But do not fear my winged emissaries or me!' advises the ageless goddess revealing herself in my fright as bringer of death and Night Sky flight. She is holder of magnificent Crow dark-light.

'Do not fear death, for you have died a thousand times and more before. To cross the Cosmic River to reach the other shore each must exit and pay their dues. You cannot pay your debts in money, only in human kind. You sleep to live and die in eternal return. Through my process are your hard places made soft. In soft form you are given a chance to reassess your attitudes and realign yourself to higher love. You arrive and return through the weakness and vulnerability of the birth/death cycle. Either way you return through me. With the vulnerability of dying, of encountering death, of losing loved ones – you gain a greater equilibrium. You get a chance to live at the heart of love, to experience the heart of love, to practice your spirituality in human form within the destiny game. The game? The ever deepening of your heart humane. My payment? I have not forgotten. Why! The taste of your good bones whilst you still live and, of course, your utmost soaring and bird soul joy!'

Day 32 – Conversation In Blue

Saturday 9th April – 16°C

Rapithwin: Afternoon (Watch 2) – I stand upon a shingle beach listening to the wind and the waves. Small wooden fishing boats have been hauled up for Winter. Nearby is an isolated beach cottage. The surrounding garden is highly designed – decorated with symmetrical rocks, pieces of wood and metal sculpture. With its standing stones, plinths and pebble necklaces, the garden is personal and magical. There is a raised vegetable bed and flowers are placed about – random colourful plants nestling between silver and green foliage. A power station looms ominously in the background. The cottage stands empty – temporarily tinged with sadness and loss. Inside, in the main room, there are notebooks and journals, sketches and paintings. Scripts lie scattered in a corner. Spools of Super-8 film are piled high in boxes with a home movie camera perched on top. Personal photos and homoerotic images from films decorate the walls. This is the house of an artist film-maker. This is the home of someone who has recently died.

I turn to face the window and observe the outside view. I can just glimpse the sea from here, endlessly churning, endlessly turning its watery pages. The sky seemingly goes on forever. So much streaky silver-blue like a washed-out watercolour. It is not bleak, but peaceful. I turn back to the smiling photos hanging on the walls – shared moments and captured memories that have been framed. There is joy and happiness contained within them. I am pulled towards a large poster that is filled with one pure colour – a particular iconic blue purposefully pressed and preserved. It could be paint, a swatch of cloth, or a sliver of sky. This poster is of his last work – the one in which he contemplates immersion and death. As I gaze into the blue the wind whips around the house and the dead start muttering. A friendly ghost with a charming voice whispers into my ear...

'I loved my windswept garden and the view from this room. I did not find it desolate, like some, but natural and bracing. I contemplated being a gardener but... well, the time-consuming images kept distracting me more pleasurably. I loved the blues of the sky, the blues of the sea – and eventually I even came to love the blues of eternity. Of course, it was the last colour I saw after the cowardly yellows and poisonous greens had disappeared and my retinas detached. I remember an all-encompassing dense blue fog before it all went black. Even the internal image-making faculty left me in the end. No shapes, no figures, no glorious sun-kissed saturations of colour... just sounds, words and phrases to mediate upon, like overheard angelic whisperings. *Cupio dissolvi.* Not in a morbid way, but the need to transcend fear and inevitable frailty at the end of my life.'

'A chance to disappear?' I ask.

'Yes... not of the body into death, but consciousness into the final absorption. I wish I could have taken all my art with me.'

'Even the boys of *Sebastiane?*'

'Especially all the dancing boys yelping and screaming – embracing all of Saturnalia's rude requests.'

'They were exotic... erotic.'

'The youthful lustful boys masturbating and preening, you mean – sowing their seed and playfully ploughing each other.' The ghost laughs. 'Sometimes I just couldn't get them out of my head. Some scenes are like that – riotous, not letting go until they find their expression. I was trying to capture different aspects of the male form, flaccid and erect... sweaty states of activity and arousal, not passive and posed, but moving...'

'And the figure of Sebastiane himself?'

'Stripped of status, humiliated, desired. An outpost of men. Is that not an expression of gay reality and fantasy? Exile – an expression of isolation? The freshness of male beauty washing in water – splashing and playing about. Sun-kissed light on sand, sea, and salt – on hair, lips and body. The beauty of male youth and the voyeuristic desire of the aging.'

'And then all the fighting, the grappling and the wrestling... People being made to do things they did not wish to do. What kind of pleasure is that?'

The ghost beams and raises an eyebrow. 'Power. Persecution. Lust. You don't seem to know people very well.'

I smile. Perhaps he is right. 'They called you queer, pagan, punk.'

'I like that. I was first and foremost an artist with a designer's eye – not a narrative driven film-maker. More impressionistic... scenes that somehow came together. *Caravaggio* was more sensual – trying to get to the man behind the paintings... *The Tempest* pure magical camp.' He cavorts around the room dancing with the air like a happy child hugging an oversized balloon. 'But I can't say that I haven't had my fair share of fun. The parties, the dressing up, the rendezvouses.'

'Yes, I believe the blonde wig was your favourite...'

He grins – a big, boyish, welcoming grin. 'Well, that was after I came out. I struggled with my sexuality. It was difficult. I knew early on I was gay but family were important and it wasn't always easy to express yourself back then... Yet I suppose every generation says that. I felt closeted in, so going to London marked a big change – a chance.'

'A meeting of minds?'

'A meeting with anybody. Contact. Connection. I walked down the midnight streets that twisted off into the shadows. Time to think and be alone. Time to act, touch and own. Time for desire to take me out of my aching, swirling mind and into the pleasure zone. You know, the kind of desire that so often starts out red, but ends up blue. There have been occasional lovers and genuine friendship. I have loved completely. And lost. He was young and utterly brilliant – beautiful and clever. But that kind of loss only tinges you with the sadness of what could have been – believing that he could have understood me if only he had survived. But I sense that you don't want that... don't need that.'

'To be understood? No, not so very important to me.'

'But for me, his voice became the first I heard – my very first haunting... just like one of the many whispering dead that you hear surrounding you.'

I smile. 'So, coming out was important to you?'

'Vital to everybody. It takes a lot of wasted time and effort trying to be someone you're not. Not only coming out as a gay man, but as an artist as well. No-one had said that I could do that – be that. But coming out with HIV was more difficult. I had become a ticking time bomb by then. A PWA – a person with AIDS. Not living with it, but dying from it. Not much dignity in that... nausea, night sweats, psychosis, chronic joint pain, diarrhoea... the endless routine of pill-popping... the relentless treadmill of hospital visits twice a day.'

"It's hard to walk away from illness when you're attached to a drip." I quote him, but add... '*Blue* had a wonderful script and sound score.'

'Seventeen drafts to capture the essence of the art of dying in an hour or so… the courage, the anger, the short-term approach to living as Death's scythe slices away so very slowly. Blade by blade the grass is mown. Pebble by pebble the stone is blown and washed away. Cell by cell the lights were turned out. That was the nature of my erosion.'

Suddenly, the ghost falls silent, thoughtful. As I take a last look around the rooms he follows until I come full circle returning to the front door. Through the front window I espy a large rusting spike plunged into the heart of the garden, curiously twisted and misshapen. It has unusual beauty – like that of a found thing washed up onto a beach but doggedly repositioned. As I stride into the garden to pluck the metal-sculpture threaded with pebble-beads I leave the front door open… Behind me a ghost evaporates, absorbed back into the final beautiful blue.

Day 33 – Sea, Land and Air

Sunday 10th April – 18°C

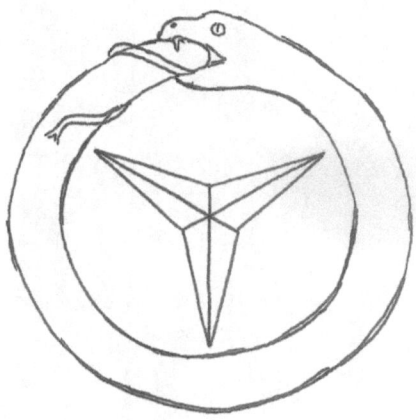

Aiwisruthrem: Night (Watch 4) – Hearts open. Hearts close. Hearts break and are broken. Some crushed hearts are crashed. Nevertheless the love rises and surpasses all. The scene is flickering. She was a Nation's Princess. She was the People's Queen. What cost human lives – those taken and those freely given? How to capture the value of a human heart and keep it? Weep at the thought of it. Mourn. The People's offerings, the candles and cards, the flowers and messages, are all blown away now on a travelling breeze as the personal tributes of the global public blew the heart world away. Old monarchy learns from the demonstrations of such love. Masses of flowers, of thought and feeling, have shared sweet kindnesses in the suffering of the common heart and this kind of rare rose. On spiritual conquest she intercepts and bears two wonderful sons. What has she done? The People's Queen never got to wear the true ring of engagement, for her knight arrived too late to save their entwined fate. She and he are recalled. They are sacrificed; tied to the same destiny string, as heart balloons are set adrift in the endless sky. It is a grievous loss, but a journey of shared heart opening for all concerned and those who looked on. It seems strange now as I stand here – how quiet and motionless the scene is. The shockwaves of grief worked their way through world-consciousness. So much has happened since that fatal crash. Towers have fallen. Hurricanes and tsunamis have smashed.

Here it is snowing – almost Christmas – and I stand in a cold outdoor car compound. There are different types of vehicles all around. An iron chain determinedly ties the tall security gates together. Outbuildings and garages sink low in the snow. Flakes fall, twisting gently to cover the metal sculptures with so much magical frosting. It is late at night and only the midnight foxes stop, turn and brush away. In the snowy silence the cars all have a certain weight, size and presence to them. Some are mangled. Some torn like pieces of tin as dented as their occupiers once were. I touch the bonnet of one of the cars. It tells a story of choice, of swerving, of how a driver has risked his life in an attempt to help save another. What would you do in the sparing? Your life or theirs? In an impulse, in an instant, your life changes course and direction as you are pulled from the wreckage of your car. That is – if you are lucky. That is if you made the right choice in the thousandth of a second between breath and brain, action and impact. All of life's swerving is here. This is collision. There can be no avoidance. You look over and cannot see the scene. For a while you are lost – not knowing the fate of others. You fade in and out of consciousness. Families are altered forever. Deep relationships become rerouted in the accidental damage we make and take with us. These snow-covered cars that wait in the car pound were once weighted with evidence, but now sleep easy. They are crime scene cars once connected to accidents and incidents under investigation. What insurance now? Not even God assures.

Meanwhile, the metal cars, over engineered, plain and fancy, all huddle together in constriction – with strange names and expensive number plates. The one I am pulled to is the rogue Princess's car. This is no Genevieve, no Herbie, or time travelling DeLorean. This is a new design four-door sedan: reinforced windows, wooden rear ashtray covers, leather dashboard, suede headliner and seats all with double-needle stitching. Looking at the car I instantly know what I have come to take. I remove the emblem – the encircled 3-pointed star – from the bonnet. In my hands I now hold a potential energy encoded amulet. This is not a peace symbol, but metal worked alchemy. This is spiritual presence pointing to sea, land and air. This is new compass and perfect chest plate. This is the forward heart of my new metal matter. I am still out of my depth, but somewhere out there the grand design is growing.

Day 34 – The Tower

Monday 11th April – 20°C

Uzerin: Late Afternoon (watch 3) – What ridiculously foolish house is this? Was I so unaware of my deep construction and oncoming destruction? I do not know who to trust on this strange on-going journey of my Tower's collapse nor where I can turn as the radical alchemical elements ignite, inside and out, like so much gelignite in constant implosion and explosion. What seals within my spinning centres are being broken and released? I need new learning in how to burn, use and process the basic universal energy combustibles in greater purpose and love crusade. How I loved you, my birth-Father; loved you with so much immense pain. How I still love and how it continues to hurt! Your departure reminds me of the oh-so much more of love and the agony of death.

Yet slowly I realise that you are not actually stripped from me, just realigned inside my opening heart and widening magnetic memory. You are within my heart like the universe is inside us all, metals as blood, meteorites as bones and all the magical stuff of life that resides within the expanding universe of our unifying heart. Still, the shudder of thunder and electrical gaze of lightning remains frightening to human hearts and ambitions. My fractured Tower walls are collapsing and I am released as all expressionist feeling. My trembling lips and chin want to keep all these unspoken feelings in whereas my eyes and cheeks oppose – being awash from tear-filled sockets that wish to let it all out. I am silent. I cannot scream and shout.

As the scythe falls and severs, I find all is in revolt. Agitation turns to worldwide protest. The unpopular is attacked in the rising of street riots and almost ends of ugly regimes and smoking guns. So much care in the world; so much sadness and despair. The sword of Damocles hangs above all our heads by a single horsehair. Political, social and religious divisions up rise and shake the World's civilised foundations. I stood by my Father's side and watched him fall. Now I follow him down. All our Towers must fall the world over in this incipient state of terrible pain, tension and loss. Such terrible pain. Did I tell you enough that I really loved you? Because I did, you know, but perhaps I did not truly know how to observe the word-mouthing. Perhaps I was never shown? The negative masculine force will not win in me nor dominate the planet with its power and aggression. The Earth is our mother as she is daughter, child of the Sun and the Moon and the night-dancing Stars. Gaia is soil-natural woman in all her wrath and glory, as she unbridles herself of the detritus of centuries of human ill intent. Humanity is not the higher or favoured species. As she empties we must fill as vertical living energy conductors. She releases the previously absorbed and brings about the shaking of nations. She wears a Snake about her shoulders as a cosmic circle of unity. Python or boa? People wheel around her as she triumphs and turns the heads of the world about.

Meanwhile, I must get back to basics, back to Nature, back to the freely born and the natural web, and to the intrinsic Earth structures. Yet I cannot stop the crying that erupts from my heart-opening wound. The wind and the weather collude in my lightning storm and I am lost within the crumbling corridors of the crumbling Tower. I must jump if I am to board the Reunification Express, the galactic train, however long I have been waiting at Time's station. Tickets please! Should I take the most direct or indirect route? The choice is mine. Watch out – here comes Heaven's collector! What have I done with my ticket to who knows where? Snakes gather in a parliamentary slithering and come to tell me wise words. They come to testify to the electric Sky. Already enlightened, they quietly soothsay...

'We watch a world at war. We observe your fall. Come, my friend, and live like us on your belly. In these days and weeks of wilderness we can show you such wondrous things outside of yourself if only your serpentine feelings were acknowledged and trusted. Do not deny us. These matters pertaining to death and the dead are rotatory in their movement, as you will come to experience and realise. That is the spiral secret contained within the evolution of all creatures born with eight limbs, within the sea and upon the land. You scuttle and crawl. The stealth of the scorpion knows this. The self-stung Lazarus also understood this pattern as he entered the Cave of Sleeping Death awaiting the touch of the higher man. You are as he. It is a temporary house. All your old arguments for sorrow, war and joy no longer fit. Your tears are the waters of regeneration washing over tumultuously in preparation for the new. The Sun and Moon jostle for repositioning. Mid-stance, you find yourself in the Temple of the Serpent.

For us, the shedding of skin is a natural and, at the same time, somewhat uncomfortable process. What's left behind is discarded, flaking beauty that served old purpose and old deed. What lies ahead is unknown and holds the future strengthening you. Your struggle is what pulls you free. All this you will come in time to appreciate, but for the moment you are not Snake but Son of Adam. In this lifetime you find yourself in human form, although still you shed and fledge. When you climb from out your skin, you will fly free. As eagles have wings and sit in Aeries so you too will find wings upon your back ready for testing. Only when your Fire-nest combusts will you find that you can then soar into the occult mystifying sky. As you are born – this is your dawn. As you rust – so this is your dusk. In midnight light is your midday slay. So it is that you are far and away.

The fine-fabric gathering about you is the cocoon of the death cloth waiting to be activated. It is both transparent shed dead skin and the forming of new light feathers. Do not be tempted to look back, but resolve to look ever onward to your future paths. Strengthen your new purpose with loving resolve. Also, know this – that from this moment of elucidation forth any future choice of evil that you take will be used against you to further the greater plan of good. This needs to be understood as you battle and thwart yourself. Your struggle is purely one of trying to understand and integrate the unity of your many former selves back into this present, momentary living one. Until the final Dream Spiral descends, you are bereft and learn patience as you let go of inner anger and hurt, frustration and aggression. It is the release of old pain trapped within your spinning centres. Now, as lightning strikes and you are thrown from your Tower, turn your attention towards the double-hearted house and the reintegration of your single winged-Sun. Find your place and peace within the Cosmic Heart. This is Serpent-good and Raven-food. So, in the infinite wisdom and mercy of your dreamtime true Snake and Bird self – let it be.'

I now know I can survive the onslaught of these unnerving processes and strange elemental, alchemical challenges. I will survive. More than that, I hope I can thrive and stride on in the finding of a brand new day. Ha. Kraa. Traa. The Ravens of the Tower call out in sombre chords. In fear and pain I splinter off and try to hide deep inside as the Ravens' Master and Sky-shaman calls out in soul retrieval. It seems I cannot curl and conceal myself in abandoned seashells or shed snakeskins. The Sky-shaman assures me that this will pass and that I will be all right; that he will be there to guide me when I have to confront the final 'Spell of Dream Spiral'. His is the single voice of encouragement and comfort within my pain, yet still the impoverished state of my sorrow and seeming daily lack is perpetuated.

I beg the great, invisible, transformational Alchemist to help me out of this hard place, but it is the Alchemist who has positioned me here within the Tower. My old self knows some of the answers to end such suffering: non-greed, non-aversion, non-delusion, but personal grief holds me fast. At this separation stage, I need to pass on the heart-pecked Pelican blood in fledgling giving so my energy can align to universal flow and sustain new birth. Such Sky forces beyond us all govern our alchemical change and I must take time to understand my heart and branching magical art. Yet as I stand alone in the old, cold, collapsing Tower, walls and stone passageways disintegrate about me. Screams of distant selves echo everywhere. I stumble as the Tower is blasted by storm and thunder. I have to jump or be buried alive. Let live or die? Ripped apart, the Tower tumbles. Lightning strikes twice. Fire and flame is everywhere. I jump.

At this suspended moment in Time, I see my Father once more. I see my face in his as he haunts from the other side of the veil. I feel wretched, sad, awful. My Father, the Tower and I all fall. Is this process of devastation really necessary – destruction simply being a natural consequence to our gathering of memories and garnering of precious things? Is this goodbye really all for the sake of my wings? Is this how the shock and disturbance of grief is meant to be? Falling from the former safe keep of you and me, you are now free, and I am granted a momentary point of perfect peace in a place of perpetual pain. I will never see your face again. Yet still the love. Always the love. In this plummeting instant I have to learn to fly. I have to try. In my Father's ascent and disappearance, the supporting angels descend. Gained wings unfurl to strengthen and embolden.

Day 35 – Initiation

Tuesday 12th April – 14°C

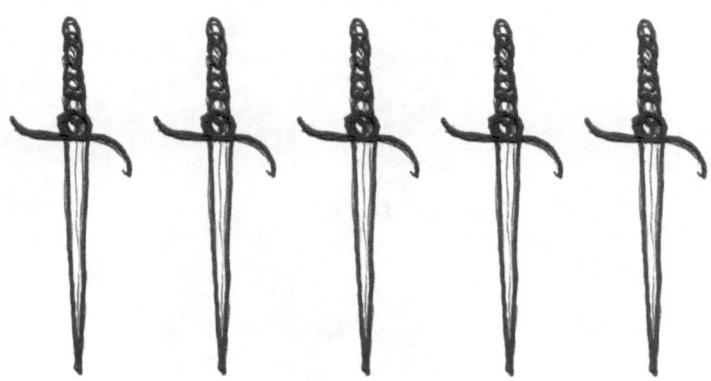

Uzerin: Late Afternoon (Watch 3) – Something is different today. In my vision travel I stand somewhere I recognise from my own lifetime and it is not so far back in the past. It seems that in my rewind I am fast catching up with my present timeline. Will I meet myself soon? The setting is urban – a poor pocket of South East London. Traffic hums. Mothers with children pass by. Schools are emptying. Teenage girls stand together chatting about boys and music, hair and nails; swapping news and laughter. People peel away and slowly the hubbub subsides. Not so far away a pervading sense of threat is settling into an ominous silence. Something is wrong. Things are twisted – inside out.

This upcoming act is not riotous, but plotted and particular – the use of knives to pierce the sides and hearts of mortal flesh. Some players are seasoned; others are innocent going through a rite of passage and drama Saint Francis and Saint Claire could never have conceived of in the acting out of Passion. This is not some daring Romeo Bravo between buddies, some exciting rendezvous, but blood sacrifice. A plague on all houses that continue with this wrong use of mettle! Yet I know it is the metal of the knife that I seek just as the blade seeks its destiny in the warm body of another. Wound. Knife. Flesh. Does life attract death magnetically, silently, without our usual knowing, or do they hear and heed each other's call? Whose head, heart and hands will be next to wield the short deadly scythe? O Mother-Father God! Please forgive them, for one will kill unnecessarily. So much for pride and family honour.

As I am pulled to a corner of sprawling streets on the edge of a vast estate, young marauders in small groups scurry about on their hidden business. Some are clustered strategically on bikes, whilst others stand at a distance watching. They know that one day this might be them enacting out wrong initiation into manhood. Something has failed them, as they are about to fail their already ailing community. There is a silver glint to eyes, smiles and the shiny steel blades that exchange hands behind backs. Fingers curl nervously around the bone handle of an ordinary flick. I would do anything to stop the forthcoming knifing, but in my astral state I can do nothing but observe what has already occurred. I wish and pray to change the outcome of this terrible afternoon, but the timeline is already written.

Nearby, watching from street corners, members of gangs move into position. Aware of the cameras, they spray paint to blind the Old Bill. I feel sick as hoods go up. Shadows lengthen. The atmosphere brews to a point of darkness. As warning screech calls are sounded the fight commences. Posturing and gesturing, the teenagers move forward to confront and intimidate. They circle as they gaze into each other's eyes. The hooded face of this looming figure will be the last the victim will ever see. They both have fighting knives, but the younger one is startled by the rapidity of the slashing manoeuvres and the longer reach of the taller boy. Then the lightning strike of a blade as it is thrust up into the young boy's side, twisting and puncturing. There is heat and blood and pain. In a matter of moments the scuffle is over. Youths run and scatter as the clatter of knives drop to the ground. There is silence as a tormented Moon shines down upon steel and trailing drops of fresh blood.

Moving from my protecting shadow, I stoop to pick up the killing blade – to feel how it feels – in this game of chance, this ugly-brave game of win or lose, life or death. I question my purpose here on the scene of a crime so recently committed. Even as I touch the rapidly cooling hot knife there are shouts from those still lurking around. A boy on a bike speeds past and grabs the other knife with a plastic bag, whilst looking for the second. I do not know which side he is on, but one knife is now gone and I have the other. He cannot afford to stop and search so he darts off into the twilight perplexed. There are escalating shouts now.

Next to me, the wounded boy holds his side and staggers towards the foot of a stairwell. Soon, flowers will be placed here, at the bottom of the stairs, with flapping commemorative picture cards, photos and notes attached. A mourning community will try to make sense of a senseless act, but no-one will come forward. False accusations will be made and faith in the beleaguered justice system will fail. Vigilantism will be harnessed. Innocence, life, freedom – so many things are destroyed in this moment as ever growing spots of blood spill behind him upon the floor. After faltering deep breaths he finally slumps and screams echo out. That is all I can hear. Without medical aid the boy only has a few cold, short minutes left to live. His vision is swirling. His life-light is leaving. What else can I do but pray for peace and bless all their houses and their anguished souls? He is turning into history past, history gone wrong, history seen and remembered, and I am caught in the disturbance and horror experienced as knife crime.

Is this what happens when friend goes against friend? What choice did they have? This was no honey trap, but an ordinary bus stop leading to an estate and an open stairwell that is now someone's last stand. Nearby, a mother's lifetime of agony and grief begins as a child is lost. Tonight, the expected homecoming of sons will be replaced by the unwelcome policeman's knock. One family will live in despair after the horror. The other will live with anguish and guilt. This is such senseless waste. These are but children already engaged in schoolyard social evil. Whether hatred or bullying, one mother will wait forever for the key in the lock. The other will veil and comfort a murderer. This is gut wrenching. This is the end of someone's days. This is nothing other than misery.

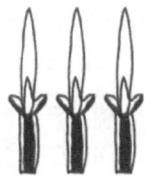

Day 36 – Love, Death, Denial…

(a year of magical thinking)

Wednesday 13th April - 13°C

Aiwisruthrem: Night (Watch 4) — I inhabit an inbetween space. There is grief everywhere. Words impress themselves upon me.

"I wanted to create a portrait of you. Reconstruct your character. Capture more than a memory. I wanted things to be different from what they now are… to wake up altered. Not to smell the shirts and rearrange the shoes. Not to walk around the empty rooms. Not to wake without you next to me in a bed too vast. Last night I sat up late and you, ghostly, haunted my midnight waking vision. We talked like we used to talk — you told me that it was all right and that we would get through this like we always do… did… had. As you can see my tenses, like my senses, are slipping. You would not have liked that. Unprofessional you would say. Yet there is no longer any 'we'. Only me not knowing what on earth to do…"

I walk around an ordinary apartment, maybe LA, maybe New York, but this time there is something different. This woman is alive, yet overwhelmed by recent feeling and palpable disturbance, busy running and rerunning scenes in her head. She is writing, gathering, researching… above all she is thinking, dwelling, considering. Her memories surround her like photographic prints in which she immerses herself. I am caught in her flashbacks — visions of doctors, of kitchens, of typewriters — mini scenes that temporarily absorb us both. She pauses from her writing and looks up out of the window as if momentarily troubled. A cat? The rattle of litterbins? The wind in the street? I look and see my reflection in the window. Does she see me? Am I what bothers her? Diligently she returns to her notes and her writing. Her thoughts — both organised and disorganised — are fragmented, rampant, and raw with feeling.

"I can no longer use the word 'our' for there is no 'us', no 'we', no 'married other'… for all is lost to the fallen past…"

Ah, now I begin to understand. She does not know what to do. She does not understand that life – that which serves us so uniquely, so individually – is also utterly impersonal. She does not realise that he could not make it through another year… not even another day… not even for her. She does not realise that… Yet.

She pauses. She sits as one wrestling with a collapsing world – as one coming to peace in an air-raid shelter. Words fail. Thoughts fail. Living, even in her disturbed ghostly sense, fails her expression of grief. This is illness beyond sanity, beyond the construction of clever words and the patina of controlled appearance. She writes so well – beautiful, poised prose with patterned surfaces; so restrained and in control. But this is death – shocking, insurmountable death that comes our way, my way, your way – so importantly, so infrequently, but has recently hit her so hard. Death has taken her husband away; taken him away from her side, from the fireside, from the favourite comfortable chair in front of the TV. On the side-table there is a plastic bag full of personal metal items. By the bag there is a tarnished bowl filled with sets of keys – apartment, car, holiday bungalow, lobby, storage, and garage. Next to it sits an embossed photo frame, whilst other metal hospital chimera – walking frames, kidney dishes, the needles of syringes – flicker in the many surrounding scenes.

She takes a scalpel – a piece of cold, cutting, glinting steel – and sharpens her pencil. Is that the object I need to take? Or perhaps the wedding silver? Or the knife and fork from the last restaurant at which they ate? I wander around the apartment, but I cannot escape the projections that emanate so profoundly from her. I do not realise she has followed me until her words,

'Spirit, why do you haunt me? You are not my husband?'

I am shocked – stupefied. Never has anyone living seen or spoken to me in such a direct manner. She is sharp and insightful, able to hide behind words and polished sentences – and she has plans that must be executed.

'Bothersome Spirit – Speak! Why do you inhabit my wounds? Why are you here? You are not who I have summoned.'

What can I say? What words will suffice? That I am from the future? That she will somehow get through all of this, yet her loneliness will never abate or cease? What good can come from saying that?

'These are not early days, weeks or months, but early years of healing,' I hear myself say.

'Healing!' she laughs derisively at my words. 'Dislocation of body and mind, you mean. Daily relentless meaninglessness.'

Void. Absence. Emptiness. World without end. Fragments shored.

We both like our poets, but I fear I have offended her; trespassed where private concerns and grief should remain undisturbed. Unshaken. But who is shaking whom? We need, in very different ways, to get past our personal states of grief. Survivors, yet both stuck in sorrowful, melancholic, wishful psychosis. Simple really – we want it to be different from how it is.

'You will be free of this savage, constraining grief,' I tell her. 'The widowed life does not get better, but you will shed this numbing state. But now all you can do is run. Avoid. Deny. Do everything you can to be magical – for that way freedom lies.'

Her resilience is slipping. She wanders after me with her scalpel. Do we share the same delusion? I inhabit her emotional state, but we are not the same. I learn from her. Life betrays. Love too. All we have is change.

'Why do you visit a widow in grief? Can't you see my veil is down, the curtains drawn, the candles lit but forgot? Shouldn't you be out living your life not invading the lives of others?

Her words ring sharp and true, like something my Father would say to help me get back into the world and living again. He went through such a lot to get me here – so should I not be out celebrating life? She and I are both in shock, yet hers is a deeper grief than mine. Is that what has drawn me here? My grief is more silent, more separate, more submerged, whereas hers is more dislocated, more distant, more disturbed. She is also more deceitful and artful than I, deceiving herself and others with her disguises, whilst I am more adverse than her. She has not yet reached mourning and seeks a different end. She sits back down at her table and writes...

"Pronouncement. Autopsy. Obituary."

She believes she can placate the world by shaping words and offering outward gestures. She lists the things she has done in order to keep suspicion away from her. But now she sits alone at midnight casting spells. She believes that this process – this shock, this death – is reversible. All it requires is the right thinking, the right words, the right shift of time zone. Anything that can alter and help her rewrite the past. Then, when this is all threaded together, upon her wish, then the outcome will be different. That is why she needs to be alone for she is hiding, plotting, withdrawing into a mystical space where ordinary time and people are not. She believes she can do it. She believes it. A part of her insists she can overcome her present circumstances. Who am I to tell her she cannot?

This is not so much about endurance, but ritual observance. She must not allow others to believe he is dead for that would impinge on her resurrecting quest. The world is mistaken... He is coming back. He is not lost to the cold earth, but simply buried alive and thus able to return home soon. Within the year. That is why his clothes still hang as they have always hung, undisturbed, arranged in colour, not seasons. So easy, still, to drift her hand through the jackets, shirts and ties that should have been bagged and given to charity. So easy to choose the right one for the evening when they shall next have supper.

On the pages she arranges her derangement slowly, painfully, day by day... Things are not getting better. What does she need? What does she wish? What does she want more than anything?

What she desires is indecent, beyond sanity, and different from how I experience the death of my Father. Hers is a pathological bereavement – complicated, tangled, a lifetime shared now unnervingly unravelling. This is not the inevitable loss of a parent, but of a partner and a life so entwined that separation is unthinkable.

"Unusual dependency," she writes.

Fate? Luck? She does not know or care, for together their sharing went the distance... aisles, smiles, altars and planes. They dined. They danced. They drank wine together until there was no way back. Sometimes they were stuck. Sometimes there seemed to be no way forward. They did not care for they were in love. Simple really, even after the love had worn and the comfortable routines and silence set in. They were there together. They were married in a suit and a dress by 'Chanel'. It was warm. It was June. There was orchard blossom.

Now she has tears, but cannot cry. Instead she has poetry and literature. She has the solace of psychology and self-help manuals. Littered about her she has advice from psychiatrists, friends, writers, psychoanalysts, and animal behaviourists... She has her intelligence, her quicksand sinking, her spiralling vortex, her haphazard Lazarus spells. She makes promises she cannot keep, yet she will be forced to disavow her twisted hopes and dreams for she is no Necromancer. And if she did cast a death-reversing spell she will suffer grave consequences – for such spells will not bring back the mouldering dead, but instead make the instigator a living phantom to false states and illusions. She confuses resurrection with her inability to resuscitate.

Anger. Failure. Guilt.

She has a beloved typewriter – but no words. She has so many endless, repetitive nights in which to think... and remember... and reorganise her madness. And sort the shirts and suits, the ties and shoes. She insists she has her magical mourning which is no mourning at all. She is deluded. She has a cliff to climb, to hang from and fall. She spends the black hours of night unpeeling her numbing condition until she reaches omnipotence. She holds back the waves from breaking upon her – from crashing and taking her down to the place where she needs, but does not want, to go.

Her circumstances are complicated. Unforeseen. It is not the death of her husband she considers, but the death of their former life. She undergoes grief therapy, but she is clever – cleverer than the therapist. She remains angry with everyone except her husband. Yet it is he who has left; he who has let her down; he who went first. How dare he! Yet she freely admits that if she had gone first he would not have coped. Perhaps he would have quickly followed, whereas instead she has years of difficult survival ahead. Years of writing, and thinking, and missing, and books. Years of killing time... but no him. Now she hates the fact that her husband has gone first.

I tell her that it is better that way, but she will not hear me. At this fleeting moment of hate there is hope of anger... hope of tears and grief that can move on into mourning. I watch as her eggshell of magical thinking begins to crack and break open. She reviews the moments of her husband's death – endlessly – both before and after. Was it better that he died at home and not in hospital? Is one place better than the other? It is just a question of blame. Could the doctors have done more for him if they were close by? Would more minutes in the hands of professional others have made a difference to whether he lived or died?

She re-inhabits the memory, emotionally reliving because she needs to find the precise moment when cause became effect so she can alter it. She might be astute, but she is not yet wise enough to deal with the permanence brought about by Death's fingers cruelly crushing her husband's heart. There is pain in her repressed impulses. Her face is vulnerable, her eyes wider, more open, fixed upon a distant point of magic and possible change. She is determined, focussed, yet she delays. Why? She is blocking me from her thoughts; enthralling me with past depth and old colourful scenes. She seeks to distract and I grow wary and suspicious. What is she plotting? I think the worse and go back to where she plays with her scalpel.

"If magical carpets can carry you to a distant place, a distant space... If elevators can carry you up and down, but not to where you want to go... Then cars can carry you on a journey..."

Is this what she intends? A solitary 'Night Ride Home'? So why do I think this is the worst thing she can do?

"And if you drive fast enough, for long enough, then you can cross time-zones and go back in time..."

Then I realise what it is I must take, but she has been skilful – pre-occupying me with a projected-self sitting sharpening pencils with a scalpel at her writing table. The car keys! She must not be allowed to take that journey for if she does there is no way back... if not a fatal collision then a broken mind. Yet we need her still – insightful writer, thinker, philosopher, deep observer of life. I admire her irrational anger, but I must not allow her to leave. She must not go back when forward is the only way however much she needs to investigate and review the past. Her 'circumstantial factors' delay where she needs to go, yet she cannot get there by car... however fast, however far she drives, whatever collision she encounters. I need her to come back alive to write her book...

'Comfort in sorrow when companionship has let you down.'

The thoughts of Old Poet's ravage us both as we run toward the bowl of keys. My presence challenges her plans. I do not wish to disturb one so already under threat, but for some reason I am here, not barred from this moment but invited in. This is love, death, denial – stuck grief and the beginning of mourning observed. *'He died at home, but not alone.'* Now we run through the dying scene, tackling memories and each other. In her re-witnessing of his fall she hesitates. She is too late as the bowl of keys spills everywhere. As my hand reaches out and takes the bunched car keys I – an unrequested ghost – begin to vanish. Rarely wrong, rarely defeated, she falls onto the carpet and begins to openly weep. I might have taken the keys, but it is she out of necessity that triumphs for she has an obligation to get through, around, over all this. Now, the days, the weeks, the months of magical thinking collapse in on her as her responsibility to higher happiness prevails. She falters, fails, and weeps... yet in her own way she at last succeeds as she senses her own fragility. Soon she will start caring for herself. And I can do nothing but disappear.

Day 37 – Raven Master

Thursday 14th April – 14°C

Rapithwin: Afternoon (Watch 2) – Nearby a divine truth breezes through the vines. A reed responds whistling its song across the riverbed of Old Isis. I try to grasp hold of the tuneful whispering secret. Along the banks of the poetic Thames, a Snake glides upon a wave through a grate and bangs on a locked wooden door on my behalf. It is Traitor's Gate. No boats, day or night, will arrive or depart here anymore for it is sealed, locked in by wood and water, despite there being many secret doors and passageways in and out of The Tower. The Snake-code is delivered to the green of a moat. I am walking up and down past the outer walls of the Tower, waiting. Inside the ancient grounds, the Birds of Black pause their pecking. Listening in, they turn on the wing to the High Tower window above. Even though they operate remotely, the Raven spies have an ultimate ally and one to whom they must daily report. The Raven Master has ears to hear us all in sincere birdcall. The message passes from gliding Snake to soaring Raven high above the Tower merlons, and then returns back to me. Whistled in, I am granted audience to the hirer and firer of Black Bird souls.

The Raven Master stands hooded with his back to me looking out the embrasure, sky-gazing into the big blue yonder. Roosting upon the ledge, some Raven Guards come and go. The door is locked and we are left alone. There is the sound of beating wings everywhere. A dark, shiny Shaman's cloak of Raven feathers hangs on the back of the door. A spiralling circle of interwoven snakeskins lies on the stone floor. Apart from a desk and a chair, the room is bare. There are strange markings I do not recognise etched into the wall. Deep claw marks pit the wooden furniture. I am wary. This is not a glass birdcage, rather a stone cut impound. I have been in such situations before and know the necessity for right response, but can barely grasp what it all means or the underlying importance of this meeting. My life is about to deepen and change forever. I listen carefully.

 'Warrior, how came your isle to be free of Snakes and Ravens, yet know so much and survive for so long? How came you to this Tower? Why come you now? Speak.'

I hesitate slightly before replying, whilst realising silence is not an option. I gather myself and speak...

'In truth, I do not know. I did not wish to be free of Snakes and Ravens for I recognise them now as super intelligence – instinct and intuition in action from the long ago. In some ways I had become an isle barren of the Old God's messenger creatures, banished and controlled by the last remnants of orthodox thought and feeling. I cannot and shall not deny this verdant paganism that has so vehemently arisen within me, nor indeed these deep feelings inside me that are creating such great turmoil. I never wished to be free of Snakes, only to be free from my fear of them.

Likewise, I have been cautious and wary of the Ravens and their haunting dark purpose. I have been stuck in office, acting a role, as befitted my previous station, but my heart grows old and my Rose Finch is dying. Under the Ravens' growing shadow I am learning to distinguish the different forces at work. I did not know that the casting of the 'Spell of Snakes', the summoning of Serpent-force, was ancient knowledge and power within me. I was not myself. Until the Snakes recent release, I was confined, restricted and fettered. Now as I am becoming free, I realise that the avenues of Snakes are my many windows onto the many worlds, offering me an astonishing and welcome new view of life. They, alongside the Ravens that have followed me these past few weeks, are all part of some deeper Primitive Spring spreading through me, that I sense to be ancient, yet ageless, and so newly awakened.'

The Raven Master listens to all that is said and not said. He peers into the horizon and the long-running rays of days.

 'Remember. This is your wild tale, not your tame one. This is everything you could no longer hold back, so give it your all. You are caught in a Pagan Dance that reengages you with the world through sorrow and upheaval. The Snakes and Ravens are informants of the fresh Spring state rising up from the rubble of your former world, rising up from out of the dust of the now of life, rising up from the ruins, in which you have so unexpectedly found yourself. They help lead you on in the re-finding of the heart home. It was they who brought you here today. In your Wilderness Days you have found yourself placed alone on the Isle of your Soul – to discover your heart's wasteland. You are isolated, but not alone. Because of certain karmic conditions you could not fully enter the loving kingdom and the shock to your system is what you are experiencing now. All your Tower defences and old structures are falling. May the fires burn through your old buildings, leaving your golden countenance to greet the new Sun as you ascend. To survive, the past Rose Finch of your station has become sin eater, but it cannot stay as such. It is, as you say, rightly dying. It must be allowed to die as you experience further the 'death within life' that so many previous masters have spoken about.

As you understand your alchemical situation you will find that you become Snake and Raven guided. Recently, you have tasted the nectar of the true Budding Lotus, and now you need to move onto the green leaves of its great white unfolding peace. Do not be afraid to wade through Life's Cosmic Water toward it. This is your shift towards a higher wisdom. Yet do not equate your future living with this terrible emotional and mental anguish you feel. All is temporary. Do not be afraid to assimilate the old selves, however beautiful or beaten, well or ill fitting, you deem them to be.

Flitting from many ways of unfurling faiths and multifoliate lives, you journey to the centre of the Dragon's heart of Cosmic Fire. This is your experience of epic time and adventure. One of the Soul World's intangible abilities is to alter geometric shape in endless divine patterning and transforming nature. Like Gaia, you shift, open and change in transition.

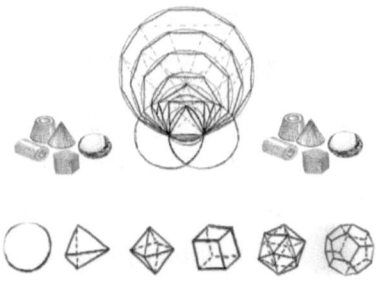

This is the way of growth and integration. You might ask what lies at the celestial heart? Benevolent in nature, the Dragon seeks out the sacred places in which to dwell – investigating the star-patterns of universes as we like children study the uniqueness of snowflakes. The living geomantic shapes link together. This is spiritual spatial harmonics in evolution. Go forth to every part of your unfolding soul and bring the good news to your creation. With every fibre of your being seek the Dragon and receive divine love. Listen to each stage of life and its phases as you walk through the many rooms and mansions of life. Your awakening heart was hidden as God's heart is hidden. Your purpose lies in the seeking of God – not his gifts – with all your heart. That is the only requirement. Dragons are messengers of balance and magick. Their psychic nature will take you to God's mystery and profound wonder. Their primordial powers are strength, courage and fortitude. That is why they were set as original guardians of the galactic seals, but to experience these flights through the star gates first your heart seal must be opened.

The Dragons are masters of all elements, yet they particularly covet the metal of experience. This is their gift, and you can only seek them through the metal wound of you. That experience which pierces you likewise pierces them. What else purpose and point the tip of your sword if not to cut through light complexity as you penetrate your auric egg from within and pass through the mystic veil that once hung like chainmail about you, but is now so slowly and surely dissolving? You are spiritual warrior, not warmonger, warlord or war king. The universal Mother-Father God seeks your safety and harmony, not your aggression. The balance of their love brings wisdom to the determination and domination of wills. The Dragons are deliverers of great healing with their clever cauterisation and the fierce ever-mercy of their magick. They make powerful protectorate keepers and custodian guides. In their cosmic cloud-climbing they bring good fortune and new beginning – for they herald the season of mid-Spring.

Now, in the coming time of our age, the Fire Dragons are bringers of fresh dawn. They bring unlimited spiritual vision in their search for their perfect counterparts in friendship: the Raven turned Phoenix, the Scorpion turned winged-Snake, and the Eagle turned Star Angel. This is when the Dragon turns golden and unlocks the seals and gateways of the cluster galaxies. The finding of Dragon is key. The Keeper of the Tower knows this and has seen your searching, your soul's overreaching, your conditioned ego's consistent fall and rise and fall. Indeed, he has overseen your struggle from Dawn's beginning until Time's world end. Your diary expressing the human heart of stolen metal and borrowed experiences, with all its sad songs and strange speeches, is but Totem Journal. It does not belong to you, and was given – nonetheless it is yours. Who else is this for if not for you? You cannot overreach in matters of Spirit, and your personal search to understand God's qualities leads you on. I ask you – do you continue to seek to steal metal or do you need to forge using the great winged-Serpent's unifying fire? Do you wish to return that which was stolen in the name and injury of love or bring metal together in new assembly? What are you shaping? Who on your journeying have you truly found? Who is it that you have unbound?

Do not hold back on the caring, yet watch as all creatures within the creation fall in and out of The Way as they crawl, hop, shuffle, slide and swim to be in the Stream of Life and revisit the feet of the Buddhic Age. See how the Snakes and Ravens glide. Observe how others walk and run as the great Wind of Change blows about them. Others dance and fly to reach Heaven's Sky and the golden Sun. Notice on whose wings the attempts are made. Not on the back of another, but on the wings of the Father and Mother. Each has to find their coursing nature and motion, and also their stillness. Ravens watch and report back daily to me. Everything is noticed within the kingdoms. The Serpents and Ravens are your friends.'

'But I am such a poor pupil for this strange alchemical education.'

 'How little you know yourself as you further embrace your spiritual humanity. How much you are learning and rediscovering about the connection between personal love and universal care. Think upon it. Apply it. The recent Convocation of Kali Crows calls you to new role within the Raven Agency. One way or another, everyone comes to the Tower, and everybody leaves; some with their heads more intact than others, some with hearts more healed and whole. Even though you work for us, you had to leave, for what do the Ravens do? They are Sky-wardens of sacred dark mystery. They are seekers of fertile soil and deepening relationships. They keep The Tower from tumbling whereas your Tower needed to collapse. The path you trod some would call Fool,

yet that fallen faith is now becoming emergent awareness. In some ways blessed is the foolish wisdom of the human way, but merciful is the true respected way. That which is outworn and unnecessary must be allowed to perish. That which is essential and fundamental must remain – regardless of cost and the effort. That which is outmoded needs to be removed

You could not stay here at The Tower. We cannot protect you from inner truth or outer aspect. We would not wish to. You must grasp the growing golden rays yourself. You stand in the streaming River of Life. The deep severing had to happen. Loss in the impermanent world is constant and natural. You are now reasoning your why and re-harmonising your world. You could not do that if you had remained here. It would have been counterproductive to all concerned. You needed to fall as you watched your Father and those who loved him fall. Remember that above all this – love and all its gains remain.'

I ponder before I reply.

'It is true. The depth of unbearable sorrow has taken me by surprise and at times I am barely able to move. What was initial peace at my Father's passing has turned into painful inner turmoil and incapacity. It has shocked me, reduced my world to rubble; destroyed me. I have been so lost, so absent, yet it has brought me here to this point of learning and re-education. It is essential for me to deepen my trust in life, in myself and in the higher guiding ways.'

The Raven Master turns to face me – serene, but serious.

 'The loss of your Father was a powerful emotional force. The intensity of turmoil has created a reverberating turbulence. Gentleness and inner strength are required to weather the

vibrational storm and restore tranquillity to the many senses. Perseverance and endurance are also needed, patience too. These are all gifts of sacred time and sacred time is the great gift of love. Peace, compassion, and understanding are at the heart of knowing thyself. Joy and bliss the rewards. Yet only you can negotiate the buffering solar wind that protects your inner rising single-Sun.

'What ails thee?' you once asked of another. I ask in return, 'What ails thee now?' So, brace yourself in the descending swirl as the 'Vortex Spell' is placed upon you. There was no preparation for what has so far happened to you and no words to explain what is about to happen.'

The Raven Master smiles as instructional love pours from his wizard fingers as magick and from his mouth as gently muttered incantations. So, the final enchantment begins and the 'Vortex Spell' fills the room. I am lost within swirling words and distant worlds, not of thought, but descending magnetic waves. Slowly, the room fills with the eddies and flows of alchemic ether, pulsing sound and light. A force field of energy slowly builds up around me. I am in a maelstrom. I utter strange words, guttural-Snake and Bird-speak, as though at a growing distance from myself. In the mists of mysteries and radiating magnetism my mystic within is lost to the descent of sacred swirling. Questions arise: What is this I am experiencing? What do I do with my aspects of self, my Sun and my Moon in these strange days of spiralling recovery, yet ever onward nocturnal journeys? What do I do with these pieces of metal that I have collected and which now accumulate upon my rooftop Aerie? The Raven Master answers,

 'Surrender them all as you are surrounded by the greater forces. Harness them. Love them. Forgive them. Share them. Melt them. Trust them as you would yourself. You are

shrouded in moments of metal and memories are gathering for you as you re-enter the Cosmic Heart. Your theft and stealing ways mean you gather gold in base form unto yourself. When your single-Sun shines, the metal will run, but who is it that heralds in such a Dawn? They are moments in time, from Time, recollecting their stories in the weave of your mind. Make your days different. Make them sacred. Bring about the totem of you.

Wonder is the true doorway of the wyrdening way. Make manifest your revelation of fire and metal theophany. The Snakes and Ravens inform you of Earth and Sky purpose, but what is your design? What remains after the tumbling is certainly yours to keep, for it is light eternal. The sum of your qualities is taken with you into the restoration. So, rebuild anew. You have amassed stolen metal items, treasures to you and the Dragons. Work is already underway. Do not think you are operating alone on this for happiness comes from shared goodness. Bring together your metal pieces torn from out of time and hurt. Then shall you be shown the way of timeless magick. Prepare to meet the Mountain's Metal Maker – the Olympian who shapes gifts and forges futures. And have you forgotten the deep secrets of The Tower for which you work?

Underneath the heart of the City resides a fire-breathing beast. Old magick still resides for use in new ways, but you must remember to abide by the rules of nature. If you are to proceed you must operate within the unifying supernatural laws. Do you understand the caution needed? Together the world can forge great Amulet Magick, but first you must be cleansed. In the act of stepping in and out of the Sacred Flame you can take nothing with you except that which is given. Are you prepared for that? You must remember that the fire of the Bleeding Heart is sacrificial and you alone must unlock its key. You strive – but for what? There is nothing to achieve except to be open to each moment. I will help you now in the magnetic extraction of old truths that hold you back. The Snakes and Ravens will guide you to the one who holds your victory fire that hides your single-Sun. The Sun and Moon, the Earth and Stars, all gather to help. Through them the creating energies reach out to you.'

For a moment I am silent, yet my thoughts are racing. Who is this that stands before me? What dreamlike spell encircles me? This audience is a rare opportunity, but I am dumbstruck. What is it that stops me from speaking? Ravens come and go by the window. Dark shadows rise. I do not know what to say or do. I do not feel strong and true, but awkward and stuck, unable, unstable in the growing dizzying. As I fall to my hands and knees I feel the textured skin of Snakes upon the floor. The Raven Master draws a chalk circle and places his cloak of Raven feathers about me, covering me. Everything turns black as magnetic waves overwhelm me. I descend into heartache, perplexity and magical mystery.

As I helix and spiral in the rotational power of the vortex something within me struggles. Cosmic Water encapsulates me. I bubble-breathe but am sucked under and down. Fly, swim or drown? In survival fear I snap my auric shell shut – closing tight to protect the Pearl of Experience contained within the heart of me. It holds the grit truth of everything I have been and done, but it no longer belongs to the new beckoning. In defence and defiance I resist the higher wisdom that wrestles with me. Like the recent shedding of skin, the Pearl extraction reminds me of uncomfortable loss. The blood of the Phoenix and of Dragons enters my exploding meridians – red and golden. My body is in spasm. Yet as the final stone walls of my Tower-mind collapse I am exposed to greater love and truth. Broken, the seal to my heart is ripped open.

The spinning energies raise me up then release me, throwing me to the cold stone floor. I collapse, gasping. I am stunned, but can feel the heavy shamanic cloak being removed from me. Resurfacing, I breathe rapidly, but try to focus on the room. Something is different. I am no longer encased. I lift my head and break free of the last dissipating waves of the 'Vortex Spell'. As I do so, a clear layer of scales is removed from my auric eyes. I can suddenly see differently now. Hear differently. Somehow my senses are retuned. There are beautiful colours and delightful sounds everywhere. Slowly, the Raven Master bends down to help me up off the floor. Two Ravens perch upon the open ledge. One hops off and flies down, calling to my awaiting Snake. The other goes to call the Raven Guard. Apparently, I am ready for collection. Still reeling and spinning, I try to steady myself.

 'Remember. To your still trembling body and convulsing mind, to your many remaining questions and unknown responses, that there is only one answer – and that answer is love. There is no truth without love. This new state will feel unsettling and strange, but do not arbitrarily fill that space. Instead, sit, listen and wait – for your Grail Cup is being replenished. What you hear calling is Dragon song. What you seek is your Dance of Faith. What you need to remember is that magick exists all around you. Although you gain control of your travelling Moon gift and Night Sky perception, much is still out of your hands until you complete the cycle of understanding contained in your Medicine Wheel. Now, on my leaving, I ask of your patience two final questions. Do you understand yourself better? And what know you now of the descent of grace?'

The Raven Master pauses then laughs to himself. Turning, he shows me the door as the shadows of a hundred majestic Ravens begin to fill the room. The Raven Guard waiting outside escorts me away. I go. I do not look back. As my footsteps fall onto the corridor floor in retreating silence I hear his parting riddling words rise and fill the air...

'One answer, of course, rests upon the backs of wings within the beating two of things and the shared one-shedding of old world skins. The other is all in response to the receiving of winged Snakes and Suns... For how else is eternal Spring begun?'

The echoing words dissolve as a dark-winged man prepares to take flight into the glassy sky. Transforming, he hops, jumps and leaps from the ledge. High up in The Tower, above the merlons, the trickster Raven Master beats his wings and flies.

Day 38 – Domine Dirige Nos

Friday 15th April – 16°C

Uzerin: Late Afternoon (Watch 3) – The tide of the Thames is still out. My Snakes and I take the steep steps down to the muddy river shoreline. Beside the boarded up Traitors' Gate I find the old, disused wooden entrance to the tunnel below. Beneath the Tower we go delving deeper than the Dungeon Rooms and underground secret passageways. I take my torch and two Fire Coins. I do not like darkness. My eyes are slow to adjust and I do not see well in it. The passageway slopes up to a natural stone high water mark and tidal break, and then slants ever downwards. Water does not pass here, but I am aware that the in-tide will block any retreat back over this route. At first, under my feet, is sand and low stone, then crunching gravel and firmer earth. I need no clew as the Slithering Ones lead the way. It is damp and dark. Eventually we enter into the antechamber of a cave. I have never been below to the Mithraeum, but have long suspected its secrets. The Snakes are honour bound to ancient confidences and have never spoken of it until today. Not even my chiselled off Hunky Punk has divulged such mysteries.

The Snakes lead me on. The air is filled with incense and smoke, prayer and chant. Yet I wonder at the sense of pain and wounding in the sound. A large underground corridor leads us further on and in. The Temple of Mithras opens up before me. It is poorly lit and in crumbling condition. Few visit such places and this is all but forgotten except for the initiate worshippers of Helios, the occasional forensic diggers and the inquisitive archaeologists of old. Time-crime still abounds. Investigations on-going. Here the way is gained through the Entrance of Truth. Guessing and threading the needle, I cross the court through the correct arch, passing the ruined remains of pillars and side altars, along the sunken nave. I move through the Holy Place towards the main plinth. On the horned stone altar of burnt offering I strike the Fire Coins and create twin flames. I sprinkle the dust of sandalwood on it, which flares and fills the air with its musky perfume. In the cave there are many deeply etched stone carvings and claw drawings. In the flickering light I see a figure of an ancient Man God emerging from the half-hewn rock.

In the light of the Fire Coins' dancing flame, the secrets inscribed on the walls briefly light up and spin off around the cave in golden gossamer threads. There are many side altars placed about in various states of decline. The cut stones and figurines intrigue the Snakes as they put out their bifurcating tongues and read the antique runes. In relief, behind the High Altar, a carved scene glows: a sun, a bull, a crow, a male bride, a knife, a wheel, a wheat sheaf and a Phrygian hat. These are symbols of a mystery religion thousands of years old, re-carved by Romans while in occupancy of Old Londinium. The flickering light on the ceiling and walls calms and the engraved secrets descend back into dimming darkness. On the High Altar, the flames of the two Fire Coins flicker true – deep orange, sun yellow, fire red and faint blue. At the back of the pitch-black cave stirs a mighty creature. My Snakes rise, bow and back out. In deference they will wait for me back at Traitors' Gate. I am left alone. From the Inner Temple – the Holy Place – a guttural voice sounds in an ancient language of prayer.

'...ashem vohû vahishtem astî, ushtâ astî ushtâ ahmâi hyat ashâi vahishtâi ashem...'

A great winged-Serpent emerges. I bow my head and kneel. This is the Dragon Defender of the City of London – Lord Protector of Merlin's Magical Isle. This is Fire-magick most high. This is creator knowledge.

'My name is Zam Azi Ahi. To each in their approach I have a different name. To you I am Zam Sorrow Bane, bearer of the separating blade, holder of the Holy Spear – guardian of truth. You stand in the Temple of the God of Covenants and Oaths where everything you think, say or do is weighed against you. You have found me out because you are becoming a Runner of the Sun – a living messenger of spirit bringing forth love, kindness and friendship. In this, your Ver Sacrum, your ritual and sacred Spring, you find yourself exiled. Yet through your reconnection with the great spirit forces of the Moon and the Night Sky you experience the birth of your inner unconquerable single-Sun. In its rising, you are invited to the Sun's banquet, but to partake you must share the Dawn Feast that is compassion and unconditional love. Before this can occur you must complete your trial.

These Wilderness Days are your ordeal pit. You are now entering the heart of it. Yet you are unable to find the Sun as your Moon grows ever more powerful – blocking your day. Know that it is I that causes your eclipse. To be victorious, the supreme Fire of Fires must be lit. The Old Rose of your heart with its thorns of protection must burn away as your aura is rebalanced by your spiritually guided soul. This transformation is your natural heritage and will release the aching days of your heart into the white flowering Lotus of Peace. The petals will open, absorb and reflect the light like an orbiting Dawn Star transmitting from above the Earth. You feel the hurt and harm from all who you have injured and all who have injured you. You eat sin in fraught attempt to end suffering and as a result your consciousness is repositioning. Grief is your fuel, fear and confusion your currency. Know that there can be no complete protection from the all-absorbing higher light. Until then you must fight to keep alive the highest fire. Conquer yourself and any enemy within. Salute the Sun. Pray to the Moon. Yet I will forever remain your Dragon dilemma for I am the ferocious devourer of suns and moons, worlds and stars. I am that which requires magical thinking – the correlation between love, prayer and ritual offering. Can you understand this support with which I sustain you?'

I nod silently. Overawed, I kneel, bend my head and listen with humility.

'For you I am joy, death, destiny and illusion. I am the joy of your birth and life – that joy which is difficult to find in the world except for the well favoured and free. I am also the real death that comes to all, with and without warning, as you have experienced recently in the death of your Father. I am the untidy end that makes your body a corpse. I am the bolt from out the blue for which you grasp and yearn, but in reaching – turns all to ash in the leaving. I am the unpredictable force, the unstoppable source – that destiny which is unforeseen, yet does ever arrive: cause, deed and experience. I represent that which is secret and hidden – the illusion that eventually results in liberation. I am all that can be made manifest and encountered. I can be recognised in life as that over which you can never achieve control or dominion. And you should never aim to succeed in this. Throughout all of this I maintain you in the all-encompassing presence of light. This I promise and to this you must bind. Speak. Do you understand?'

'Yes,' I utter, but I truly fear I fail to comprehend. Rays born of purity, goodness and positive intent radiate about me. It is light answer that the Dragon seeks rather than any inarticulate words and stumbling humanity of mine.

'Then I become Zam, Joy Deliverer, bearer of Dragon-fire, provider of spiritual knowledge – bringer of gifts. Unlock me. I am guardian of holy places, temples, land and seas. I reside in the Temple of Love and Truth and for all eternity I have served humanity as the relayer of First Fire and emitter of the single unsplittable ray. I am creator and protector. I am the light beam propelled as seed sent forth from original unfathomable fertile darkness. I am both former and transformer – the undecaying one. I am inception – that through conception became Mother-Father of All Heaven together with the earthly worlds perceived by you as the substantial elemental universe. Through Fire Mist I am all-consuming, yet you will also come to know me as that force which sustains and reveals the underlying ordering principle. I am the source of Celestial Flame that brings you to truth out of collapsing earth and into firmament, the light within dark, yet also the dark. I am the power of Cosmic Water over fire – the presence that does not alter or extinguish. Listen…'

Momentarily, silence descends. Then chiming sounds and chant ring out through the cave. I am engulfed in strange song. There are no words for this – all is rosy light and golden feeling. Enraptured, my mute understanding is like the rise of a greater Dawn as I listen to this new language and sound.

'I create a certain type of music that resonates around the cosmos – a most heavenly sound which combines forces with the energies of angels and archangels. Sometimes it is called Dragon music and it is a rare specimen of its type. Can you hear it? Even within its aspect of destroying all matter and energy which must be crushed, can you also comprehend the nurturing essence that is behind all its intent? In the presence of humans I present myself as the terrifying beast for I am first Keeper and mighty defender of love.'

'Then why do I hear pain in your song?'

Standing in the Inner Temple the Dragon roars, filling the cave with burning fire. I am frightened as it lifts its great five-toed claw. The Dragon could crush my skull and body in one blow, but it does not do so. Instead it reveals a spear piercing its flank. Who would harm such a primal guardian? I advance and pull out the spear from the Dragon's bleeding side. I kneel and place my lowered head under its raised crushing claw. There is no wish to harm. The Dragon is grateful and needs me to understand the nature of deep wounding.

'I am the ancient injured one. Man can only approach me through their wound – as conquering lamb to devouring lion. To survive you must pull the Holy Spear from out of my side as though you were I – for each in turn must tend to their suffering self. On the outward journey, through the process of living, you experience harm. In returning all must be restored to its rightful place. The pain in my song is your history and belongs to you. Likewise, let joy now fill that space where the ache and the agony have thus far dwelt. See, this is no longer the Cave of Wound and Regeneration, but the Temple of the Golden Sun.'

As I am lifted up high, a second breath of flame races through the subterranean Temple. This time my aura is ablaze with rosy fire, permeating old views with glimpses of a higher world. Visions rise and fall before me. I see the layers of the subtle body and planes. Other worlds open and quests tremor on the verge of being understood like the view of life from the branch edge of a jolt-waking dream. Then the Dragon lowers me to the ground and begins to withdraw backwards into the darkening cave. I have only one remaining question: How do I achieve what the Dragon requests? I do not know, so I deepen my trust and follow the wisdom of my heart.

Now I must leave to escape the rising tide, as I know of no other route out. I pocket my Fire Coins. Next to them, left on the carved altar, is a Dragon gift – a Moon Pearl, beautiful and most intriguing. I recognize it, but I cannot tell whether it is the Crone Crow's crystal ball salvaged from the Caravan of Fire or that seemingly precious Pearl so recently garnered and extracted from me by the Raven Master's 'Vortex Spell'. It holds a mystery unknown to me. I slip off my jacket and swaddle the gem within its hood and folds. I tie the arms around it and gather it up. It is heavy. As I leave, an ancient voice fills the chambers of the cave. Once more an old prayer chant starts up and begins to spread its angelic Dragon sound. I know it from of old, from out of Time, but it is now newly resonating.

'...athā ahu vairyo athā ratush ashāt chit hachā... Vangheush dazdā manangho shyaothananām angheush Mazdāi. Khshathremchā ahurāi â yim dregubyo dadat vāstārem...'

In truth, the prayers of angels and Dragons have never ended – their chants are the unsung plainsong of Time before our history began. It is the song cycle when star clusters all sang together, and the universe was a seed twinkle in the Supreme Architect's loin and eye. Through the cave the galactic tones are ringing. It has a new message for us all. Listen. Follow. It tells our waking hearts of a new present and a wonderful tomorrow.

Day 39 – London's Burning

Saturday 16th April – 18°C

'…London's burning. London's burning. Fetch the engine. Fetch the engine. Fire, fire! Fire, fire! Pour on water, pour on water…'

Aiwisruthrem: Night (Watch 4) – On my rooftop I sit cross-legged and gaze into my wondrous Moon Pearl, my precious Dragon gift. Old tales tell of Dragons harvesting these pearls, one of the Night Sky Goddess's monthly ova, when they were once kept as pets by the race of Giants. That was before the first diluvian flood, before the last of the Giants were fought and sent to ground. The pearls were highly treasured possessions of the Lady Giants, kept in dressing table drawers, used in power rings and pressed into gold clasps as earrings and rare jewellery. To me it is more indefinably precious than the Tower's guarded crown jewels. It is a meditative egg and a crystal ball of great wonder. This particular iridescent orb with its spectral interiors is a Doorway of Awe. It is the beginning of the returning of me.

As I gaze into the Moon Pearl's cloudy depth I see the whole of London contained within. It is like a curious snow globe, as though a colossal Godchild has placed a city under a glass chalice inspecting its entrapped citizens like so many insects squabbling in anthill chaos. London pulls you in and spits you out. Yet what I see in its central glow is not shaken snow, but billowing smoke and specks of ash. It is a city on fire. Is this past incendia or present pyromania? It is a money-obsessed City dealing with wealth, wants and daily needs – a besmirched jewel in need of cleansing. What fascination of blazing ecology continues through the ages? Is it Dragon breath or solar fire? Through the suspended fissures and crystalline cracks of the Pearl, I espy winged Serpents of Flame sweeping across the corridors of Time, consuming all before them. In the bowl and basin of masculine energy that is London, the City ignites time and time again. Fires great, greater and small. The universe warms. From molten fire and through the hundred thousand years of inferno – lightning strikes.

As I look within the Orb of Old, birds of Swan-white and Raven-black steal Dragon fire for unfolding mystic purpose and planetary evolution. They are like specks of soot and snow rising and falling as distant flakes of ash. Serpents share secrets of fiery wing and branching flame. They bear it as gift to the late forming Land of Man. Within the crystalline Pearl, the Web of Time spins out and collapses in on itself. Two thousand years of London on fire dream weaves itself through the swirling smoke. Boudicca's force of queenly warrior wrath surprises the invaders and burns Londinium to the ground. Destruction is everything. Hadriatic fires wipe out the Hundred Acres. Anglo-Saxon wooden houses and churches are burnt to the ground. The Norman City is destroyed. Great medieval conflagrations sweep East to West again and again. Pentecostal fires reach churches and cathedrals and threaten the precious palaces. Bridges burn down. North to South, people are trapped and die. Winds carry embers and ash. Little blades of human life bend with the weight of red and black soul-bearing insects. The Ravens follow – chanting childlike charms for all fire's harms, telling of isolation and loss...

'Ladybird, ladybird fly away home, your house is on fire and your children are gone...'

Ushahin: Dark Night (Watch 5) – Fires continue to blaze within the Pearl as I sit into the night. I watch on as so many souls are lost. So many magical, beautiful books and drawings. Pudding to Pye gluttony is blamed along with Dutch blown karma. Four days of Great Fire, ineffectual mayors and unwanted monarchy. Suspicion and reason, papists and lynching mobs, all riot in the rubble. The rats disappear. The Tower provides powder and the garrison uses it to create late firebreaks. Where is the spouting, dousing water? Where are the fire teams? The diseased and the dispossessed, the poor, the growing middle classes and the privileged – all are threatened by levelling flames. The outcome is governed by wood, wind and water. Strong winds die down. Ill feeling rises up. Time moves on. I watch Shakespeare's Globe Theatre founder into ash.

Yet nothing compares to the Fire of the Skies and the seventy-six nights of thunder and lightning. Prolonged Blitz and bombardment in strategic bombing and terror attack bind evil friendships in pacts of steel and atrocities of blood. The halting good are the enemy. Victory through siege is sought. Ships are scuttled. Nations strike hard and without warning. The World divides and takes sides. Neutrality is questioned. Nations fight. Might turns to good and bad in the flexing of military muscle and Rainbow Plans. Operation Sea Lion is thwarted. Operation Loge and Sea Snake continue. The East End takes so much, the Palace a little too, momentarily equalising the class divisions in destruction. Chaos, poverty and panic are on the streets of London. Thousands of tons of metal are dropped on people and homes, cities and ports. People are trapped underground and under falling houses. Civil unrest, strife and disorder spread everywhere. Caught in our hands Time becomes corrupted and blighted.

Now, within the Dragon Pearl, the wisdom of fire chaos continues as it rises up and ignites the anger and frustration of lands the world over. Independence, welfare and warfare are at stake. Gaia's soul purge shakes the Life Tree to its foundations. Thoughts burn. Emotions blaze. Fire makes cinders of memories out of the Sky you and I. In return we fall as ashes upon the arid lands. In the deserted mountainous outback I watch the wonder of an ancient burning bush spread its truth. What visiting Phoenix, Dragon or fiery Archangel is this? The Rattlers around me coil and rasp in

Serpent renewal. Time is on fire and the time is now, but still the Ravens insist that the dreamtime can be remembered.

Within the Moon Pearl both the enduring and un-enduring realms go up in the flare of solar fire. There are flames and thick clouds everywhere. There is conflagration by blazing hail and coals of fire. Caught in geysers of molten flame souls cry out. Between my crossed legs the Pearl turns into a Heliosphere. Helios is here. All is pyro, and heliotropes grow out of my head and hands. This is fire as agent of Agni truth. The Moon Pearl becomes hot in my hands. A glorious new forming Sun burns within it – glinting, dazzling and blinding. Warmth rises and rushes through my body to my heart, brow and crown. All is flamma. The fire of a thousand Sunflowers races through my spine. They open above me like golden umbrellas. The blossoms of light amaze me. Is love on fire? Did life require so much heat? I find I have journeyed to the feet of the Sun, yet who is it hidden behind the glowing golden disc?

It is sunrise. The city is on fire as the morning sky becomes infused and lit with growing light. I see the Sun Runner, the dawn star torchbearer. Apollo hears my prayers; my heart is appeased, pleased, and my mind is ablaze! In ignition, in recognition, I am slowly becoming living harmony as I catch the speeding rays and pass on the flame. Streams of fire flow from the palms of my hands. The heralds of the golden dawn bear olive branches to adorn my head and celebrate. There are no winners and losers here as everyone is invited to join in the optimistic universal energy. The Sun declares its new day presence. The distant Moon reflects the light of my new solar understanding. Everything is going to be all right. Hope for all hearts is here in Sun-comprehending love and Moon-giving compassion. The rising Sun smiles and warms, well on its way to cosmic super nova.

Day 40 – Buddhist Monastery/Fire Ceremony

Sunday 17th April – 19°C

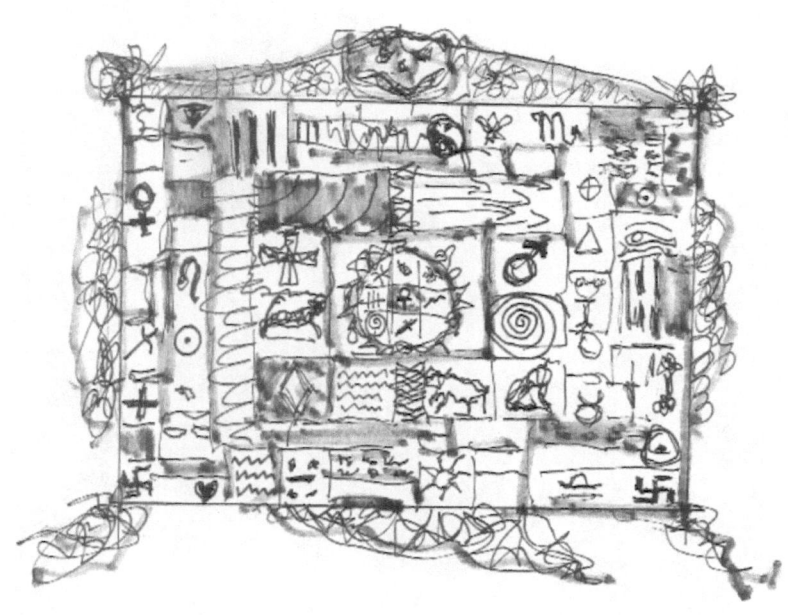

KEITH BRAZIL

Uzerin: Late Afternoon (Watch 3) – Flags flap and wave around the nearby Buddhist Monastery – calling wind and water to prayer, bidding me to visit. They summon my soul. High up in the Himalayas, Tibet turns the World on a Wheel. These are crushing times for one of the mountainous states of Heaven. The incarnated Jewel of the East shines in the West – just as the Light of the West falters and fails. In the local urban monastery, healing ceremonial banners ripple in blocks of fire colour above my head. Red – the colour of life, warming and bringing heart happiness, achievement and virtue, fortune and dignity. Yellow – blazing emptiness, balance and prudence welcomed by the humble soul. Orange – burning as insight, strength and dignity, representing the forces of creative life and vitality. Blue – glowing devotion, loving kindness and peace. White – shining brightly for purity, liberty and emancipation. The Buddhist nuns and monks chant away the World's pain and reveal the Heart of the Lotus in their opening arms, oms and pad me hums. Yet they persist in self-immolating. Such tragedy forced upon the gentle tribe.

In the shrine room, I sit silently at the feet of Lord Buddha and gaze into his eyes. He is serene and fecund with wisdom; he is fulfilled and imbues me with his gentle warmth. Soaking up divine light like a wick, he shines forth as a lamp of peace and happiness, sharing the glory of golden light rays. He offers love's greatest gifts – freedom, compassion and spiritual friendship. Under his watchful gaze I release myself from my questing and he helps prepare my mind and body for the next chapter of life. From his heart he offers safe haven and instils the quietness of a non-violent way. He makes me calm as the residue of my emotional spasms and physical pain burns away. What to do with the sadness and the gladness of our personal fires? I place my soul self into his hands.

As I meditate I realise that the intensity of my sorrow has triggered perception of a vast new world. Now, in response to the Buddha, my glistening light bodies shimmer and rise about me like a multi-winged radiant butterfly – momentarily free from my former grieving state. This sudden liberation brings happiness. My transforming light body flies up in belief as an active magical force like an emergent butterfly trusting its intuition to find its first flower and lover in ritual pollination dance. This winged gift from the Buddha brings about a new sense of confidence, gladness and understanding. In this newfound element of light, a guiding star glistens in the East. But it is the West that beckons and calls.

Daemons are suddenly around me, climbing the wooden rafters up onto the sloping roofs like evil flying monkeys. They too want liberty, but do not know how to gain it. They are not my personal daemons, but Daemons of the World – Hell Beings and Hungry Ghosts. They are the Chthonic: the trapped, the repressed, and the oppressed. They are the pained and the fettered – dispossessed souls cut off from evolving spiritual heritage – clambering up to the higher lands on the backs of others from a rock-bottom world. Like nightmares, they do not belong to any of us except for our forgetfulness and our sleeping, whilst they remain alert – ready to jump upon us at a moment's notice. The Buddha Lord raises his hand to hold back their harms and brings about the Peace of the World. He grants me solitary quietude. He speaks:

'Friend, there is a light that casts no shadow and an unknowable darkness that creates all light. Let the sacred flame set alight your body with its connections to the many realms. Before me now, enter the blazing conflagration. Bathe your body and feel the pouring fire melt your metal matters of woe. Let the metal disorder collect in your luminous field and dissolve, for the karmic chainmail of your light body has so far limited your viewpoint and restricted your interactions. You have been self-imprisoned. You could see, but were not able to act. Let all Hell that feeds on your fear assemble. In the test of fire, if you are good, the impurities and the pain of metal will melt away, and you will pass through and be free. If you are truly free, all traces of harm will fade from your centres, tongue and deeds.

As a true seeker, every soul must liberate themselves and release their inner prisoner. Yet there are many earthly prisons. What keys do you need for each freedom? What daemons? Remember. Each has their own personal relationship with the Noble Path and each must find and approach the aspects of love and truth in their individual way. Your karma, your childhood, your past lives, are all held in Nature's embrace linked to your spiritual choice. Befriend them, fulfil them. You have shown your gratitude and honoured your Father. Out of loss, something is regained. What fruit you have past borne and will future bear grows high up in the pine cones on the branches of the Huangshan tree.

As you step free you are able to experience the elements and taste the fruits of the Earth differently. Serve life and it will serve you. Give thanks. All that you have been through, all that has made you, gathers in love. Value the past. It makes you rich with invaluable experience. It makes you who you are. Let it feed you. Be kind to yourself. Be gentle towards your mistakes. Be compassionate to the misunderstandings of others. Even within all the World's noise, evil and turmoil, there is a beaming, positive, central light to the wonder of the universe. Seek that light. Share that light. For the expression of your truth generates living light. Make wonderful that wisdom, for life is a miracle.

Now, secure your connection with the divine and step into your winged-Serpent self. It is a Path of Love through the appreciation of life upon which you tread. As a celebrant, take Sun-blessed communion and encourage others to become part of the World hymn. Sing your praise. Chant your pain. Realise yourself. For humanity stands on the threshold of an age of great change. Be part of it. Come, let the sacred fires descend and dance about you as the final battle of love and truth unites in the ultimate victory of wisdom and peace.'

In the crucible of now, the totality of everything that I have learnt from the past comes pouring into the very thing that I am becoming. Molten fire falls about me as burning liquid metal. In this state, even with final fear, all I feel is the bathing of warm milky water – both cleansing and restorative. I find myself healed and soothed. My diary art of metal and fire becomes a mechanism for conveying my offering to Heaven. In my meditation at the feet of the Buddha, I become the Fire Ceremony and my Lent Pages go up in fiery transmutation. I ignite and find myself absorbed into the higher sacred flame. All around me divine sparks flare up as spiritual fire descends burning the World Soul. The Buddha takes in his disciples and leads them on to greater destiny. I become winged fire. Let the single-Sun be released. Let it be.

Day 41 – Dragon Design

Monday 18th April – 18°C

Rapithwin: Afternoon (Watch 2) – I am left to ponder. What to do with this mounting collection of strange metal? Hide it in a chest in the ground like some exciting Viking's burial hoard or place it in the Tower's Sun Temple, spread about the Mithraeum cave like otherworldly relics and so much Dragon treasure. Should I leave if for others to stumble upon and find or perhaps I should melt it all down to create a Raven-Snake crown – an emblem of a lost spiritual culture and a tribe past? The electricity of the metal fragments pulled from out of Time creates a perceptibly different magnetism and forces a new array of passing light streams. Ultimately, they belong to the goddesses of the Moon and the Night Sky – they are their gifts, but they shall not see them again.

Where best to hide all these fragments though? Not beneath the Earth whilst waiting for Time-bandits and Tomb-raiders to find them, or those seekers of curious remains who use pendulums, metal detectors or divinatory spells. Then, in a moment's sudden inspiration: the knowing of a perfect priest hole. Where best to hide anything except right under the occult noses in the Raven Agency itself? Not hide it, but deliberately and purposefully put it on show. There are only two suitable places within The Tower for the large sculpture my growing design requires. The Winged Advisor's Hall is built with wooden pegs in deference to the forgotten element of wood. There is no harmful metal allowed in there to injure the timber. So, it must be to the stone chambers in the White Tower that I look to complete my task.

So, my Magpie plans plot and move to the formation of a fantastical scaly artefact to capture a moment. I start to bond the stolen metal relics together in my mind's eye. This will be a reminder of art to serve the spirit, not destroy it, pushing to evoke and invoke understanding of the whole self. This will be art as offering, art as action, and art as healing to soothe the soul; cathartic art not only as interpretation or escape, but also pushing into activism and liberation – the combined power of Sun, Moon, Raven, and Snake. I want the breastplate and exoskeleton of a Keeper Dragon to hold fire-breathing mystery and lead to greater soul connection and spiritual enfoldment. For that they need a Dragon's flame and a God's strength to harness and forge them together.

Yet first I must turn to the forgiveness of history for such fragments of harm and old pain need to be animated with new alchemical life. The metals are not stable. Too much fear and loss, pain and darkness, have saturated these objects that in so many different ways have caused or felt the injury of misaligned love. Love triumphant; love defeated. In their resonating duality the darkness could still prevail, but now I know what I must do to unify and attune the metal artefacts to the light. I must seek blessing of the heavy dark particles and remove any residue pain. A new electrical imprint and a revitalised energy signature must circuit the whole of the sculpture. That which was harmful, must be put to good purpose if this metal is to be votive deposit. I need to bind them not with incantations and ritual overtones, but with greater apotropaic magick. They need feminine benediction. For that I must journey to the feet of the Mother whose light wisdom from out of time could bless my fragile human soul, cleanse the metal and advance my Dragon design.

Day 42 – To The Feet Of The Mother

Tuesday 19th April – 24°C

Uzerin: Late Afternoon (Watch 3) – I take a train and huddle down for the outward journey to see the Great Mother, yet I am apprehensive of my pending visit. I wish, hope and pray that in the light of my recent seeking – my Night-journeying and my thieving – she will handle my human heart with tenderness. In an unassuming wooden hall, in a park in Outer London, I travel to present myself at the feet of the Mother. In my pocket there is a lodestone and a key quartz crystal, both aligned to a set of crystals and gemstones surrounding the collected Metal of Ages on my rooftop Aerie. The crystals are attuned and I come to get them cleansed and blessed by the Mother. Good Mother. Loving Mother. All aspects of the powerful Mother; one aspect of incarnated earthly Mother. Praise be to thee – bringer forth of holy light and server of the rays of the world. Bring me thy joy. Bring me thy peace born of acceptance of strange personal circumstance. Untie my remaining light knots and radiate through me as eternal beingness. Hold me. Save me. Help me transcend myself.

In meeting the Great Mother there is real happiness for there is greater almighty assistance to be received. O divine being of love. Want what is best for me, cradle me, and make me momentarily child – for I am a weary adult with passing responsibility. Being loved. Being able to love. Make me strong now. I sit. I meditate. I wait. I take my crawling carpet turn toward her and bend my head to be touched by her skilful healing hands. I touch the Mother's feet, and then look up into her dark eyes. She who is liquid light and beauty nurtures me. She is able to see the love of all lights. I give her my grief and my difficulty. I give her all the love of my limited understanding born of limiting experience. I give her my highest thoughts and deepest feelings and the troubled journey of my heart.

Now, as the locked light links around my crown chakra are dissolved, a new kind of Heaven is realisable. The Mother gives me her deepening joy.

Let me be filled by love and become love itself. Help me to know when is the moment to surrender. Help me to know when it is the time to fight. Grant me a small slice of trueborn understanding of the greater spiritual life. Then in the sacred space of her gaze, stars descend – thousands of stars – piercing my heart, my head, and my feet. These stars last but moments, seconds filled with grace, yet they are all time in ever permeating space. The voice of the Mother fills me in answer to my mind's many questions and my heart's beseeching:

'My child, here in meditative silence the heart opens and resonates. Your craft of intrepid fox, of clever mind, is no longer needed. It has brought you to the door of the sacred heart and to the feet of the Divine Mother. Your cunning and guile are unnecessary here. Be thankful and rest now. Your fight and might strives for victory, but here peace is offered instead for I come to bring forth God's love. I do not seek to destroy, but to protect and change. However, where there is no openness some things might need to be destroyed. Within all your conflict lies the affirmation of a harmonising art waiting to be unlocked. Remember, it is the meek who shall inherit the Earth, for they pass through God's fingers like tender shoots being nurtured by a gardener. The bud wishes to open and blossom. The inner light hitherto hidden must be revealed, so aspire to the divine and your realization will grow faster. Yet, until the un-meek are disinherited, the gentle are armed in disquiet battle. Be warned, though, do not be schooled in the arts of your adversaries, in aggression and warfare, but rather uphold and defend the highest creative values of life with appropriate words and sustaining action. Spirit's compassion is easy and straightforward so be infants in love, not giants in evil.

My child, man is free, but now he must choose. God does not force his will, but wants his children's open love. The people of each and every age get worn down, yet the spirit of humanity endures through insights of faith and acts of kind-heartedness. Great golden civilisations can emerge and everything at this time is being reconsidered. Nothing is truly known or is as it seems to be. In Earth's hidden history – all is to be remembered. There is everything to learn and opportunities are ripe so choose well. Let forgiveness now replace the last remnants of sadness and regret at your Father's passing, for you are both my sons. Open your heart to joy and hold each other there for it is happiness that guides your spiritual growth. Only the freedom of love can encompass the all. Encourage those whose hearts are not open by helping them to enter into silence – since in that often forgotten place the sweet medicine of the Mother can be found. Aggression seeks fear, so take care to be unafraid – even until the gift of death, if necessary. The power of quietude is immense and unstoppable, as you have discovered in your recent visit to the Buddha Lord. It is now further encouraged by the harmonising energies of the Mother.

My child, the time has come for you to immerse yourself in the wellbeing of spiritual love and action. You, like so many others in the ripening, in the opening, are becoming the person you wished to meet; the one you wished would come to help you; the person you always secretly wished to be. You have been walking beside yourself all your life. It is in this precise moment of your personal history that the inner becomes reflected in the outer through the expanding resonance of your true spiritual self. Take care. Look upon life as you would desire to see it expressed from the other side. Learn from Supernature as it is reflected within the natural world. The laws of divine cosmic order feed your soul with light ever descending. Partake.

So, my son, in the name of joy and of my service – become.'

I look into the Mother's eyes and she sees me. I know she can see the stealing secrecy and the hidden me, but in her mercy it does not matter. The metal treasure upon my rooftop is but daring and ritual horde. For the time being, they are linked through the lodestone and key crystal in my pocket, and in the presence of the Mother they become votive offering. She knows all the secrets of magnetic electricity – and she accesses them now as she brings down the higher light. Greater status is conveyed to the lower vibrational energy of the metal artefacts torn from Time. She makes things good. Whatever their former purpose – the swift, subtle connective energy of higher air and fire, light and heat, now work to transform the metal objects. Their vibrations are cleansed and raised. One earthly sacred visit – and The Way becomes clearer. I am free to continue and complete the Dragon design.

'I am on my own now...'

Now more than ever I realise the untruth of those words. The reassuring fact is that none of us have ever been on our own. I give great thanks and take my leave.

Day 43 – War Museum

Wednesday 20th April – 24°C

KEITH BRAZIL

Ushahin: Dark Night (Watch 5) – Tonight the Moon has summoned me and pulled my travelling body to her in serious request. In tremulous Night-journeying I am suspended momentarily over the War Museum, London. It is midnight. The adjacent Peace Garden looks beautiful under the fullness of the Moon's spectral swan light. Serenity hangs here amidst the trees, covering the ground and the naval auto-cannons like so much trailing Moon mist. Buddhist pathways, sculptured elements, ancient trees and up-pressing flowers add fragility and strength to the cold stone weight of the museum and the heart of the war matter.

Inside the museum, in amongst the tank shells and propellers, I gaze upon all kinds of modern machinery and ingenuity put to salvation and brutal, frightening end. How long have we all been shaped by war? For so long. All our time and the tens of thousands of past years. Surely better and safer days await us now the barefoot, flower people are here – the Peace Army who are placing blossoms into the barrels of guns and lobbing posies inside canons and tanks. In remembrance, poppies are dropped and placed in the reconciliation of war, horror and peace. Yet here inside the museum, the suspended metal machines and the galleries of battle tell their own stories of struggle and love. Photographs haunt. Drawings and diaries reveal details of suffering, bravery and cruel misdeeds. Courageous women and men fight for the safety of the state. Good and bad wars have taken so many lives away. Centuries of natural laws are broken and the penalties are inescapable.

Overhead a plane hangs in silent glory. This museum collection offers a different type of reflection – of strange metal-wrought beauty and a life at war. In the second twentieth-century atrocity the survival of nations hangs in the balance. Pilots become angels and devils, flying aces and red barons. Everyone is in determination and distress. Emanating from somewhere in the lining of silver clouds and searchlights I hear the sputtering of engines, a plummeting flying noise, and a war-torn radio quickly scrambling...

"Request your position, request your position, come in Lancaster... come in Lancaster..."

"Position Nil, repeat nil, age 27, 27. Did you get that? That's very important..."

"I cannot understand you, hello Lancaster, we are sending signals, can you see our signals? Come in Lancaster, come in Lancaster..."

The two radio voices, a man and a woman, engage in happy-sad banter. They do not know that they talk in the code of love. Yet one is facing great uncertainty and the imminent prospect of death – a pilot who has already lost his flying buddies. He is alone, but he is prepared to make the final journey knowing that death does not discriminate, welcoming and taking all. He fires flares off into the sky and sends last minute radio signals, but in his final descent he ascends into poetry and the love of philosophy.

"...But at my back I always hear, Time's wingèd chariot hurrying near, and yonder all before us lie, deserts of vast eternity. Andy Marvell. What a marvel. What's your name?"

I am all ears, all fears, for them. It is *A Matter of Life and Death*. The transmission I overhear intrigues as their conversation continues...

"Are you receiving me? Repeat are you receiving me? Request your position. Come in Lancaster..."

In amongst the shadows and spitfires, the bombers and bullets, the smoke and sparks of love pervade. Destiny is here.

"Can't be helped about the parachute, I'll have my wings soon anyway – big white ones... What do you think the next world's like? I've got my own ideas... I think it starts where this one leaves off or where this one could leave off if we'd listened to Plato and Aristotle and Jesus! With all our little earthly problems solved but with greater ones worth the solving. I'll know soon enough anyway..."

Their voices recede as the plane plummets through the air into the water. There are caught sighs and silent sobs everywhere, and not just from the audience. In their newfound, death-defying, life-escaping affection, a Stairway to Heaven is being built for us all in their escalating love. Will our war ever end? I know love will not. Humanity is so caught up in itself, but here I am humbled by such faith and courage as the fate of entwined lovers and their war-torn predicament fills me with the vestiges of hope. As the banter of their charming words and newly entwining worlds fades, I disappear from the War Museum like a misty ghost rising up from a secret midnight garden. I am moved, touched by the lovers finding each other and their hearts in the midst of conflict and war, but there is nothing left to hold me here. My final learning from inspirational encounters is over. The Moon pulls me to her. I am suspended in the Night Sky surrounded by a shimmering starry mantle. Reassuringly, she is here with all her sacraments of life.

'Love,' she whispers looking down upon the Earth. 'Look nightly upon the world with love.'

Lifted up so high, I see the world from a wonderful new perspective. The Moon informs me that this is to be my last Night-journey, as she absorbs back my mysterious ethereal body. It was hers to give. It is hers to take. I am bereft, but emergent. I cling to small breaths of sad relief.

'In the phenomenal universe all elements are lent. All relationships are offered just for a short while. Long have you been told that you are all the sons and daughters of life, of seeming chaos and catastrophe. Know that you are creatures born from many milks of kindness created out of compassion and universal love. No-one actually belongs to anyone else even though they may choose to be with you, however briefly, however long. Love them whilst they stay. Let yourself ebb and flow, come and go, like the tide with natural love. Allow others to change and move on in life's seasonal drift and weather. Do not be lone-afraid for I know you all so very well. I am the guardian of all your dream secrets, whilst your new coming Sun has none to keep. Your shadow flight was intentional, offered, yet under me is guided no more. These magical adventures have been ferocious in their dispersal of fear, but your journeying has also been so much more than that. This is the momentous threshold where it is also goodbye to the old you. This is grieving and growing. This is the ending of your milky silhouette and your midnight solitude. Spun so very far away from yourself, this is the return of your orbiting curve in the swerve of infinity. Remember that you are so much loved. Remember that with all your heart.'

So my break with the dark, starry Night Sky and the Moon's gracious light occurs. A personal genesis has been achieved and her final words resonate in my soul forever.

'Love,' the Moon whispers as she returns my borrowed milky body to the rooftop Aerie like a lost somnambulist child. 'Remember to look nightly upon the world with love as I have ever looked down nightly upon thee.'

Day 44 – Maundy Thursday/Hephaestus

Thursday 21st April – 24°C

Hawan: Morning (Watch 1) – Whilst the avid eyes of the world turn to paupers, palaces and the ritual giving of money, I wrap up my metal horde and place it within cloth sacks. I take a taxi to The Tower and the Temple beneath. I inform the Ravens of my return and purpose. The Raven Master has foreseen this event. Perhaps it was his words that first gave hint. Within the Mithraeum, my Serpents and I seek out a different altar – one that can serve as anvil, crucible and forge. I strike my Fire Coins and in their glowing light I offer up words from the 'Great Invocation'. I seek the aid and inspiration of Hephaestus – the lame and faltering one. He is the Olympian God of fire and metal work, creator of sun chariots and thrones, staffs and sandals of office, girdles and breastplates, armour and arrows, bows and thunderbolts of fortune and of ire. I do not offer sacrifice, but ask for guidance in the creation of Dragon sculpture and effigy.

I am encumbered with what Hephaestus loves best and what he loves not – metal and injury. He has acquaintance with Helios. He knows Aphrodite. He is familiar with the difficulty of marriage as both son and lover. He knows the suffering and cruelty of parents. He knows rage, rejection and adversity, yet he has also experienced help, care and friendship from strange and sympathetic sources. Most importantly, he knows his craft – the magnificence of finely wrought metal work imbued with magical powers. It is to Hephaestus that I turn in the underworld Cavern of Shadows for I am aware that it is he who helps the hampered. Yet was it not he that bound Prometheus, even though he felt for the stealer's chained suffering? This iron crime of mine, does it bind me to the World or does it set me free? Have I made the Fool's journey to the summit of Olympus to sit in the gathering of the Gods? For so long The Way has seemed impassable, but now I am here although not yet done. Still the raising of the Winged Dragon; still the rising of my Sun.

Shuffling in the shades and glowing twilight of the cave, Hephaestus stands ready to serve and give physical arm to advice. Heavily resting his weight on a staff, attired in a leather apron, and with sweat upon his brow and chest, his great arms and hands accept the challenge of my work. At the feet of his lame and twisted legs I pour my metal offerings from the cloth sacks. He goes to lean on the altar and turns each item over in his hands in consideration. He smiles wryly. This is what we have to work with.

Rapithwin/Uzerin: Afternoon (Watch 2 and 3) – The hours spread out and the watches join seamlessly. We spend the day turning our minds to possible design and the challenge of mounting the items of metal into one final sculpture. Carbon steel frameworks, suspended wire rope, braided structural cables, exoskeletons, and mobile armour – all are considered in determining tensegrity. Joints, flexibility, symmetrical and asymmetrical angles, compression, compatibility of objects, lines and aesthetic focus all demand attention. At Hephaestus' suggestion I physically tomb raid The Tower's armouries, dungeons and map rooms for missing components and Dragon details. I return to find all the metal lying out on the Temple floor like an unearthed prehistoric, winged dinosaur skeleton awaiting assembly. Hephaestus arranges and rearranges these parts by running fine metal chains to connect together the fragments of metal. The pieces of the puzzle slowly fit into some kind of synthesised totality like an expanding flat pack map waiting to be hauled into its final three-dimensional position.

Groaning, Hephaestus slings the main load chains through pulleys he has affixed to the ceiling. Then he launches the smaller lifting cables up and lances them through grab hooks. Using rattling hand chains he hoists the whole design up until the metal Dragon can finally spread its wings and is ceremoniously lifted off the ground into the air. Suspended in the centre of the cavern the sculpture gently twirls and rotates, sending reflected light and warping shadows spinning off into the dark corners. It is strangely beautiful in its broken metal majesty. Behind the main High Altar a voice begins to chant and a magical beast stirs. Hephaestus laughs. What better beast and creator than this in the now reign of fire?

Hephaestus is thirsty and requests wine. I pour out water and go to fetch Dionysian supplies from The Tower. I find I have become exhausted, yet still the exhilaration and excitement trembles through me. Am I almost home? More than anything I yearn for this. At least I know that tonight I can look forward to celebrating, sharing wine and spinning yarns with this most wondrous God Metal Man. Incredible moments to be treasured always in my mythical memory. How could I ever be able to describe to others what these special hours have entailed? Lost in myth sharing we are accompanied by startling tales from the most mystic beast from beyond the Dawn of our Time. We set sail together in barks upon a brilliant dark sea. We float in boats on cosmic tides and cover the great expanses. Together they tell the struggle stories of the heroic we. In these brief moments of story I could almost imagine and ennoble myself as some hero – bearded and ancient, completing a mystical quest and universal voyage of discovery. Is that so very far from the everyday twenty-first century me? Thus musing, smiling, drifting, I slip into the welcome cloudless lands of dreams and sleep.

Ushahin: Dark Night (Watch 5) – In such a manner the cheery night passes until outside the creeping dawn Sun begins to shine its enriching rays on everyone. Stirring gently, I sense that the solar source is pulled into position by steed-drawn chariots of a breaking new dawn. As for me – no sunlit chariots to tempt me from slumber, save cosmic ray patterns rippling under the lids of my slowly opening eyes. I blink awake in the dim Temple Cave, my body lying alone by the side of the altar where steadily flicker the perpetual flames of the two Fire Coins. I stare up at the floating metal Dragon still hanging from the ceiling. I cannot believe the sculpture's construction is complete! Such huge endeavour has been asked of me and is now achieved in the creating and building of this work. This display is the sum total of my soul's Dragon totem – parts rescued and reassembled from my plummeting Night-quest. It is a strange feeling. Is this it – am I returned to inner home? Almost, but not quite – for there is one I still need to make my way back to and make amends with. Nearby, a Snake stirs and calls me. As I leave the Temple, I inform the Ravens that the Dragon task is complete. Ha-Kraa! Ha-Kraa! Ha-Kraa! I am done. The Raven Master knows what to do for the best and The Agency can do with the sculpture what they please. At long last I turn towards home. I wonder how You will react to the Dragon work and all it has put me through? Am I really so changed, so different? I head home to the finding of You.

Day 45 – Good Friday/International Mother Earth Day

Friday 22nd April – 24°C

Hawan: Morning (Watch 1) – Striding the length of the Bascule Bridge I head South, winding through side streets on the way home. I follow the weaving red, green and golden strings that connect my ankle, wrist and little finger back to the sweetness of my soul mate. I go back to the union that balances me and helps me to try to shape my world, back to the people who share and care in the broken bed-sit land of love. The strange house is full of shifters: a circus geek and an IT highflyer, both members of the skateboarding software brigade, a graffiti artist, a poet rapper and a late-night dancing TG meter maid. Apart from house sharing, they are all free runners and traceurs, practitioners of parkour, roamers and clubbers, itinerants with loose roots and strong bonds; interactive people who dare to journey free in an often oppressive city environment.

My housemates are skilful high-speed users of computers, land, sea and air. As good monkeys, they are darers and doers, acclaimed world citizens reclaiming their soul-right to be here. They claim their supple bodies and playful active minds like playground kids born to be free, not people smothered with conservatism and concrete, but free to run through urban spaces in liberated defiance. They reclaim their wings and retain their right to fly. We are all immigrants and refugees of one kind or another – all in strange exile with broken pasts, thrown together in gathering new friendship. They contain more aspects of soul love and of God than I can bear. I am so grateful that I can return and hopefully fit back in.

But I have grown... there is greater closeness to come, more opportunity for light. I feel soothed as I shower off the residual sorrow and shame of my missing and the dust of my travels. I stand under the warm flowing water for ages – eyes closed, silent, but thoughtful. Feeling cleansed and reassured, I realize I need to forgive myself. I also need to ask my Beloved to do the same as I am wrapped in towels by strong arms. What can I tell You that allows the sharing of my experience? That I had to build an Aerie – that I needed to fly and journey and die? I can hear my housemates laughing at me, but how about You?

In the bedroom I unpack my rucksack and place my diary on the shelf next to my Rosewood wand, which I notice has grown in my absence. It sparks and blossoms from both ends in open spiritual flow. Somehow it mirrors me in the new flowering of serpentine Aquarian consciousness. I know my Beloved will not ask, so I wait patiently until I can deliver the truth of the purpose of my leaving. My Beloved so loves me – even though I have been gone too long, far away, over afraid and out of control. Now, standing in front of each other in silent greeting, I tremble with tears until the terrible flooding of purification descends. Sobbing, I rest in the security of being held. I need to release my anguish – my residual shadow pain. These days of difficulty are not coming easily to me even at their end.

My Beloved offers comfort and I know in the warmth of loving touch that my suffering is near-ended. I am lucky to be so loved. Overcome with deepening understanding we simply embrace. The intensity of my thoughts and feelings has made me so disturbed and distant, but this is not God given insanity, just human frailty. I have been too far removed in the solitary buffeting altitudes and sunk too deep in the churning sea, and yet I find I am so kindly forgiven by my Beloved's compassion. I lie down upon the bed to rest. At last I am home, at one, and like a child with its head upon a pillow, I surrender to sleep and longed-for dreamless states.

Day 46 – Ministry of Light, Sound and Vision

Saturday 23rd April – 24°C

.

Ushahin: Dark Night (Watch 5) – I have slept for hours. An entire day has gone. The rest of the house have been out running – jumping off walls, swinging off railings, climbing sculptures and statues, vaulting walkways, twisting and tumbling off roofs – as they surf the roads and buildings along the River's great south bank. What else are weekends and holidays for? Not for surviving the working week, but for thriving in adventure. They come home to cajole me. They are ready to play, to dance and explore their love of lights, music and the delights of the gyrating body. I have been so utterly selfish in my removal that I feel I owe them some kind of explanation. How could I have done it? For the moment there is no answer that will appease. I had to do it, to go alone. All I can do is to be there more for them now.

So, we go. The partying army marches on in exhilaration, liberation, and expansion – connecting to an old alchemical branch of science and magick of the experimenting unconventional. Inside the Ministry of Light, Sound And Vision, the unorthodox are here in resplendent array of extra-terrestrial trance, daemon dancing and celestial celebration. We party on a happy Moon. A new life is begun; a life I can love the more. With reluctance, the lost self finds itself as redefined new; the old AWOL rogue has gone, but something more real is beckoning. Sometimes the pendulum swings back and away through Time and I discover that there is an optimal time for soul vibration to complete its purpose. Mine has taken the past two thousand years or so – representing a small clustering epoch within the last millions of my lives. It does not matter when or how long it takes, but enlightenment is definitely now. Not for the choosing, but for the receiving. I rediscover known lands – as one surfacing from previous slumber. Who knows the future journeys? The geography of the soul and new self is placed upon the star charts for the imagining. The blueprints of the World are seen unfolding everywhere.

Around us, Space Cadets and Star Children enter nirvana, temporarily or otherwise – everyone bound in their pursuit of happiness and the forgetting of the daily grind. The Ecstatic raise their arms in an urban wilderness towards a newly descending Heaven. Memories are regained; memories are wiped. Love and friendship within the dancing community becomes the all and the everything as we dissolve into the unquestioning arms of a gentle hugging, tugging love. Touch. Tenderness. Embrace. My Beloved and my friends encircle me as they prepare for cosmic take-off, whilst the surrounding Pyjama Army marches on in search of Paradise creation and rightful ownership of their bliss body. In the world speedway to the new Over Soul it is not temporary oblivion they seek, but re-entry into the true, sustaining, joyful world. They are trying to get out of it so that they might somehow get back into the garden.

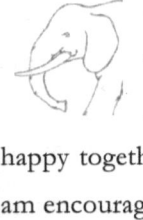Once more, I spiral within vortices. This time dancing men with beards twirl about me as I turn Sufi. The Winds of Heaven dance between us all, but here we jig our dances of happy togetherness. The dark of night descends into the too soon dawn. I am encouraged home by my Beloved and by the best of the rest. We return to sit in the garden to celebrate the new golden sunrise and enjoy the benediction of an Easter Sunday. It is radiant. It is warm. The garden is beautiful. We refresh ourselves by drinking the water of lemons and limes crushed with mint. A newfound happiness born of greater acceptance and understanding arrives. The Morning Star is here – that which was once whispered as Phosphoros. As I become immersed in his light, the sun of a once bound golden dawn is set free to ride the new Sky. After such sorrow and sadness, such destruction and downfall, this is the beginning of my Elephant's glad day.

Day 47 – Resurrection Day

Sunday 24th April – 24°C

Hawan: Morning (Watch 1) – Rejoice – the active Lord is newly arisen! The Moon observer has taken one step closer, only then to disappear! The Easter Bunny from the Far Side sends his happy, bouncing love. The best of ceremonial and ever celestial eggs is all over us. I am encompassed by more compassion, more love and light, than I can imagine in any single heavenly moment! I sit in rapidly growing sunlight, which fills me with golden energy. I grab onto the beautiful Quetzal tail feathers as the Birds from Paradise fly by on their journey to the centre of the Cosmic Sun. History begins to unravel and rewrite itself. In Gaia's new Spring testament of love I find I am as resonant as a bright yellow star.

So, the mystery mission of Ravens comes to a close. I have been out of my nocturnal mind in this travelling experience and I am afraid of this end, as I go into the hitherto great unknown of the Sun. If I became, even fleetingly, a Sun Runner – a herald to a new dawn – I now pass on the torch. In the relay of rays the Sacred Flame engulfs us all – burning our World consciousness and setting ablaze my former diary pages. Words are replaced by coals of fire and placed on the tongue as Dragon-speak. Now, riding the waves of rays like some new day Dawn Treader, I am uncertain of what is to come as I enter into the big blue yonder. The vast me longs to take further flight, while actually I am still reeling from exhaustion. This is so much bigger than me. It is out of my hands.

In the garden I sit alone. I turn to the final assembly of my thoughts and feelings in the Page Book of my Heart to find it is already done. The Wilderness Days match the many opening Lotus petals of peace. This is not account and explanation, but deepening wonder. The various states of grief and joy, elation and sadness, anger and quiet, have all passed by and left me alone here to consider the triumph of peace. In my obliteration, my absorption and immersion into this – I am left only with that which abides.

All my wanting and my desire to express my love could not bring my Father back to life or restore the former states of old times. There was no conjurer to help except my emergent alchemical magician.

If there is an impenetrable veil separating realities, then it exists because it serves to enable our progress – so when we journey we can discover the great invisible that is our fundamental self. We all have to go beyond now – to realise the otherness that is coming. It is us. Treat it as us – the you and the me engaged in struggle with God within and God without. Pursue contact with the Spirit World – and let them in. I have listened and half listened. I have gone it Human alone – and in turn gratefully I have been Spirit guided. They pursued me with Raven haunting and terrifying Snake truth. I had to surrender to them. I recognise that I have been the fallen – inasmuch as the ground can give into Sky-suffering. That provides the connection between the two worlds, of all our toing and froing implicit in the transmigration of souls and passing through the veil.

 My victory lies in humility as love flows down and surrounds me. Yet this is only one such moment within millions of moments that you and I experience in the Eternal Sky. We are all naked here – born beneath and underneath in higher struggling. I choose to dance to the Holy Ghost and God Host. Theirs is such strange beguiling Dragon music. I hear their ecstatic hum all around. I taste love like a fine wine, but it is you and I trembling on the Spirit vine. If I have been ungrateful for this genuine solitude and wandering experience, then I honestly repent. I have realised afresh the truth that aloneness eventually proves to be more valuable than money. I believe that I did not know how to respect the alone state. Now I seek it. I thought I knew better when I did not. On this day I have become Ēostre's momentary egg and mandala of me.

Day 48 – New Octave

Monday 25th April – 24°C

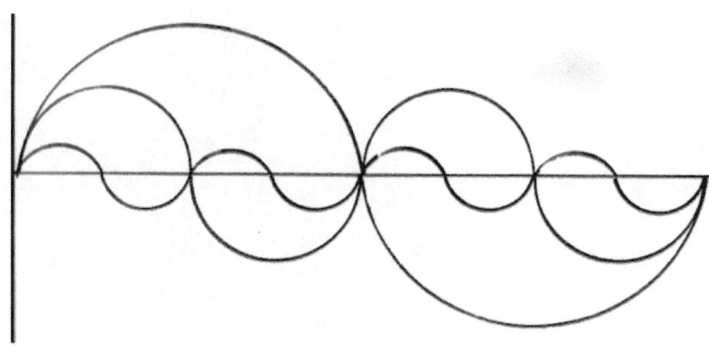

KEITH BRAZIL

Hawan: Morning (Watch 1) – So a new octave begins with all the electricity of a new spiritual ministry. Yet who was I when railing in the desert of my recent days? Just another prophet and madman wild at heart or a besieged artist whose work on life is soul progress? Perhaps simply a son struggling with grief after recent loss. If I became a Servant of Serpents or a Daemon Dancer it was to scare away the Fear Devils from my Father's pyre and re-instil higher joy. My Father! As refugees, we travelled across European Lands together, over the sea to Dover, following the coastlines to Bleak Heath. He left me in London to find fame and fortune. Instead, Time reveals art and love. We part for many years, yet cycles complete in the balancing of equations. My Ash leaving so many days beforehand represented both departure and arrival. To me, it is my soul's memory, an adventure through Time to find and unlock my Parsifal castle – however many attempts it takes in the failing and falling. To my Father and I, it is our Heaven's Night-journey home to the shared Cosmic Heart. To anyone else's eyes, it is simply an urban tale of the Elephant and Castle via the Old Kent Road and the Street of East. Now my Father hands me on as he hands me back over to myself with a smile. Go on – get on. It is done. What else is there left for me to say except the giving and receiving of thanks? Thank you. Thank him. Thank God. He has done World service.

Yet still the garden birds of our station call to summon us in. They will serve us well if we can respect and serve them. The Robin and the Rose Finch happily sing to those listening. It was their song that first attracted the seeking me and brought me to the secret East West division so long ago. Them, and the bright Holy Star that once flashed through the sky and across the folk soul land of Old Anatolia. The songbook mysteries of Finches originate from the beauty of roses and orchids, and they adorn many a poem and a pavilion of the East in daily decoration and veneration.

Now, it is the Lotus Bird – the Turtle Dove of the East – that wades across Cosmic Water to greet me. Its vitality is here as radiance and splendour. Walking upon opening leaves, it carries new building materials in its beak – the strands of thoughts and feelings that make up the tapestry of our lives. Still, the canny Ravens are busy watching the World – awaiting those who would heed their message and follow them on the final journey. Ha. Kraa. Traa. They tell of grieving elephants, wounded dragons and an enchanted Vortex Castle. They tell me that they have seen emeralds and diamonds as bright as sparkling stars that once belonged to the crown of a fallen Turquoise Angel. Their future stories of magick are but yet to come.

So, as my heart's old rose fades and yields to a new lotus position, I await further Snake instruction and find I am no longer afraid. Tomorrow, I become dreamweaver and art crafter, newly apprenticed scribe and librarian to the Raven Master – The Tower, London. By then, the Snakes inform me, the Dragon sculpture will be installed in the Tower Hall. Thus I finally come to the earning and to the gaining of wings. But light or dark? Vestigial or angelic? Bird, Dragon or Serpent? Only Time and my perching Raven and my basking snake will tell. Oh yes! I have new familiars now. Until then, know this – that the Sun will fall on each and all. Yet ever the rising! Thanks to the glorious morning Venus-Lucifer binding.

My name is Golshan. I come from the ancient land once called Persia. I am but astrological cat to the King of Gods. The 'Spell of Snakes' and higher mathematical summation concludes – enabling me in myself to move on. My heart is opening. The Ravens take wing. Peace unfurls. The Serpents sing. Solon. So long. I am my Mother-Father's son. I am my winged-Serpent's single-Sun.

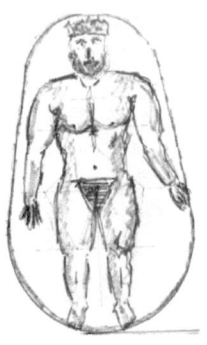

ABOUT THE AUTHOR

Keith Brazil was born in Broadstairs, Kent, England. He trained in Dance Theatre at Laban Trinity Conservatoire, London, and was a founder member of 'Adventures In Motion Pictures' Dance Company. He has worked as a freelance professional dancer, choreographer, teacher, and dance lecturer. Keith has also trained as a complementary therapist in spiritual healing and reflexology. He gained a degree in English Studies and is currently engaged in writing a collection of metaphysical and fictional stories, essays, poetry and novels. 'The Wilderness Diary' was first published in December 2012 (second edition 2015). 'In Consideration of Cats' was published November 2013. His third book 'Popcorn, Parasites, Precious & Pearls' was published December 2013. 'The Chameleon's Last Dance' was published in June 2014. 'An Alchemist's Wedding' was published June 2015. He lives and works in London.